This Bud of Love

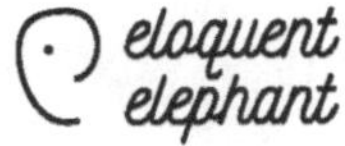

To Andy.
"Every love story is beautiful, but ours is my favourite."

'This bud of love, by summer's ripening breath,
May prove a beauteous flower when next we meet.'
William Shakespeare, Romeo and Juliet

Autumn

Lil

Do you ever feel like things that happened when you were seventeen were more real, more vivid, more *technicolour* than your adult daily reality now?

Samuel Park moved in next door in the summer when I was seventeen. Between travelling with my family, and getting ready for school, I didn't really meet him properly until church, a week before school restarted. That's when I realised that his dad was the new minister.

The Parks looked like a nice family, although marked by suffering. Reverend Simon Park was a strong, energetic man, who wore lumberjack shirts and jeans and eschewed the traditional suit-and-tie culture, which I liked. His wife, Meredith, seemed pale and fragile. Apparently the youngest child, Annabelle, had a rare immune deficiency, and had spent a lot of time in and out of hospital. She was fifteen, the same age as my sister Darcy, but she looked much younger. Meredith home schooled her and I never saw them apart. Sam, by contrast, looked… normal. He was tall, looked good in long shorts and a T-shirt, and he had a nice smile. His face was freckled and his brown hair was longer at the front, short at the back.

To be honest, it was a relief to have someone else my age at the church.

I started going to church on my own, about two years before the Parks arrived. My parents had never been very interested in going, but I just… felt compelled. Cross Street Baptist was not a 'trendy' church with flashing disco lights, but they were my family and it felt like home. No one asked awkward questions when I turned up at various events alone; they just drew up a chair and made sure I was never left out.

The minister at the time, Steve, explained the Bible so clearly that it finally made sense to me. I went to a beginners' course, and then got baptised when I was sixteen. My parents did come to that service, to support me. They've never stopped me from coming, but they just… never really got involved themselves. Same with my friends, really. I hung out with the musical group at school: Shannon, Beth and Clare. We were all in the choir and the school productions every year. On the weekends, all they seemed to want to do was drink and find boys, so I found myself passing up their invitations. I was looking forward to school restarting.

I shook Reverend Park's hand on my way out of church.

'I'm Lil, and I live next door to you.'

'Oh, that's great!' he grinned. 'Hey, I was thinking we could have a barbecue and invite your family—you know, get to know each other.'

'I'm sure they'd love that.'

'They don't come to church?' he asked, looking over my shoulder as if expecting to see them.

'No,' I said sadly. 'Not yet, anyway.'

'Keep praying,' he said. 'God hears.'

Later that day, as I watched my little sister Darcy obsess over her phone, and my dad leave to play golf and my mum drive off for a shopping trip, I felt a totally irrational anger at Sam Park for having a family who went to church, shared one faith together. I wished that I could have a different life, a different situation. I wished that I could have had his life.

Sam

The first thing I noticed about Lil was her style.

In a Baptist church with a heavy majority blue-rinse brigade, to see a teenage girl with a long denim shirt, beaded necklaces and red hair down to her waist was enough to make my jaw drop. I was supposed to be listening to Mrs Hart, the church treasurer, but she noticed the direction of my eyes and smiled wryly.

'That's Lil,' she said. 'She's seventeen.'

My heart literally jumped. I cleared my throat and coughed awkwardly.

'You should go and say hello,' Mrs Hart continued. 'She lives next door to you.'

What? How had I not seen her before? I tried to breathe normally. *Don't be a psycho.*

I kept my distance, figuring out a hundred different ways to speak to her, and watched as she spoke to my father. Her smile was dazzling. I was swooning and I hadn't even introduced myself yet. It was such a new, intoxicating feeling. I'd never been interested in a girl before. At my last school, they were totally inaccessible, going around in packs, and none of them shared my faith. Dad drilled into me the importance of being wise with relationships, so I just… never had any. It was lonely. Sometimes it felt like I was the only guy who was single in my entire year group.

If I was honest, sometimes I wondered if there was any point to following my dad's advice. He preached that being Christian wasn't about following rules, but under his roof, there were a lot of do's and don'ts to obey. Sometimes I felt like we had tried so hard, done everything right, and it still wasn't good enough. Things had been difficult at our last church and in the end, Dad felt it was best to move on. Uprooting right before my last year of school hadn't been ideal, and I was feeling quite disillusioned as we started all over again in Cross Street.

But then I saw Lil.

And I knew that God didn't 'owe' me anything, and that just because she went to my church and she might be a Christian didn't mean that she was right for me, and that even though she was next door could be a complete coincidence… But I felt excited. I felt hopeful. Maybe God did know what He was doing, bringing us here. Maybe there was a plan after all.

Sam

It was surprisingly difficult to meet Lil without seeming like a stalker.

I hovered; I twitched curtains; I spent far too long staring out of my bedroom window into her back yard. No joy.

When Dad mentioned they were coming over for a barbecue, I had to sit on my hands to stop myself jumping around shrieking 'hallelujah!' He looked at me suspiciously.

'Do we need to have a talk about this?' he asked.

'What?' I asked innocently.

'I saw you staring at her. Be careful, Sam.'

'You invited them over, not me,' I pointed out.

'I want to get to know them… as our *neighbours*,' Dad said, his warning clear. 'She's the only one who comes to church.'

'Is she a Christian?' I asked, desperate enough for information that I threw caution to the wind.

'She was baptised a year ago,' Dad said, his eyes narrowing at me. 'She's on the membership list Mrs Hart gave me.'

This was a good sign. Or so I thought, until Dad added,

'That's not a green light, Sam. We don't know her, we don't know the family, and she must be a baby Christian who needs a lot of support…'

'I don't get you,' I interrupted, shaking my head impatiently. 'All this time, you said "wait for a Christian girl." And now we're here and there's one living next door, and you say she's not good enough!'

'That's not what I—'

'I don't know why I'm surprised,' I continued, building momentum. 'I'm never good enough for you either.'

'Samuel!' my mother said, shocked.

'I'm going out for a walk,' I said, grabbing my raincoat on my way out of the door.

That was one awesome thing about this neighbourhood: we lived right next to a bunch of fields, with a path winding through and leading out to a hill which overlooked the whole area. There was a river, too, further beyond the fields. I loved getting out from the reach of the streetlights and the hum of traffic. The air felt clearer.

I prayed as I walked, trying to calm down. I loved my parents, but they were slowly suffocating me. Maybe it was partly the result of Annabelle's illness—their need to clamp down and control everything in their power. But part of me thought that they would probably have been like this anyway. The irony of their rules and over-protectiveness? It made me want to rebel.

I'm not proud of my own arrogance. But growing up is about being able to make decisions for yourself, and at this rate, my mum was going to be cutting up my food for me at my own wedding.

If I ever got married.

Lil

I'd be lying if I said I didn't make an effort to dress for the barbecue.

It was the tail end of summer, and I put on my favourite floral print dress with sandals. I hadn't met Sam properly yet, only heard the sound of his music through the walls. I figured Annabelle wasn't into rock.

Our houses were semi-detached, a mirror image of each other. Both had back yards with patio doors leading out from the kitchens, and then steps leading up to the rest of the back gardens. We went round to their front door, and Meredith ushered us through to the yard, where Reverend Park was brandishing barbecue tongs, and Sam was standing, smiling as soon as he saw me. As if he *knew* me already.

'Nice to meet you,' he said, clasping my hand.

A piece of my heart was his from that moment.

'And you,' I echoed, feeling my breath catch at his touch.

His eyes were a brilliant blue, and it was like my life flashed before my eyes, but instead, it was a montage of possibilities. The way he was looking at me, it was as if he could see it too.

'Sam, do you want to sort some drinks?' Reverend Park's voice cut into the moment.

Sam smiled, a smile only for me.

'Come into the kitchen,' he said, dropping my hand and beckoning me to follow him.

We passed Darcy, striking up a conversation with Annabelle, and I overheard Meredith explaining her condition to my mum. My dad was standing with Reverend Park by the barbecue. Inside the kitchen, there was a glass jug filled with punch, fresh strawberry and lime slices, and ice cubes.

'I made this,' Sam said, pouring me a cup and handing it over. 'No refunds.'

And that was it: we were friends.

Sam

It felt like I'd been waiting for her my whole life—I had sixteen years of Lil Harper to catch up on. Talking to her was like drinking water when you'd been in a drought for over a decade. I couldn't get enough of her.

She liked salad. She didn't like mustard. She preferred burgers to hotdogs. Her laugh was infectious, and a dimple appeared in her left cheek when she smiled. Her music taste was eclectic: blues, rock and soul. She told me she heard my music through the wall. I tried not to look too excited—didn't want to freak her out—but I was thinking *yes!* If her room was next to mine, it meant we were closer. I already wanted to protect her—although I had no idea from what. I already saw her as mine.

Lil

'Tell me about Avon High,' he asked.

'It's alright,' I shrugged. 'Depends what subjects you're taking.'

'Biology, Geography and Religious Studies,' he said.

'I'm doing RS too!' I said.

His eyes lit up.

'What else are you doing?'

'English and Drama.'

'I would have loved to do Drama,' he said wistfully.

'Why didn't you take it?' I asked.

'I couldn't do separate Science if I chose it,' he explained. 'My dad thought I should keep my options open in case I wanted to do Medicine.'

'Wow.' He must be so brainy. Swoon! 'And do you want to do Medicine?'

'No.' He shook his head. 'I want to work outdoors. Do you realise how awesome it is that you can walk straight from your front door and be by the river in forty minutes?'

'The river?' I asked. 'I don't think I've ever gone there.'

My parents weren't into walking. If they wanted a pint of milk from the corner shop, they drove.

'What?' he asked in mock horror. 'We have to go, then. When are you free?'

I giggled and tried to hide my elation.

'We start school tomorrow,' I reminded him.

'After school, then,' he said without missing a beat. 'What time do you normally get back?'

'The bus usually gets in at about three-thirty.'

'Bus?' He wrinkled his nose. 'Don't you want to walk? It's not even forecast to rain.'

'Wouldn't it take ages?'

'Forty minutes,' he said. 'I checked on Google maps.'

'I've been at Avon for five years and I've never walked.'

'First time for everything.'

And that was how it all started.

Sam

My first day at Avon, I called for Lil in the morning. It was strange seeing her in the uniform, both of us in white shirts with the school tie, a bright shade of lime green. It was a fresh, dewy morning where the air smelled of cut grass, and we needed the charcoal blazer jackets for warmth.

'Hey,' I said.

'Hey yourself,' she said. 'First day. You nervous?'

'Not really,' I answered. Honestly, now that I knew her, I wasn't.

We fell into step together, Lil hugging the straps of her rucksack tighter onto her shoulders.

'You're not nervous, are you?' I asked her.

'I've got that fluttery excitement you get when you're on a rollercoaster, about to drop,' she said, grinning.

'You know the teachers already,' I pointed out. 'What about your friends? Are they all coming back?'

'Yeah, mostly,' she said, but her voice lost some of its enthusiasm.

'What's up?' I asked.

'I think it's going to be a bit awkward with them,' she said, sighing. 'They were meeting up over the summer to go out partying, and I turned them down a lot. So I'll probably be completely out of touch with them all and they might be mad at me.'

'Sounds tough,' I said. It also sounded like she needed some new friends.

'I'll need you to introduce me to everyone,' I said. 'No pressure.'

'Well, knowing you for twenty-four hours definitely qualifies me for that privilege,' she quipped.

'It only takes a minute, girl.' I broke into full-on Take That, and she threw back her head and laughed. It was probably good that I stopped there and laughed with her, because if I said (well, sang) *to fall in love*, that would seem premature. But as I stared at her eyes shining with joy, her nerves forgotten, I could have finished the whole song for her in that moment. And I would have meant every word.

Lil

I hardly noticed time passing as we walked to school for the first time together. Sam had a way of making conversation feel easy and effortless. I was hypnotised by his eyes, the way they sparkled with fun, and it was impossible not to mirror his grin.

He'd looked up different possible routes, and chosen a quiet canal path. He seemed happiest when he was away from traffic and town life. I didn't mind. It was nice to have him to myself. As the concrete outline of Avon High came into view, I thought about how I'd have to introduce him to everyone. I took him to the Common Room, and I could see heads turning with interest and eyebrows raising as they saw us together. We weren't holding hands or anything, but I felt myself blushing because it was obvious that everyone assumed we were a couple. This was reinforced immediately when Shannon, Clare and Beth ambushed me.

'Lil!' Shannon cried, pulling on my arm. 'Where have you *been*?'

'Who's the guy?' Clare hissed, not very subtly.

'Calm down,' I said, trying to laugh.

I took a step back so that I was next to Sam.

'Everyone, this is Sam. Sam, this is Shannon, Clare and Beth.'

Thankfully there wasn't long to make conversation, because the head of Sixth Form, Miss Carr, sent us all to form rooms to collect our timetables.

'You need to tell us everything,' Beth muttered to me with a meaningful look at Sam, before heading in the direction of the Science lab.

'Miss Carr?' I called out. 'This is Sam Park—he's new. Can he join my form room? He doesn't know anyone else.'

'Hi, Sam,' she said with a smile. 'Welcome to Avon High. Yes, I don't see why not. I'll make sure your timetable gets dropped off to the right place.'

'Come on,' I grinned at Sam. 'I'll give you a full tour.'

Sam

I was in a total daze as I followed Lil around the school: partly because I had no idea where anything was, and partly because she was so beautiful and I was falling harder for her with every passing minute.

There weren't many classes because it was mainly an admin day, and Miss Carr gave us an assembly about working hard for our exams, constant revision, and applying for university. I hadn't really given it much thought. As a family, we'd been totally focused on moving house over the summer. My mum worried a lot, and I didn't want to give her more stress by mentioning open days and applications. Money was tight, and the world of student finance would totally invoke emotional meltdown for her. Lil, on the other hand, knew exactly what she wanted to do.

'I'm going to Exeter for Liberal Arts,' she said. 'If I get accepted.'

'What's that?' I asked.

'It's basically made up of Humanities subjects, and I can pick different modules,' she said. 'I can study English, Drama, Creative Writing and Sociology. I can major in English.'

'Wow, you've got it all figured out,' I said.

'Well, you know you want to work outdoors,' she said. 'So that's going to narrow down your options a bit.'

It melted my heart that she actually listened to what I said.

'I need to do some research,' I said, adding it to my mental to-do list.

'Oh, look at this!' Lil dragged on my sleeve, pulling me towards a noticeboard in the school hall.

There was a huge 'auditions' poster with *Romeo and Juliet* on it.

'I love Shakespeare!' Lil said, clapping her hands with joy.

'Are there many people who take part?' I asked her, feeling an instant longing to be involved.

'Lots of girls,' she said, raising her eyebrow. 'If you audition, you'll get a lead, no question.'

'Glad to know you have faith in me,' I joked.

'There's a meeting after school tomorrow with more information,' she said. 'Let's go together. Maybe we can audition together too.'

I'm pretty sure by this point, massive heart emojis were floating in the air above my head.

Lil

As far as first days back went, everything was fine. Better than fine, with Sam around. When we started the walk home at the end of the day, the sun was high in the sky. The canal path was shaded and peaceful, with only the ducks to accompany us. Sam sighed.

'It's so good to be in the quiet again after the noise.'

'Maybe I should stop talking, then,' I teased.

He laughed and shook his head.

'I don't mind *your* voice,' he said. 'You don't stress me out.'

'Yet,' I said. 'I've been told I'm very demanding, you know.'

'Really?' he asked incredulously. 'By who?'

'Oh…' I shrugged, wishing I hadn't turned the conversation in this direction. 'Just… guys.'

'Any in particular?' he asked, with a raised eyebrow. 'And… you don't have a boyfriend, do you?'

'Why?' I asked, deliberately ignoring his first question.

'I don't want to get into trouble,' he said. 'Well, I know you don't, because I would have seen him by now, surely?'

'Unless he's someone I met at another church and I just meet up with him on the weekends.'

Sam's face fell, and I laughed, unable to keep it up.

'I'm joking, Sam.'

'Oh.' He clutched at his heart dramatically. 'Don't do that to me!'

I held my phone up.

'I've been inundated with messages asking me who my cute boyfriend is.'

'People think we're together?' Sam definitely looked pleased at that.

'I suppose it's the natural conclusion when a boy walks around with a girl all day.'

'Are you getting annoyed at me trailing you?' he asked.

'No,' I said, shaking my head. 'Plus, you'll be very useful whenever I need to reach something high up.'

He laughed, a rich sound that made me want to throw my arms around him. I just about managed to restrain myself.

'You know, we should probably talk about the whole dating thing,' Sam said.

'What do you mean?'

He flushed slightly.

'My dad is quite anti-dating.'

'What?'

'I know.' He sighs. 'It comes from a good place. He just wants to protect me.'

'So you're not allowed to date anyone?'

'I don't know if he would say it exactly like that…' Sam ran a hand through his hair. 'He gave me this book to read about it. You can borrow it if you like, see what you think. It basically suggests that we need to guard our hearts before marriage, and so we shouldn't date someone unless we're considering marrying them.'

'Right…' I frowned, turning this over. 'So your dad doesn't think I'm good enough for you?'

Sam hesitated for a second before answering.

'I think he would just say that we're too young to get married, so therefore we're too young to date each other.'

'And what do you think?'

I stopped in my tracks, crossing my arms in front of my chest. I didn't want to be messed around.

'I think I would be lying if I said I only wanted to be *friends* with you.'

A small smile played on my lips when he said that, but then I straightened out my expression.

'Sam, your dad's going to notice if we're more than just friends,' I pointed out. 'The entire school is talking about us already. We're in the same church. We're neighbours! What are you going to do, have a secret relationship with me?'

'No,' he said, frowning and shaking his head emphatically. 'I just want you to understand that it's not going to be straightforward with him. It's nothing personal against you.'

'Hmm,' I said, expressing my skepticism.

'He'll need to get used to the idea,' Sam continued.

'You realise we're talking about this but you haven't even asked me out yet,' I said.

'Oh.' Sam blushed. 'I'm not very good at this.'

'Have you ever asked anyone out before?' I asked, although I could guess the answer.

'No.' He gave me a sudden grin. 'Never been anyone worth asking before you.'

'Smooth,' I said, starting to walk forwards again. He fell into step beside me.

'Are you mad at me?' he asked.

'Maybe.'

'Do you feel I've lured you here under false pretences?'

I gave him a playful shove.

'Don't overdo it.'

We reached the end of the canal path, and turned into the field that led to the river. It was a meadow of long grass, a little wild and overgrown, and we pushed our way through to the stile.

'Here.'

He held out his hand to help me. I took it, raising my eyebrows again.

'I'm getting mixed messages from you,' I told him.

I scrabbled over the stile in as ladylike a fashion as possible, then he nimbly jumped over.

'Just being chivalrous.'

'Would your dad be horrified to know we were out here... alone?' I teased.

He shrugged.

'Possibly.'

'I don't want to deceive him. He's my pastor, remember?'

'That doesn't mean he always right,' Sam muttered, then indicated to the path. 'Go ahead, we're almost there.'

I followed the dirt track and the sound of the gushing water, and walked down the steep bank to a tiny strip of pebbles at the edge of the river. Sam held my hand, ostensibly to help me down the bank, but I think there were ulterior motives. I wasn't complaining.

We sat together, backs against the rocks, and watched the river.

'It's the best sound, isn't it?' he said, in a raised voice so I could hear him.

'Like that bit in Revelation: *his voice like the sound of many waters*,' I said.

He looked at me in surprise.

'You know Revelation?'

'It's one of my favourite books of the Bible,' I told him. 'So much poetic imagery.'

'Wow,' he said. 'Most people find it pretty confusing.'

'When Steve was pastor, he did a series on it,' I explained. 'He made it much clearer for me.'

He was quiet for a moment. I watched him, trying to read his thoughts.

'What's your favourite part of the Bible?' I asked him.

'Probably the Psalms,' he said. 'When everything seems dry, I always go back to them. I've been feeling pretty dry lately.'

'Why?' I asked.

He sighed, then looked at me with a pained expression.

'It's been pretty stressful, with the move. Sometimes I read the Bible but I'm just going through the motions. Typical pastor's son.'

'You don't realise how blessed you are,' I said. 'I wish my family were Christians too.'

'I know,' he said. 'But Lil, just because my family are believers, it doesn't mean that we have a perfect life, or get it right all the time.'

We watched the white foam of the river crash over and over, our hands on the ground, just touching.

Sam

Miss Raine taught English and Drama, wore flipflops and three-quarter trousers with a striped shirt, and clearly loved Lil as much as I did.

A cluster of students gathered for the meeting about the auditions. Lil chose a seat right at the front, so I sat next to her. She was right about the lack of guys. There was one boy who also took Biology, so we nodded at each other. He was quite short, with dark hair and a big voice. I hoped he wouldn't pip me to the post with the part of Romeo, because then it would be torture to watch him pretend to be in love with Lil.

Let's face it, if I got the part, I wasn't going to need to act at all.

'This play is very well known,' Miss Raine said. 'But I hope you can make it your own. I've chosen a section of Act 2 Scene 2, the famous balcony scene, for the audition script. I want to go through the text with you all now, to explain the meaning and make sure you understand what's happening at this point in the play.'

She handed out sheets of paper, and I scanned through it. Already I was imagining Lil and me, on the stage, speaking these famous words of love to each other. Part of me was afraid of what my dad would think, and part of me wanted to show him that I was old enough to make my own choices.

'By overhearing Juliet's declaration of love, Romeo is able to bypass the usual rituals of courtly love and confess his love directly to her,' Miss Raine was saying. 'Juliet's main concern here is: is this real? It's too easy for Romeo to try out his well-worn phrases on her. She wants something different, something unique.'

My mind wandered to my conversation with Lil at the river yesterday. The whole no-dating thing didn't go down well… I could see how she was justified in feeling annoyed at my behaviour contradicting my words. The truth was, I was all over the place. I didn't know how to fit what I'd been taught with these new feelings I was experiencing. What did I actually want from Lil? People already thought I was her boyfriend. I didn't want her to contradict them. But I felt terrified of actually telling my parents that we were a couple. I just didn't know how my dad would react.

Well, it would be bad.

'When do you want to rehearse?' Lil asked me, at the end of the meeting.

'Tonight?' I suggested. 'Where's a good place?'

'You could come over mine,' she said.

'Won't that be awkward, if your mum walks in?'

'We can go in my room,' she said with a shrug.

I shook my head.

'My dad would go berserk if I stepped across the threshold of your bedroom. Or if you came anywhere near mine.'

'Oh,' she said, looking deflated.

'What about the garden?' I suggested. 'Don't you have a treehouse?'

'You noticed that?' she asked. 'Yeah, I sometimes go there to write when I need peace and quiet.'

'How about you go up there and drop the ladder over my side of the fence, then I can climb up.'

'That's very Rapunzel,' Lil said, rolling her eyes. 'Sure.'

After dinner, my dad left the house for a meeting, and my mum settled on the sofa with Annabelle for soaps. I sneaked out of the back door, and made my way up to the top of the garden.

'You up there, Lil?'

A rope ladder came down in response. Feeling like I was already playing my Shakespearean hero part, I clambered up into the tree.

It was quite a large Rowan tree, and the treehouse was made with wooden pallets. It wasn't much more than two metres squared, but there were cushions and blankets on the floor, and fairy lights twinkling from the branches. Lil was sitting, her hair long over her shoulders, holding her script with a highlighter in hand.

'This is cool,' I said.

She grinned.

'A secret hideaway.'

'Thanks for sharing it with me,' I said.

She patted a cushion and I sat down, folding my legs.

'Let's read through it,' she said.

It struck me that for the first time, I understood this play. Before, I would have said it was crazy to meet someone, marry them and die for them within a few days. It had only been a few days since the barbecue, and yet, if we had been older, I could quite easily have proposed or suggested an elopement like in the period dramas my mum and sister watched. I understood Romeo's certainty.

'*Although I joy in thee*,' Lil read. '*I have no joy of this contract tonight. It is too rash, too unadvised, too sudden,/ Too like the lightning, which doth cease to be/ Ere one can say 'It lightens.'*'

She paused, and lowered her script.

'You know, maybe there's wisdom in what your dad says. We *are* young, we *have* only just met.'

'True,' I said. 'But I've never felt like this about anyone before. Have you?'

'That's not the point,' she said, resuming her speech.

We ran through it several times, and she directed me a few times, with comments like 'you need to make that funnier'.

'We are going to have to think about our actions and movements,' I pointed out.

'We can do that tomorrow,' she said. 'How about we go over the field after school?'

'I'll try to learn the lines tonight,' I promised.

Lil

Considering I hadn't even met Sam a few weeks ago, we settled into a routine of walking to and from school together with an ease I could never have anticipated. It was our time to tell each other silly stories, anecdotes, or share useless information. Sam was particularly talented at impressions, and made me laugh with his impersonations of different teachers on the way home. He had met all of his classes and I thought he was incredibly chilled out, given that he was transferring to a new school at a really bad time, academically speaking. He just seemed to take it all in his stride.

After our conversation about university, he looked up an Ecology degree at Plymouth.

'I always wanted to be by the sea,' he said.

Plus, it would only be a short journey to Exeter… I wondered if that was a factor at all.

'How about we go to check it out together?' I suggested. 'I can ask my mum to borrow her car.'

'You can drive?' he asked, impressed.

'My dad's a driving instructor,' I told him.

'Wow,' he said. 'That's another thing on my to-do list. Along with getting a job to pay for driving lessons.'

'I work at the library on Saturdays. The café next door has a sign up for part time staff.'

'You know, you're starting to put my PA out of a job.'

Thankfully, the summer weather was stretching out and it hadn't rained on our walks. We headed to the fields after school, and I felt a tingling excitement about rehearsing for the audition together. We dumped our blazers and our bags, and I pulled out my script.

'What's this?' Sam pulled at it playfully. 'Haven't you learnt your lines yet?'

'You're not telling me you have.'

'I'm a fast learner,' he said.

I rolled my eyes.

'Shall we do a read-through first before we block it?'

'All right, you can test me to see how much I remember.'

We went through it. He faltered a couple of times, but he knew most of the lines.

'I'm impressed.'

'I think you should ditch the script,' he said, trying to snatch it out of my hand.

'But what if I get it wrong?'

'Improvise!'

'This is one of the most famous scenes in history. You can't just make it up!'

'Come on,' he said, stepping back and gesturing. 'Take it from the top.'

'*By whose direction found'st thou out this place?*' I began.

'*By love, that first did prompt me to inquire,*' he returned.

He walked back and forth, spacing around me as if I were on a balcony, and then we talked about using a desk or some chairs to create height for the audition.

'I think I should climb closer to you, so that by the end, we're practically on the same level,' he said.

'How are you going to do that?'

'Maybe I could make a joke out of it. Use some chairs. I just think that line *wilt thou leave me so unsatisfied?* would be more powerful if our faces were, like, *this* close and then Juliet pulls away.'

He leaned in close enough that I could smell his skin. My eyes were turning black and I couldn't concentrate on anything else.

'What do you think?' he said softly, his face still inches from mine.

'Sure,' I squeaked, blushing and taking a step back to compose myself.

It was just for the play, right?

Sam

'You seem so happy at your new school,' my mum said, lifting the pan of potatoes to drain them over the sink.

Annabelle took the opportunity while her back was turned to flutter her eyelashes and mouth 'Lil', puckering her lips. I gave her a death stare in response.

'I'm so glad this move has worked out well for everyone,' Mum continued, clattering with the saucepans at the hob. 'Annabelle, lay the table, please. Sam, get the drinks.'

'I have a job interview tomorrow at the café in town,' I told her. 'I'm hoping to start on Saturday, if I get it.'

'As long as you make time for studying, too,' Mum warned. 'I don't know where you've been half the time this week.'

'Mum, can I invite Darcy over?' Annabelle asked.

'Sure,' she said. 'Hey, she can join us for soaps on Friday if she wants?'

'Uh, I was thinking we could hang out... on our own,' Annabelle said.

I concentrated on filling up the glasses.

'Well, as long as you remember to—'

'Take my medicine,' Annabelle finished, with a sigh. 'Mum, we've been through this. I'm not a child anymore.'

'Technically, you are. You're under eighteen. You're not even sixteen yet.'

'I would like to think that you trust me enough to start acting like a normal teenager.'

'It's not that I don't trust you,' Mum began, 'it's just that I don't trust other people to look after you like I can.'

'Mum, you'll still be here if she needs you,' I pointed out, not able to resist chipping in. 'No offence, but you don't have to be a doctor to take meds. Diabetics have to inject insulin—at least she doesn't have to do any of that.'

'No, she just has to go to hospital every time she gets ill,' Mum snaps. 'You have no idea what it's like—'

'I've lived in this family for seventeen years,' I frowned. 'Of course I know what it's like.'

'I don't want to be a burden,' Annabelle said, cutting in. 'To any of you. I want to start looking after myself more. And Mum, it was your anniversary last week. Why don't you and Dad go out on a date?'

'What's this?'

Dad walked into the kitchen at that moment, and an awkward silence fell. Mum looked on the verge of an anxiety attack just at the *thought* of going out and leaving Annabelle behind. Annabelle sighed and set the table.

'What were you talking about?' Dad asked me, suspiciously.

Great—the dating radar was sounding.

'Annabelle suggested that you and Mum could go out to celebrate your anniversary,' I explained.

Dad's face softened.

'Mer, we could,' he said, taking a step towards her.

'I'll think about it,' Mum said, in a tone that shut down the conversation.

Later, I was drying dishes with Annabelle, and we heard raised voices coming from the lounge. I kicked the kitchen door shut.

'If their marriage fails, it'll all be my fault,' Annabelle said glumly.

'What?'

I tossed the tea towel to one side, and gave her a bear hug.

'Listen, you can't control their choices. That's on them.'

'I've ruined their lives,' she said, in a matter-of-fact way.

'How could you even think that?' I shook my head.

'And I don't even *have* a life,' she continued.

'Your heart's still beating, isn't it?'

'You know what I mean,' she said.

She sank down onto one of the kitchen chairs and sighed.

'You get to go to school, make friends, get a job… and I'm just stuck here, watching from the sidelines.'

'You *are* younger than me,' I pointed out. 'I wasn't doing much when I was your age.'

'When are you going to tell them about Lil?' she asked, looking directly into my eyes.

I shrugged.

'Dad already guessed that I like her.'

'And I bet he told you not to ask her out until you're twenty-one.'

'You know what Dad's like.'

She shook her head slowly.

'Want to know what I think?' she said.

I gave a nod.

'Life is short,' she said. 'Life is hard. If you find someone who makes you happy, then don't wait. You should be together.'

'When did you get so philosophical?' I teased.

'When I nearly died.'

I give her another bear hug. That was a close call, about two years ago.

'I mean it, Sam,' she said, giving me a squeeze and then letting go. 'You can't control their choices, but you can control yours.'

Lil

In many ways, Sam was a golden boy. Things just seemed to fall into place for him, without much effort on his part at all. He got the job at the café, and started the next day. It was fairly certain that he was going to land a major role in the play… and I hoped it would be the two of us as Romeo and Juliet. He'd never even done much acting before. He'd decided he liked me (or so I thought, anyway), and we'd pretty much immediately started doing everything together. I still didn't have much clarity on what we were. I'd been reading the anti-dating book, and he hadn't asked me out officially, but we spent a lot of time alone together. The way he looked at me was definitely more than just friends.

There were unspoken rules. We generally didn't hold hands, unless he was helping me over a stile or something similar. We didn't go inside each other's houses; we hung out in the fields or the treehouse. We didn't kiss.

Maybe if we got the lead roles, then he'd *have* to kiss me.

On Sunday, he met me in the church entrance and sat with me for the service. He could sing. His dad spoke about the book of James and the need to ask God for wisdom. I thought about our futures, mapping out like wires crossing in a telegraph box. Anything could happen, but what if our pathways were tied together? Could we choose that?

After the final hymn, he said,

'Let's go.'

We rushed out before his father reached the door, and climbed into my mum's car.

Living in a sleepy Somerset village, we had to drive along a windy road before hitting the main carriageway. My worship songs playlist was blaring out '10000 reasons' by Matt Redman, and we both started singing along. I'd sung along to it so many times, but now there was another voice joining with mine. It gave me a thrill to look across and see Sam, sitting right next to me. Was the barbecue just a week ago? It felt like we'd crossed an unimaginable distance in that time. I felt a rush of gratitude for this moment.

Sam fed me bits of my packed lunch, passed me water at regular intervals, and asked me what I thought of the anti-dating book.

'I think there's some good points in it,' I said, taking a bite of my sandwich. 'If Christians act like everyone else when it comes to dating, then we're not showing that God's way is better. But to me, there has to be some middle ground between casual dating and then basically going from friendship to engagement at the other extreme.'

'What would the middle ground look like?' Sam asked, his eyes trained on me as I took the exit off the main road.

'Dating someone with serious intentions, not just playing around with them,' I answered, feeling my cheeks tinge with a blush. 'Respecting physical boundaries. Honouring God and the other person in the way that you treat them. Being honest about your feelings.'

'Have you ever dated someone like that before?' he asked, his voice huskier than usual.

'No,' I said, looking sideways at him.

We sat in silence for a few minutes. I waited for him to say something, until I lost patience.

'Well?' I prompted.

'I don't know if I'd be very good at it,' he said finally.

'Why?' I pressed.

'I might hurt your feelings in some way,' he answered, in a way that made me think that wasn't the real reason.

We'd crossed some distance, but there were obviously things which one week wasn't enough to reveal. I rolled my eyes, wanting to point out that he could hurt my feelings whether he called himself my boyfriend or not, but I let it go. We were arriving at Plymouth.

Sam

Plymouth was sunny, and walking around with Lil was a blissful escape from our usual reality of school, parents and homework. In front of the lighthouse, I took a selfie of the two of us and immediately set it as my new home screen on my phone. Lil raised her eyebrows but smiled.

The trip confirmed what I needed to know: it was close enough without being too close, it was right by the sea, and it wasn't a packed-out city like Bristol or Birmingham. It was also an easy distance from Exeter, where Lil was planning to go for the next three years.

Three years. As much as I agreed with what Lil said about dating in a serious way, three years did sound like a horribly long time for a relationship to be conducted in the kind of emotional limbo of high passion but no way of progressing to marriage. Looking at the golden sunlight glinting on Lil's hair, I already felt that magnetic pull towards her, wanting to be closer... wanting to be one with her completely. If I dropped my guard, if I lost grip on my self control, then in one fell swoop, I might disregard her boundaries, and do something stupid that would break our relationship forever.

The stakes felt too high.

On the journey home, I leaned my head back against the head rest, closed my eyes, and prayed, while Lil sang along softly to 'Blessed Be Your Name'.

Lord, what should I do?

Lil

When we arrived back, we got out of the car and stood facing each other on the pavement. Sam looked at me with a new, agonised expression. I instinctively opened my arms to him for a hug. He hesitated, and then stepped forward, crushing my body against his for a long moment. Then it was over. He released me, and said,

'Thanks for driving.'

The next day was the audition. We'd gone over the scene so often I could say it in my sleep (and I probably did). It was strange, performing it together with an audience this time. Miss Raine applauded loudly at the end and thanked us with a huge smile on her face.

It wasn't hard pretending to be star-crossed lovers.

We walked home, buzzing from how it went, but part of me felt sad that we weren't going to the fields to practise anymore. It was probably for the best. Now that the first week was over, all the teachers were piling on the homework. The next day, it rained. Sam called for me in the morning, holding a massive golf umbrella. I rolled my eyes but I enjoyed huddling under it with him. I wondered at what point the weather would get so bad (or cold) that we would finally cave and get the bus instead.

The cast list was pinned up on the board at break time. We got the leads! Sam shouted and punched the air with excitement, then swung me around in his arms. I laughed, despite the dirty looks some of the girls gave me. Perhaps they felt they would have been more likely to get Juliet if they had auditioned with Sam.

Now things were really going to get busy. With studying, play rehearsals, working and church, our free time evaporated. At least some of those activities were together. We had a long, ongoing text chat and we kept up the walks to and from school. Sam called it his 'decompression time'. I felt privileged that he was willing to share it with me.

The dating thing didn't get mentioned again. So we were friends, but a bit more than friends, without the official title of being in a relationship. Maybe visiting Plymouth had brought it home to Sam that we were going to be spending three years apart, even though the holidays were long and it would be easy enough to visit on weekends. To me, it wasn't an issue. But I didn't want to make things weird between us. I didn't want to ask for more than he felt comfortable to give. So I settled for being Sam's non-girlfriend girlfriend. I didn't want to give him up, so I let him draw the lines of our relationship. We both knew that's what it was.

Lil

Religious Studies was never my favourite lesson compared to English or Drama, but with Sam in the class, the dynamic had definitely shifted. Mr Jones, the teacher, didn't follow any particular religion himself, and encouraged lively debate. I had been the only Christian in the class, until Sam joined. We sat together and he shared my highlighters.

'In church history, the question of whether man has free will has been a hotly debated topic,' Mr Jones said. 'Does God choose some to be saved, and some to be damned? Does he know everything, and also control everything? Do humans have freedom to choose faith? What does everyone think?'

A few students shrugged. For those who didn't have much certainty about God, it was a bit of a moot point.

'Sam, what about you?' Mr Jones asked.

I looked at him as he replaced the lid on his pen and set it down on the table.

'You make it sound like the free will of man and the sovereignty of God are polar opposites,' Sam said. 'What if they are both true and necessary: a paradox?'

'Excellent,' Mr Jones said, impressed. 'Yin and yang both need the other in order to exist.'

'Well, I don't think God needs us to exist,' Sam disputed. 'However, love by definition cannot be forced or controlled. As soon as it is, it is no longer love. If God is love, and wants us to love Him, then we have to be free to make that choice. Even though it's impossible for us to love God without Him loving us first.'

'We could draw a parallel to that,' Mr Jones said, 'if we consider the cultural custom of arranged marriage. Many would argue that after making the choice of the partner, they are then free to love that person. Love follows the choice they have made. Love is a choice.'

'I thought love was a feeling.' A girl, Sarah Hook, spoke up.

'It's a very powerful emotion,' Mr Jones agreed. 'But it can be steered. For example, did anyone have a holiday romance over the summer?'

No one raised their hand.

'Well, I'm sure you can relate. You might go away and meet someone, have a nice time with them, but after you come home, you lose touch pretty quickly, because you never see each other. Your choices lead, and your feelings and emotions follow.'

People must have looked non-plussed, as Mr Jones tried again.

'Or the other way round, when you like someone, you spend more and more time with them. Your feelings for them grow, because you feed them. It's the same with parents and their children. The more time they spend together, the more they can bond, and the stronger their relationship.'

I felt Sam's eyes on me, and I blushed and looked down into my pencil case. It wasn't surprising that we'd developed feelings for each other, given the amount of time we'd spent together. It had been particularly intense, but things were settling down now.

'For homework, I'd like you to research what John Calvin believed, and then we can discuss it next lesson,' Mr Jones said.

'Meet me in the treehouse later so we can do it together?' Sam asked, as we cleared the desk.

I blinked.

'The homework, I mean,' he said, his face flushing.

'Sure,' I said.

I needed to get my brain back into gear.

Sam

'So what you're saying is that God's will always happens,' Lil said, looking over at one of my dad's books that I held open for us both to share. It had nothing to do with wanting her closer to me.

'In terms of salvation,' I corrected. 'Calvin argued that God's grace is irresistible.'

'But people don't always do what God wants them to do. Look at Jonah. He ran away instead of going to Nineveh where God told him to go.'

Lil's hair brushed my arms and it smelled of coconut. She looked at me, expecting a response, so I tried to shake myself out of my trance.

'Yes, but God intervened by getting the fish to swallow him up. Then when Jonah got back to dry land, he did go to Nineveh.'

'He did things the hard way, right?' Lil laughed, then pulled at her sock to adjust it over her ankle. 'I can relate to that.'

'Me too,' I grinned.

'Really?' Lil raised an eyebrow skeptically. 'Pastor's kid? What's the worst thing you've ever done?'

I looked at her eyes, sparkling with this challenge, and contemplated answering honestly. Of not being afraid to break her perception of me as some great Christian guy. But I chickened out.

'Not saying.' I shook my head.

'Oh, it must be *really* bad, then,' she joked. 'I bet you've never even been to a party.'

'Speaking of which,' I said, jumping on the opportunity, 'shall we go to the social on Thursday?'

'You want to go?' Lil eyed me, frowning. 'Why? Everyone just gets drunk.'

'We don't have to drink anything.'

'So why go, then?'

'I don't know.' I shrugged. 'It might be a good way of getting to know people a bit better.'

'They'll spill all their secrets and won't remember any of it the next day.'

'Doesn't part of you want to go and dance?' I dangled the carrot deliberately. Girls seemed to love dancing.

'It's just not a great atmosphere.' She sighed. 'If you really want to go, then I'll drive us.'

'Thank you,' I said.

'Now you have to answer my question about the worst thing you've ever done,' she said, grinning.

'Nope,' I argued. 'But you're forgetting something about sin. You don't have to go anywhere in particular to do it. It's in here.' I pointed to my head. 'And in here.' I pointed to my heart.

Lil's eyes turned serious, and she placed her hand over mine, while it was still on my heart. I could feel the Calvin book slipping out of my left hand, but I did nothing to stop it. I swallowed.

'You don't need to hide, Sam,' she said.

I took her hand and stretched out our palms in the air.

'*Palm to palm is holy palmers' kiss*,' I whispered.

'That's my line!' she giggled. 'Are you suggesting that we rehearse that part?'

'*If I profane with my unworthiest hand/ This holy shrine, the gentle sin is this:/ My lips, two blushing pilgrims, ready stand/ To smooth that rough touch with a tender kiss.*' I memorised the words and I'd thought of little else. Speaking them to Lil felt magical, somehow. The solar lights wound around the tree came on, as the day was waning, and the sky had the grey edge of twilight.

'*Good pilgrim, you do wrong your hand too much,/ Which mannerly devotion shows in this;/ For saints have hands that pilgrims' hands do touch,/ And palm to palm is holy palmers' kiss.*' Lil didn't break eye contact with me the whole time. My hand tingled from her touch.

'Can I kiss you, Lil?' I managed to stutter, my voice husky. My next line had gone completely out of my head and all I could think about was the action Romeo was meant to take... the exact same action I wanted to take.

'Yes,' she said, and her voice disappeared too.

I slowly lowered my hand, still holding hers, and brushed her cheek with my left hand. We were leaning in close to one another now, and I could smell her perfume as well as her shampoo, some kind of vanilla musk. I could see tiny freckles on her face. She was so beautiful.

It was the first time I ever kissed a girl, and the world tilted on its axis as I closed the distance between us and our lips finally met.

She was soft, and I was tentative because I was worried that she was fragile like porcelain, but as her lips moved against mine, the sensation took over.

Fear was replaced with need.

I ran my hand over her silken hair, from her ear down to her shoulder. Quicksilver. Mercury that could explode at any moment, *like fire and powder, Which as they kiss consume...*

Can a man scoop fire into his lap without his clothes being burned?

Remembering the proverb, my eyes snapped open.

'Are you all right, Sam?' Lil asked, stroking my cheek.

Now that I'd kissed her, my life was never going to be the same again.

Lil

It was a sweet relief that he'd finally kissed me, but Sam was looking guilty. I pulled away and tried to read his expression more clearly. Did he like the kiss? I was pretty sure that he did. It was the sort of kiss like drinking cool lemonade on a hot day: utterly addictive. One sip was never going to be enough.

'I guess it was better to do that here first, before we're in rehearsals with everyone watching,' Sam joked.

'Was that just a practice run, then?' I grinned.

'I'm going to have to figure out a way of doing that and being able to speak my lines,' he said.

'I'm beginning to think you've memorised the entire play,' I said.

'I listen to the audio version before I go to sleep,' he told me. 'Speaking of which, it's getting late.'

He rescued the abandoned Calvin book, and packed it into his bag.

'I'm excited for the party,' he said.

I wished I could have said the same.

Sixth Form Socials were notorious. They were organised every few months, in various grubby bars or social clubs. Yes, some of the students would be eighteen, but a significant number wouldn't. And everyone knew that those with ID would buy drinks for the younger ones. It was just a drinking fest and it wasn't much fun if everyone was throwing up in the toilet or kissing someone's face off.

I parked up outside the club, and hoped my car would still be in one piece when we returned to it. I stood up and pulled my dress down nervously. It was a little too high on my thighs for my liking. Sam bounced around to my side of the car with obvious excitement. He took my hand and led me to the door.

Inside, it was carnage.

It was only 8 p.m., but clearly most people had been drinking ever since school finished. The thudding music through the speakers was not as loud as a proper nightclub, but they were clearly trying their best to rival one.

'There's some guys from Biology.' Sam pointed to a group near the bar, and pulled me towards them.

I knew them in a vague way, but I'd never spoken to any of them much.

'Hey Cole,' I said.

'Hey.' He shifted over to make space for me. 'You're friends with Shannon, right?'

I nodded. Everyone knew Shannon. She was a fantastic singer and always the life and soul of the party.

'Do you think she might be interested in going out with me?' he asked.

'Uh, I'm not sure,' I stalled. I didn't think it was likely, but stranger things have happened. Scratch that—*anything* could happen at a social.

'Woooo!'

A pair of arms slung around my shoulder, and Beth pressed her cheek against mine. She smelled of cheap cider.

'Lil!' she said. 'You'rrrre out with us! Ready to party?'

'I got Owen to buy us some shots,' Clare said.

Owen was following in her wake with a silver platter and neat little glasses. In a surreal moment, I thought how similar they were to the wine cups used for communion in church. From the sacred to the profane… If Calvin were here, what would he think of me?

'Take one, Lil,' Shannon urged.

'I'm good,' I said, shaking my head.

'You have it, Sam,' she said.

I was about to open my mouth to tell her to leave him alone, when he said,

'Okay.'

He shrugged, picked it up and knocked it back, then made a face.

'What was that?'

The girls laughed hysterically.

'Parma violets gin.'

I rolled my eyes.

'Tastes like toilet cleaner,' Sam said, sipping some of my lemonade.

'It's a bit more expensive than that,' I commented.

We moved away from the bar, and Sam leaned against the wall, pulling me against him.

'Lean back,' he said, turning me to face the same direction as him.

I shifted my weight and tried to relax into his arms. It did feel good to be held by him, like a real boyfriend would, but I wished we were anywhere but here.

'I was hoping we could dance,' he said, his mouth grazing my ear. 'But this isn't really the right kind of music.'

'They're not going to play actual songs, with a beat,' I said, turning my face up to his. 'Just this pneumatic drill stuff.'

He was resting his head on mine, and when I turned, I was practically speaking against his throat. He swallowed, and his grip tightened around me.

Whether he was going to speak to me, I don't know, but I didn't move away. The next moment, we were kissing.

This didn't feel tentative, like before. It felt strong, urgent, like we were running out of time.

I twisted to face him properly and brought my hands up to touch his face, his jaw. He made a sound in his throat that I couldn't hear with the thumping bass, but I felt the vibration with my hand. It made my stomach flip. When he opened his eyes, he held my gaze with fiery intensity.

'Lil.'

He breathed my name, and it was as if we were completely alone.

If the book he lent me had rules about (not) dating and relationships, I was pretty sure we'd broken them now.

Sam

I wasn't drunk, but that shot must have gone to my head. I was dizzy and intoxicated… with Lil. How could one inch of gin do that? It must have been hormones, a rush of dopamine… Suddenly the textbook was becoming real.

I just couldn't get enough of Lil.

One kiss had turned into another, then another, and I was vaguely aware that I'd become the stereotype of the "snogger", but I didn't care. Lil and I had spent most of our time walking, or cramped in the treehouse, and in this dark bar I was finally showing her how I felt.

I was ignoring the little voice in my head, telling me that I should be careful not to get carried away. I felt like I'd lived my whole life suppressing my emotions, and now I was finally allowing them to show.

When I'd been rehearsing Romeo's early scenes, what had most struck me was Romeo's articulation of his feelings. Okay, he was a bit cliched and reliant on well-worn tropes, but he was a guy who knew how he felt and owned it. What was I? A pastor's kid who had never felt anything stronger than mild admiration for a girl. My entire emotional range could be summed up in three emojis. I was the epitome of even keel, because I had to be; my mum was up and down like a yoyo with my sister's illness, and my dad didn't need the extra stress of my emotions. Then there was the book he gave me. Essentially, its message was: Lock Up Your Heart. Now I'd met Lil, and she was offering me her heart, how could I keep my own barred? It was time to finally love someone. It was time to live!

Sure, the social wasn't the most romantic of environments. But it was an opportunity to be away from our parents, and I wanted to make the most of it.

The party definitely became rowdier as the night went on, and the drinking continued. Lil went to check on her friend in the toilets, and was gone long enough for me to start worrying that something had happened to her, but she came back looking annoyed.

'Beth's just thrown up,' she said. 'I offered to take her home, but she's refusing. Said she wants to stay.'

She shook her head and sighed.

'Shannon's kissed two different boys and is now trying to keep them apart so they don't find out about each other.'

'If one of them is Cole, then you might want to look over there.'

She followed my direction and we watched as Cole sized up to Lee, while Shannon stood in between them and tried to push them further apart.

'If they start fighting, they're going to get kicked out,' she said.

She sounded resigned, like she'd seen all this before. I suddenly felt bad for practically forcing her to bring me here.

'You want to get out of here?' I asked her.

She looked at me with instant hope.

'Really? You don't mind?'

I shook my head and squeezed her hand.

'I just want to be with you.'

That was the problem, really. I was already obsessed with her before we kissed, but after that... And I know she felt the same. Something flashed in her eyes as she looked at me. I knew, even as we walked to her car together, that a stick of dynamite had been lit.

I wasn't thinking of the destruction it might cause.

I pulled her close for a long kiss before we got in the car. She was slightly breathless as she started the engine, and I rested my hand on her thigh. Her dress had moved higher up her leg, and I couldn't resist the temptation to stroke her smooth skin. She gasped.

'How am I supposed to drive when you're doing that?'

I held my hands up in mock surrender, and she pulled out of the car park.

'You're staring at me,' she said, flicking a glance towards me and curling her lip in a sexy smile. I couldn't wait to kiss her again.

'That's because you're gorgeous.'

She laughed and shook her head, then changed gear. Her dress hitched momentarily. Watching her drive was incredibly arousing.

'You look like you want to eat me,' she said, lifting an eyebrow.

'I think you'd taste like chocolate,' I told her.

'Hopefully not the cheap, sickly kind,' she said.

'Oh, definitely not,' I said. 'Minimum, Galaxy.'

'Galaxy?' she repeated. 'I was hoping for at least something upmarket. Like a box of expensive truffles or something.'

'The ones with chocolate powder around the outside?'

'No, the ones with silky goo in the middle.' She made a small moan, then looked over to see what effect she had on me.

'You did that deliberately!' I laughed.

She laughed back.

'I'm going to get revenge,' I said. 'But you'll have to find somewhere to pull over.'

She gave me a coy look and then pulled her skirt up a little higher.

'I guess I can try to find somewhere,' she said, teasing me.

She turned down a few side streets, and finally pulled up in a part of the road where there weren't any cars, next to a darkened building. I was wild by this point and kissed her desperately, guiding her over the gearstick until she was straddling me. Her dress was stretched tight over her backside—I knew, because I was running my hands over it. I kissed her neck, and she moaned, properly this time. It nearly undid me.

'Sam,' she gasped, and I kept kissing her because the sound of my name on her lips was the best thing I'd ever heard. 'Sam!'

She gently placed her hands on my cheeks, and pulled my face up to hers.

'I'm getting mixed messages again,' she said.

I was struggling to breathe and collect any rational thought together.

'What?'

She moved off my lap back into the driver's seat, and pulled her dress back to its normal length.

'You gave me a book about not dating and now you want to kiss me in a car, at night, when we're alone?'

'Presumably you wouldn't want me to do that if there was someone in the back seat,' I joked.

'Ha ha,' she said. 'I'm serious, Sam. What's going on with you? We barely held hands and now we're... Well, I don't even know what we're doing.'

Her words pierced my heart, and I started to feel the sinking weight of guilt again.

'I'm sorry,' I said. 'I got carried away.'

I sighed and ran my fingers through my hair, tousling it.

'I just wanted to live a little. I feel like I've been stifled all my life.'

She didn't speak for a few moments, just looked at me and shook her head.

'Sam, you need to realise that feeding the pigs is just that: feeding the pigs. Your parents haven't withheld something good from you. Nor has God. I grew up being allowed to do many things which I realise now are wrong and empty.'

She gestured with her hand, and I was so lovestruck, I even thought about how much I wanted to kiss her wrist.

'I grew up always being told "no",' I said. 'For once, can't I have something I want?'

'That's the problem,' she said, her voice laced with frustration. 'You don't know what you want.'

'I want you,' I said.

'So, are we going out, then?' she asked. 'Am I your girlfriend? Because I'm a bit tired of being a friend who you kiss when you feel like it.'

'You think I'm using you?' I asked, horrified at the thought.

'Your intentions are not very clear.'

It was like a bucket of cold water over me, but I knew she was right. I had been taking the moral high ground, and because of my contradictory actions, that was worse than just having the courage to be her boyfriend.

Plus, I was a total hypocrite.

'I'm sorry, Lil,' I said, cupping my hands over my face. I couldn't cover the fact that my cheeks were burning. 'You deserve so much better than this.'

'Hey,' she said gently, taking one of my hands away from my face and holding it. 'I like you. I'm sorry for getting carried away too. I just… want to figure out how to do this the right way. I don't like the idea of sneaking around and being one person in church, then someone else at a party… God has my whole life, and my whole heart, not just pieces.'

I wished, I honestly wished, that I could say the same, but I knew that I couldn't. Lil was looking at me like she could read my silence.

'Sam?' she said. 'Next year, when you go to uni, you won't be the pastor's son anymore. No one will know who you are. If these things aren't real for you, then when you're on your own, they'll disappear. You can go out and get drunk and kiss girls and no one's going to know… But God will. So, are you going to keep pushing Him away, or are you going to get serious and own your faith for yourself?'

All I felt was guilt; I didn't appreciate the invitation of grace.

'Are you saying my faith's not good enough, just because I'm not as confident as you?' I said. I hated myself for saying it.

'No,' she said. 'But please tell me that you see what happened tonight for what it is. A ton of kids messed around drinking too much, and we weren't really any better than them.'

'We didn't get drunk,' I said, pointlessly.

'What were you planning to do if I didn't stop you?' she said. 'Because I don't want to lose my virginity in a car and get pregnant by a pastor's son who won't even call me his girlfriend because "dating is wrong".'

I closed my eyes, wincing. Truth hurts.

'Lil, I'm sorry,' I said again.

'You still haven't answered my question,' she said, her tone sharpening.

'Which one?'

'About whether I'm your girlfriend or not.'

Her voice was raised and I looked at her in misery.

'I don't know how to…' I trailed off, hopelessly, gesturing between us. 'I mean, I don't know how to do this, how to be us, without it going wrong. I don't trust myself.'

'Well that makes two of us.'

She turned away and looked out of the window onto the deserted street. Light from a few windows made warm yellow squares in the shadowy houses.

'Maybe we should just be friends,' I said, and at the same time, she said,

'We can't go back to being friends.'

We stared at each other. I swallowed.

'Why?' I asked.

'Because we're playing Romeo and Juliet together!' she shouted, hitting the steering wheel for emphasis. She groaned into her hands in frustration. 'Argh, why are you so dense?'

'I've never done this before!' I said, starting to feel annoyed too. 'They don't give you a handbook and say, *here's how to be a good Christian boyfriend*—they just tell you not to look at a girl until you're twenty-five and able to propose.'

'What am I supposed to do, then?' she asked, losing some of her anger and sounding helpless.

I reached out and touched her cheek.

'You just keep being beautiful,' I told her. 'I need to get my head straight. Can you give me some time to think, and then we'll talk?'

She nodded, and restarted the car. We drove home in silence.

Lil

A week after the social, it was my eighteenth birthday, and I was hosting a party in my back yard. I'd not had much time alone with Sam, because the rain had set in. Classic pathetic fallacy. I sat on my bed, crying as the raindrops incessantly pelted my window, and alternated between remembering the way he had kissed me, and the way he was completely messed up.

When I saw him in church, he looked pale, like he wasn't getting enough sleep. He came to sit next to me.

'How many times should I say sorry to you?' he asked softly. 'Do you think after a hundred, you might be able to forgive me?'

'I've already forgiven you,' I told him. 'Grace, remember?'

He gave a small grin at that.

'How are you doing?' I asked him.

I wanted to hug him, but I didn't know if that was the right thing to do.

'I've been doing a lot of thinking,' he said. 'You gave me a lot to think about.'

And that was all I'd got out of him. Because of the rain, we'd taken the bus to school, and you can't have a heart to heart when you're squished up with too many people in a confined space.

I was worried I'd have to cancel my party, but on the day, the sky was finally clear. It was a cold, crisp morning, and the trees were brilliant in all their red and gold glory.

'Happy birthday,' Sam said, calling for me to walk to school.

He gave me a hug, and I held on to him perhaps more tightly than necessary. He felt so warm.

'I've missed you,' I breathed.

'I've missed you too,' he said. 'Is it okay if I give you your present later?'

'You didn't have to get me anything,' I said.

'But I know how much you like gifts,' he said, waggling his eyebrows.

I smiled. It was getting easier again between us, and I liked it.

After school, we were rehearsing the Capulet ball on the stage. Miss Raine was directing from the floor, holding a clipboard, while the other Capulets were positioned in twos and threes. I stood near the front of the stage. Sam looked at me, took my hand in his, and never once broke eye contact.

'If I profane with my unworthiest hand/ This holy shrine, the gentle sin is this: / My lips, two blushing pilgrims, ready stand / To smooth that rough touch with a tender kiss.'

It was like starting again. His eyes were questioning: *is this okay? Can I kiss you?* I gave him a tentative, shy smile.

'Good pilgrim, you do wrong your hand too much, / Which mannerly devotion shows in this; / For saints have hands that pilgrims' hands do touch, / And palm to palm is holy palmers' kiss.'

He mirrored my smile, and when it came to the moment, he hesitated for a fraction of a second before pressing his lips to mine. It was brief, and chaste, but the cast whooped anyway. He broke away, giving an embarrassed grin, and I laughed.

'Perfect!' Miss Raine cried.

We walked home, crunching crisp leaves under our feet, and the ground was sodden and damp after so much rain. The sun was visible, but the air felt cold. I'd pulled a scarf out of the cupboard this morning and I wound it tightly around my neck.

'Can I hold your hand?' Sam asked me, holding his own, palm up, to me.

I blushed and smiled, placing my hand in his.

'You don't need to ask,' I said.

'After what happened, I think I do,' he said seriously.

I squeezed his hand.

'You want to talk about it?'

'Okay,' he nodded. 'I don't have much to say, other than: everything you said was right, and everything I did was wrong. I'm sorry. Please forgive me.'

'That's, like, the third time you've apologised,' I said.

'Well, sometimes it feels like words aren't enough,' he said. 'That reminds me…'

He stopped, and placed his bag on a bench. We were by the canal, and there was no one there except the ducks on the water.

'This is for you.'

He drew out a present, and handed it to me. It was wrapped in beautiful jade paper.

'Thank you,' I said, unwrapping it.

It was a hardcover edition of *Romeo and Juliet* , with gold embossed text on the front. Inside, he'd written

To Lil. Will you be my Juliet? Love, Sam. My eyes widened and I looked up at him. He held out his hand.

'Will you give me another chance?' he asked. 'Will you be my girlfriend?'

Grinning and barely suppressing a squeal, I threw my arms around his neck and hugged him as tightly as I could. He stepped back in surprise, then his arms folded around me. In that moment in his arms, I felt warm and totally safe. It was a feeling I wanted to bottle up and experience whenever I felt doubtful or unsure. As much as I was looking forward to going off to uni and for my life to begin, I was already feeling twinges of sadness and homesickness, and I hadn't even left yet. It was just the thought of *Romeo and Juliet* being my last school show, of this being my last September in school, my last birthday party with my school friends… Everyone talks about eighteen as a beginning, but it's also an ending too. The ending of your childhood.

'I'm sorry that I didn't ask you sooner,' Sam said, pulling back and looking at me apologetically. 'I should have shown more courage and thought more about your feelings. I'm so scared about getting this wrong, and I already have.'

He took my hand and we started walking again, and I enjoyed nestling close to him when I had the chance.

'So I had a couple of thoughts,' he continued. 'I won't kiss you indoors, or in a car, or somewhere where things might get out of hand. If I mess up, you can pick someone and I have to go and tell them about it.'

'Your dad,' I said immediately. The ultimate deterrent.

He winced.

'Okay. I'll be super motivated to pray for self control.'

'I need that too,' I told him. 'Only, let's not forget that rules don't stop you from sinning in your heart. I don't think any of those ideas are bad, but honouring God is more than just do's and don'ts. If we're just trying harder all the time, we've missed the point. The Holy Spirit makes us holy, not our own efforts. Which, let's face it, are pretty rubbish.'

'I just know I need to take this more seriously,' he said.

I looked across at him, and it felt like there was more he wasn't telling me. I guessed that being a guy, this wasn't a new problem for him, but I couldn't force him to open up about that. I was still worried that Sam was depending way too much on his own effort, because he hadn't really got real with God and understood grace. Again, I couldn't force that. I was willing to be with him and I hoped that at some point, things would click into place for him. It still felt like God had sent him into my life at just this moment for a reason. Amidst all the uncertainty about the future, if I had Sam, I knew we could face it together.

Sam

When we got to Lil's house, I didn't even bother going home. I helped her to set up for the party, and her parents were busy preparing food. With her speaker on the window sill, she blasted out her favourite songs, and we hung fairy lights across the yard. I lit the fire in the fire pit, and Lil spread out candles on every surface. It looked magical.

Lil hurried off to get changed, and I popped home to throw on a nice shirt and jeans. Annabelle caught me putting on cologne in the bathroom.

'Making an effort for your girlfriend?' she teased.

'Yes,' I said simply.

Her eyebrows shot up.

'So you've made it official now?'

'As of this afternoon,' I replied.

'That's awesome!'

Annabelle gave me a quick hug, and then rushed down the stairs.

'Mum! Guess what?'

I rolled my eyes and sighed, waiting for the bomb to drop. They were all coming next door to the party. Better get this part over with.

Adjusting my collar, I walked down the stairs. In the hallway, Mum was looking up at me curiously with Annabelle hopping excitedly next to her.

'Is it true, Sam?' she asked. 'Is Lil your girlfriend now?'

'Yes,' I said, blushing. 'Can we go now?'

'Simon?' she called my dad.

It took a minute until he emerged from his study. He joined us in the hallway and looked from my red cheeks, to my mum's expression, and then to Annabelle.

'What's going on?' he asked.

'Nothing, we're just going to Lil's party,' I said.

I caught Annabelle's eye and she shook her head in disapproval.

'My *girlfriend's* party,' I added.

Annabelle grinned.

'Oh?' Dad asked, raising an eyebrow.

'Let's talk about it later,' Mum said, gesturing towards the door. 'I don't want to be late.'

'It's not like we can say we were stuck in traffic!' Annabelle joked.

'Have you got enough layers?' Mum asked her.

'I'm too old for you to ask me that, Mum,' Annabelle said, her smile fading as she grabbed her coat.

They left through the front door, and I caught Dad's eye as I picked up my coat.

'I know you're growing up,' he said, like he was about to launch into a speech.

I had just reached for the door handle, and I hesitated. There was a moment of silence.

'And?' I prompted.

'That's all I wanted to say,' he said.

Weird.

I opened the door and joined Mum and Annabelle as they entered Lil's house.

'That wasn't so bad, was it?' Annabelle whispered to me.

'Hmm,' I said noncommittally.

Thankfully, my role as fire-keeper kept me busy for most of the night, and my parents were drawn into conversation with Lil's family. Lil's girl group of friends were squealing and giggling around her all the time, and they kept pointing over at me, but Lil had also invited some of my friends from Biology. We ate hotdogs and toasted marshmallows, and Lil made a point of snuggling up next to me by the fire. The sky above was clear, so the stars came out, and the yard was warm and sparkling with all the lights.

'This is definitely my best-ever birthday,' Lil murmured, her head on my shoulder.

Cole snapped a pic of the two of us, and I quickly made it my lockscreen. From the misery of last week, life had somehow turned into something beautiful.

Christmas

Lil

Time seemed to speed up. The days grew shorter and shorter, and we were at school until it was dark, rehearsing for the play. We both sent off our uni applications, and by December, we already had offers through. I was on track for a place at Exeter, and Sam seemed happy with Plymouth. Even though the distance was easily doable by train, I still felt nervous at the idea of separation. Quite simply, because we'd become inseparable.

We'd already had our school routine of walking together in place, before we officially became a couple. We were spending a huge amount of time together and with the rest of the cast of the play, although naturally, we were the ones kissing and generally looking starry-eyed, rather than star-crossed, at each other. I drove us to town for our Saturday shifts, and then we'd usually go out afterwards. We often met Sam's Biology friends for food, and sometimes for Xbox nights. When she was interested in Cole again, Shannon would tag along (they were on-off like a light switch).

The treehouse quickly became too cold and damp to use anymore, and besides, there was no point hiding. Sam started hanging out at my house, and we would cook dinner together. My mum was stressed with work and wasn't getting home till late, and my dad was always busy in the evenings with driving lessons. We kept to our rule about not going upstairs, and not kissing when we were alone—mainly because Sam did not want to have an awkward conversation with his dad.

It seemed that Reverend Park had accepted our relationship status, perhaps in a resigned way rather than in jubilation. After several long and arduous conversations, Sam persuaded his parents that we weren't going to do anything stupid. Sam and I started helping out at the church kids club together, and Reverend Park seemed happy with this. I began chatting more with Annabelle, and she invited Darcy and me over for a movie. It turned out to be really fun, and after we'd done that a few times, Meredith finally agreed that she could come over to our house. She wouldn't stretch to going out herself, but at least it was progress.

'Dad's trying to persuade Mum to go with him to a Christmas meal for local church leaders,' Sam told me. 'I said we could have a movie night with Annabelle or something.'

'I bet she was thrilled at the prospect of being babysat.'

'I get why Mum doesn't want to leave her alone,' Sam said.

'Surely she's not going to stay at home forever?' I asked. From what I'd seen, Annabelle was keen to get out more and become more independent.

'She has to be so careful, especially in the winter,' he said. 'There are so many illnesses going around.'

I'd never really thought about it from that perspective. Anyway, it didn't hinder Annabelle's enjoyment of all things festive. She gathered greenery and wove some beautiful wreaths, hanging them all over the house, on the front door and in the windows.

'You should run a workshop for this at church,' I said, watching as she tied some bright red ribbon onto her latest creation.

'Really?' she asked, then blushed and shook her head. 'I could never do something like that.'

'Why not?' I said. 'These look amazing. I want to know how you do it.'

'It's easy,' she said, with a giggle. 'You just wrap a bunch of ivy around the metal ring.'

'I don't think I'd get the same results as you,' I said, shaking my head.

'She could start up her own business,' Reverend Park said, walking past us to put the kettle on with a grin.

He drank a lot of tea, and as neither Sam nor Annabelle really liked hot drinks, it was one thing we had in common. He told me I should call him Simon, but I was struggling to get used to it.

'One for you, Lil?' he asked, but he was already reaching for another mug.

I knew he wasn't over the moon about Sam and I dating, but he was never cold or judgy towards me. I didn't spend as much time in Sam's house as he did in mine, but gradually, I was becoming more comfortable there.

Although Meredith sometimes put me on edge.

She was lovely, absolutely lovely, and there were times when I caught a glimpse of who she was underneath her 'fretting mother' persona. Annabelle's creative crafting made a lot more sense when I found out that her mum was a brilliant artist. Sam saw me admiring a painting on the wall of Glastonbury Tor.

'Mum did that,' he said proudly.

I did a double take.

'Wow,' I said. 'She is really talented.'

The picture had a wintry feel to it, with slightly subdued colours and wispy brush strokes.

'We should go there,' Sam said, slipping his arms around me from behind. I loved it when he did that.

'Bit cold, isn't it?' I said. I knew that wouldn't put Sam off.

'I'll make you a flask of tea,' he said. 'And we can take some of Mum's mince pies.'

'After the play,' I said. It felt like everything was on hold until then.

There were times, when I went over Sam's house, when the atmosphere was strained. Usually, the tension centred around Annabelle wanting to do something, and Meredith saying no.

I knew Annabelle's health was fragile, but sometimes the things she wanted to do were so basic, things I took for granted, that I completely understood her frustration. Going to the library, a shop or a cinema were turned down immediately.

'Imagine how many hands have touched those books!'

'You'd have to sanitise your hands after touching every surface.'

'Such poor ventilation; I don't think it's a good idea.'

Annabelle didn't want to argue with her mum in front of me, but frequently she ran upstairs with tears in her eyes and slammed the bedroom door. Then Meredith would start to clatter plates and saucepans around the kitchen, and Sam would alternate between trying to hug her and going upstairs after Annabelle. The latter was the worst case scenario for me as I was left to awkwardly sip my tea and look sympathetic to Meredith's stress. Which, to be honest, I felt was something she'd become so used to, it was a protective shield she couldn't lay down.

'Are they all coming to see the play?' I asked Sam, inwardly wincing at the thought of his parents watching us kiss onstage.

'Yes,' he said, and he got that look in his eye when he thought about something he wasn't happy about.

'That's nice,' I said.

'If they don't think I'm wasting my time,' he muttered.

'Why would they think that?' I said, laying a hand on his arm.

He shrugged.

'Acting in a play, learning the lines… It doesn't really do anything, does it? It doesn't change the world.'

'So you're saying there's no value in Shakespeare?' I said, my eyebrows shooting up.

'I like it,' he said. 'But I feel like they want me to be… ah, I don't even know what they want me to do.'

Having spent more time around his parents, I got it. They were always busy with church things: meetings, people, building projects. I could see how Sam felt they saw his acting as frivolous. But as we rehearsed, he made it easy for me to play the part. He seemed to understand Romeo, in a way that absolutely delighted Miss Carr.

'You see, too many people write Romeo off as impulsive and stupid,' she said. 'But you manage to present him as someone who loves deeply, whose emotional life is their heartbeat.'

I looked at Sam sideways when she said this. I'd always seen him as quite a calm, logical person. The one who always finds a solution to every problem. After witnessing the dynamic between his family, I began to realise that it was merely a role he'd been forced into, out of necessity. His passion, his depth of feeling, which I'd glimpsed that night at the social, was deeply suppressed behind the version of himself that his family needed. Part of me liked the safety of that Sam, because he wouldn't pull me onto his lap and break our rules. But part of me wanted to see the real Sam more often, because the idea of a man who loved deeply, who was in touch with his emotions… That was irresistible to me.

Sam

Mum and Annabelle both loved Christmas. It was their favourite time of year, and our tree went up embarrassingly early, along with enough fairy lights to illuminate a London high street. They roped me into hanging most of them, and rewarded me with hot chocolate and giant marshmallows. I wasn't complaining.

I think for Mum, this was one time of the year when it was acceptable, even encouraged, to stay indoors and be cosy, and so this was her happy place. Dad tolerated all of the cluttered decor, such as our wooden nativity scene on the mantelpiece, and wreaths hung on every door, because he knew it put Mum in a good mood. That meant peace and quiet for all of us.

For my sister, she loved being creative, and she started teaching Lil how to make a wreath or a greenery centrepiece. She showed Lil the glass baubles which she and Mum painted, and invited her over to join in some of the baking days they had planned. Lil was delighted, and I was relieved—and tentatively pleased—to watch her get to know my family better. She seemed to know all the right things to say, and my parents were won over by her attention to Annabelle. For so long, my sister had very few friends, and now she had both Lil and Darcy. It was opening up new possibilities for my parents, which I hoped they would embrace.

'I need to RSVP for that dinner,' Dad reminded Mum.

He was straightening his tie in the hallway mirror, about to leave for a meeting, and Mum had filled every surface of the kitchen with cooling mince pies. Lil, Annabelle and Darcy had helped to make them, and had now disappeared upstairs into Annabelle's room. I was sizing up which one I wanted to try first.

'Only one,' Mum warned me.

'Mer?' Dad prompted.

'Lil and I will both be there,' I chipped in, to help his case. It would be nice to have a movie night or something without my parents hovering around.

'I don't know what I'd wear,' Mum said, looking down at the pies and rearranging them.

'Your Christmas jumper!' Dad said, exasperated. 'You have no reason to say no. Let's do it.'

She sighed and looked up.

'All right.'

My eyes widened, as did Dad's. Mum actually agreed? This was major. Catching his eye, I legged it out of the kitchen and took the stairs two at a time. Giggles and shrieks came from Annabelle's room, and I rapped on the door. There were more shrieks, then Annabelle opened it, just enough for me to see her face.

'Yes?' she asked.

'Mum just agreed to go to the Christmas dinner with Dad.'

'Seriously?' Her jaw dropped, and she opened the door wider. Lil and Darcy were sprawled on her rug. 'We can have a parent-free night!'

She did a victory dance and Lil grinned at me.

It gave me something to look forward to, as we struggled through a mountain of homework and then long rehearsals. The play was coming together, but there were still plenty of sections where people forgot their cues, and where we mimed sword fights without any swords. The day when the props and costumes finally arrived, things started to feel real. I had a blue jacket to wear over a white shirt, and I was allowed to wear jeans. Miss Carr wanted a trace of rock-star, she said—whatever that meant. Lil wore a dress with a laced bodice, but with Doctor Marten boots. She said something about experimenting with eye liner for both of us, and

I'll admit I was too distracted to fully listen. It sunk in later—another thing to make my parents hit the roof.

I was feeling nervous about them seeing the play, in all its messy and unbridled glory, but part of me thought *game on*. Here was a side of me they never saw, and I wanted to open their eyes to the possibilities of who I could be, outside their expectations and limitations for me.

Maybe, most of all, I wanted to show myself.

Lil

I walked into Sam's hallway and smelled the now-familiar scent of cinnamon and orange. Between the baking, decorating and festive candle burning that seemed to fill Annabelle and Meredeith's days, the house was permanently christened in seasonal spices. Perhaps it would linger into the new year. I always hated the cold emptiness of January.

'Hey beautiful,' he said, taking my coat.

'Gross,' my sister said.

We'd decided to hang out with all four of us in the house while Sam's parents went to the dinner. I'd come armed with microwave popcorn and chocolate; Sam's kitchen was full of baked goods but low on sugary snacks. I'd worn my forest green dress, with long sleeves and a sweetheart neckline, and it made me think of walking with Sam through pine trees, in a world of our own.

'This is a great colour on you,' he said, eying the dress appreciatively.

'Well, you seem to love all things green and natural,' I said. 'Except sprouts.'

Christmas dinner was coming up in school, and we'd already debated the best trimmings. Pigs in blankets were top of the list.

'Hey,' Annabelle said, standing still on the stairs for a moment. She was holding the bannister and looked paler, more strained than usual. I guessed that she'd been battling Meredith all day for this to actually happen.

Darcy went forward to hug her, and Annabelle's face brightened. They went straight into the living room, while Sam took my hand and led me to the kitchen. The main lights were off, and there were four candles lit, placed around the room.

'Ooh,' I said. 'This is fancy.'

We stood next to the counter, and his arms slid round my waist, sliding over the patterned fabric. My skin tingled.

'There are advantages to it getting dark at four o'clock,' Sam grinned. 'In here, it could be five p.m. or a.m. and no one would know.'

We were facing each other, our bodies close, but our faces were some distance apart.

'Do you fancy getting stuck in a time warp together?' I asked playfully.

I was only joking, but there was a wistful look on his face.

'I'd be stuck anywhere with you,' he said. 'You're the only person I never get fed up with.'

'What an honour,' I replied.

Our faces had moved closer together. Our rules hung between us like a dead fish in the water, and I could see his train of thought without him even voicing it. If it could be five p.m. or a.m., then it could be indoors or outdoors, and if it were outdoors, kissing would be allowed…

'Bit dark in here, isn't it?'

Reverend Park hit the main light switch, and gave Sam a nod.

'All good?' he asked. 'We'll head off, then.'

I still hadn't seen Meredith. He stood at the foot of the stairs and called up.

'Come on, Mer.'

I put the kettle on and opened up the popcorn, ready to go in the microwave. Sam watched me, smiling, and trying to catch my hand every time I walked past.

Meredith came downstairs, wearing a pink and grey Fairisle jumper with tiny rows of reindeer. She paired it with a black skirt and court shoes like school uniform, but her hair was down and looked pretty. She looked younger somehow.

'Ready to go?' Reverend Park asked.

'Sam, you know where we're going,' she said, calling to the kitchen. Her forehead was furrowed.

'Yes, Mum.' Sam stepped into the kitchen doorway and nodded to reassure her.

'Okay,' she said. She was twisting her hands together and Reverend Park gently took one of them to hold.

'Let's go.'

He ushered her to the door, helping her into her winter coat. She gave a last look over her shoulder before they left.

'Phew,' I said, pouring hot water into my favourite mug from the Parks' cupboard. 'I hope they have a great time.'

'Yeah,' Sam agreed.

'Shall I put the popcorn on?'

I turned my back, sorting it out, and Sam came up behind me and put his arms around me.

'You're very huggy today,' I said, turning to face him.

'You're very beautiful today,' he returned.

He ran his fingers down my hair.

'I love the colour of your hair,' he said. 'It smells like…'

He leaned closer to inhale.

'Strawberries.'

'Just because it's red?' I teased.

'You can't call it *red*,' Sam said, stroking it again. 'It's a perfect blend, darker now it's winter, with a touch of blond in the summer. Gingerbread.'

I giggled, and the popcorn started popping, so I pulled away to grab a tray to set the snacks out.

'Are you guys coming?' Darcy called impatiently.

'Just doing the popcorn,' I called back.

Sam caught my wrist and his fingers touched the pressure point gently, then made slow circles onto my hand.

'I just want you to know how perfect you are,' he said.

'The popcorn'll burn,' I said, my eyes darting towards the microwave.

Not letting go of me, he used his other hand to turn it off.

'Happy?'

'They're waiting for us,' I said, a little breathless as he drew closer. My eyes were in line with his neck, and when I dared to lift them to his face, his eyes were gazing at me with such focused love, I couldn't look away.

Love?

Was Samuel Park in love with me?

'We're starting the movie!' Darcy shouted.

'We should go,' I whispered.

He stepped back and I opened the microwave, pouring the popcorn into a bowl, and then he took the tray while I grabbed my tea.

Darcy and Annabelle were curled up together on the main sofa, and reached for the popcorn greedily. Should have made two bowls. The second sofa was further back, and Sam pulled me down next to him. I settled into his arms, leaning onto his chest. He ran his fingers up and down my hair, from the top of my parting to the tips over my shoulders.

If you asked me what the film was, I wouldn't be able to tell you.

Sam

My heart was fit to burst.

As I sat with Lil in my arms, my sister happily chatting with Darcy, and the Christmas tree sparkling in the corner, I felt overwhelmed with blessing. For all the ups and downs my family had been through, my parents had finally gone out for an evening, and an invisible burden had lifted from my shoulders. In some imperceptible way, equilibrium had been restored. I felt keenly how we were enjoying a simple thing: a Christmas movie with popcorn; yet somehow, it was everything.

In all the battles I'd had with my parents, I'd missed how precious it was to have a home like ours. The room was covered with Annabelle's wreaths and greenery, Mum's spiced candles, and fairy lights. The wooden nativity scene on the mantelpiece drew my attention. What madness, that God would leave heaven and become a baby! That He would enter into our messy world, starting with a stable covered in manure and the stench of animals. That He would know the realities we all daily face, of pain, sorrow and the wrongness of our world. That He would be the answer.

I was lost in my thoughts, stroking Lil's silken hair, and marvelling at the fact that she was my girlfriend. Six months ago, I was so full of angry questions. Why had things gone wrong at the church? Why did we have to move right before my last year of school? But now, I wouldn't change any of it. Lil was a beautiful surprise, an unexpected gift, and I was deeply thankful.

I didn't even notice Annabelle leave to go to the bathroom, until Darcy paused the film.

'She's been gone a while now,' she said. 'Is she all right?'

'I'll go check on her,' I said, gently extricating myself from Lil and the sofa.

The stairwell was dark where we must have turned the light off earlier. As I climbed, the fog of my thoughts began to clear as the familiar worry shifted my senses onto high alert. Was my sister okay? The bathroom door was open and light poured out onto the landing.

'Annabelle?' I called.

I heard a slight sob in response.

Reaching the doorway, I found her sitting on the floor by the bathtub, leaning against it. She looked at me with red eyes, sniffing.

'I've been sick,' she said.

I frowned and leaned on the doorway.

'I'm sorry,' I said. 'Can I get you anything?'

She shook her head slowly, dropping her chin to her knees. Tears fell down her face.

'I was so looking forward to this,' she croaked. 'I know it's just a movie, and it's pathetic, but I just wanted to be well enough to enjoy it.'

I sighed and joined her on the floor, pulling her into a hug.

'It's not pathetic,' I said, rubbing her back. 'But it's not the end of the world. There will be other times.'

'It's not fair,' she continued. 'I just want to be normal.'

'Hey,' I said. 'I don't want you to be normal. Being normal sucks. God made you like this for a reason.'

It was something my dad had often said, but as I said it, I realised I believed it too.

'He made a mistake,' she said, sniffing. 'I wish I could be like Darcy, or Lil. They're pretty and cool and they can do anything they want.'

'They don't have a home and a family like ours, though,' I said. 'I know our parents are difficult sometimes. I've argued with them about everything over the past few years. And I know your condition makes things harder for you. Mum can be… well, we love her, but she's hard work too. But honestly, do you know what I was thinking downstairs? I was thinking how blessed we are. We can celebrate Christmas, and we actually know what we're celebrating. I wouldn't want to trade that for a hundred meaningless presents I don't need.'

'You've changed,' Annabelle said, looking at me closely and wiping her eyes. 'It's Lil, isn't it?'

I smiled.

'Sometimes the way you look at her pierces my heart,' Annabelle said, in sudden raw honesty. 'Because I don't think someone will ever love me like that.'

She collapsed into tears again, and I hugged her again, but her words left me reeling.

I was in love with Lil.

I supposed I knew that already, that I would have said, *of course I love her,* if anyone had asked me, but somehow, someone else seeing it made it real.

'You're not well, and you're disappointed, so you're seeing everything in black and white,' I told her, trying to refocus my attention into being a good brother. 'You're too young to decide that no one will ever love you.'

'Have you told Lil you love her?' she asked, lifting her head up again.

'Not yet,' I said.

'You should.' She sniffed and wiped away her tears. 'She deserves to hear that from you.'

'Noted,' I said, then stood up and offered her my hand. 'What do you want to do now?'

'I'd better go to bed,' she said. She looked white and washed out. 'Say sorry to Darcy from me.'

'I will,' I said, then hesitated for a moment. 'You know I should probably text Mum.'

Her eyes widened.

'No! Sam, you can't!'

'You know how much she worries…'

'That's exactly why you cannot text her,' she argued. 'This is the first time she's gone out with Dad in forever. If you send her a message saying I'm ill, she'll come straight home. It's pointless because she can't even do anything. I'm old enough to look after myself.'

'Do you think you're going to be sick again?'

I can't help but remember all the times in the past, where Annabelle was up all night, vomiting, and my parents would debate whether they should take her into hospital. There were so many times when they asked the neighbour to watch me because they both wanted to be with her. Well, perhaps it was that Dad was the only one strong enough to drive, and Mum didn't want to be left behind or separated from Annabelle.

'I don't know,' she said softly. 'I feel better now, just tired.'

She sighed.

'We went to the library today. I finally persuaded Mum because I wanted some Christmas reads and Lil told me I could use my library card to access ebooks and audiobooks on the app. If she thinks I caught something from there, she'll never let me go again.'

I felt the tussle of conscience. I had promised Mum that I'd get in touch if anything was wrong… but Annabelle seemed okay and could go and sleep it off… I didn't want my parents to cut their evening short, not unless it was really necessary… My sister was excited about joining the library and I didn't want that to be taken away from her.

'All right,' I said finally. 'You drink some water and go to bed. But you have to call me if you're sick again. I'll keep an ear out for you.'

Annabelle nodded, and gave me a last hug. I really hoped I didn't catch whatever she had.

Downstairs, I told Darcy and Lil that she was ill, and Darcy stood up to leave.

'You don't have to go, Darce,' Lil said.

'Uh, I'm not staying around you guys like third wheel,' she said, whipping her phone out and starting to text. 'I'll catch you later.'

Lil and I were left alone in the living room. Lil was still on the sofa, looking worried.

'Is she okay?' she asked. 'Do we need to call your parents?'

I picked up the remote and switched from the movie to a Christmas radio channel.

'No, I think she's fine for now. I'm going to listen out in case she's sick again.'

The familiar notes of *Last Christmas* started up.

'Want to dance?'

I held my hand out to her, and she giggled and took it, standing up.

I'd always loved dancing, although it had never exactly been encouraged by my parents. Parties with discos were my favourite, but to them it was more of a punishment to sit through them. I bopped around with Lil, turning her round and holding her waist, and she laughed and joined in.

Saying I love you, I meant it...

The lyrics caught my attention, and I felt giddy. Maybe Annabelle was right; I should tell Lil how I felt. But it was terrifying, and soon one song blurred into another: *Do They Know It's Christmas?*, *It's Beginning to Look a Lot Like Christmas...* The pace had slowed and we shifted into a slow-dance position, with Lil's arms around my neck. The candles were burning low, the fairy lights were twinkling, and I had never felt so *whole*. Lil's eyes were the warmest shade of brown, golden in the light, and she was looking at me with total trust and acceptance of who I was. She saw me, and she still loved me.

'I love you, Lil,' I said.

Her eyes widened, and her smile was dazzling.

'I love you, too, Sam,' she said.

I kissed her as gently and reverently as I could, feeling the perfect curve of her waist and the sheen of her hair, the softness of her cheek on my fingers. She was beautiful, both mine-and-not-mine, and the moment felt transcendent.

The problem was, reality always returns. With a vengeance.

Lil

By the time the Parks returned, Sam and I were creating our own Christmas playlist, and Michael Buble was featuring strongly.

Sam had gone to check on Annabelle, and she'd been asleep, so hopefully it was a one-off, something she'd eaten, rather than a full blown stomach bug.

I was loving the feeling of being in the Parks' winter wonderland lounge, with such beautiful decorations, and even more, being with Sam, his declaration of love ringing in my ears.

'Hello?' Meredith called, as they came through the front door.

She hurried into the living room, and looked around for Annabelle.

'Hey, Mum,' Sam said, getting up from the sofa. 'Annabelle's gone to bed.'

'Is she ill?' Meredith said, her face instantly creasing with worry.

'What's going on?' Reverend Park appeared in the doorway behind his wife, and gently moved her along so he could enter the room.

'Annabelle,' Meredith said, then turned and started walking upstairs.

'What's wrong with Annabelle?' Simon asked.

I saw Sam hesitate.

'She wasn't feeling well.'

'What do you mean? Did she have a temperature? Was she sick?'

'She was sick once.' Sam blurted his response like a confession.

I looked down at my mug of tea. Judging from the silence, a range of expressions were passing over Reverend Park's face.

'You didn't tell us,' he said finally.

Sam swallowed.

'She didn't want me to,' he said. 'I would have, if it had got worse…'

Reverend Park raised his eyebrows, and looked at Sam coldly. Then he turned to me.

'Thank you for coming over, Lil. I need to speak to Samuel now, if you don't mind.'

The dismissal stung, and I saw Sam's eyes flash with anger. I stood up and squeezed his hand.

'Sure,' I said.

I stepped out into the hallway, just as Meredith came down the stairs. She saw me and her face fixed in fury.

'She was sick, wasn't she?' she said.

I darted my eyes back to the living room door. I didn't want to get embroiled in a family row. Reverend Park and Sam hurried into the hallway, hearing Meredith's words.

'Meredith,' Reverend Park said.

'You wanted him to yourself, so you didn't call me,' Meredith said. The venom in her tone scared me.

'Mum!' Sam said, raising his voice.

'Do you have ANY idea of what her condition is like?' Meredith continued, walking right up to me. I couldn't help backing away.

'It's nothing to do with Lil,' Reverend Park said, taking her by the shoulders and steering her away from me, towards the stairs. 'Annabelle's fine.'

'I thought—' Meredith broke off. 'I thought—'

Reverend Park helped her to sit down on the stairs, and sat next to her as she started to sob. I turned away immediately, grabbing my coat and slipping my shoes on clumsily. Sam laid his hand on my arm. I looked up into his eyes, full of sadness and shame.

'I'm sorry,' he whispered.

I squeezed his hand.

'I have to go,' I whispered back.

Sam looked back over his shoulder at his parents, then pulled on his trainers.

'I'm coming with you.'

Sam

I followed Lil out of the front door, and closed it behind me. The cold air threw everything into sharp clarity. I zipped up my coat, while she looked at me with frightened eyes.

'Your mum…' she said.

'I'm sorry,' I said, shaking my head, and pulling Lil into a hug. 'She gets overwrought over Annabelle. It was hard for her to go out tonight. She won't forgive me for not calling her.'

Lil pulled back and stared into my eyes.

'That's not right, Sam,' she said.

'It's the way it is.' I shrugged.

'Sam?'

I heard my dad's voice from inside the hallway. I reached out for Lil's hand.

'Fancy a walk?'

'I think your dad wants to talk to you,' she said, but she still put her hand in mine.

'Well, I don't want to talk to him right now.'

We set off down the street, the yellow glow of the streetlights showing up the evening mist. In the partially clouded night sky, patches of stars were visible. This had gone from being one of the best nights of my life to an absolute disaster. I knew my family was dysfunctional (not perhaps in traditional ways), and now there was no doubt that Lil knew it, too. For my mother to accuse Lil in that way… I was internally cringing with embarrassment. I was also riddled with guilt for not calling them. Maybe there were some selfish motives involved… It was all jumbled up and I couldn't unravel it.

Walking made everything better. I could breathe more easily out of the house. I spotted the side path and turned on my phone's flashlight, leading Lil off the main road.

'Let's hope no one's waiting to ambush us,' she joked.

I tucked her arm in mine, snugly. Whenever I needed headspace, I still had infinite tolerance for Lil. She truly was my favourite person in the whole world.

We didn't speak for a while. I wasn't really thinking where I was going, but we ended up by the river. At the rushing water, I felt ready to stop. The sound was soothing.

'I'm so sorry,' I said, 'for the way both my parents spoke to you tonight.'

'It's fine,' Lil said, frowning. 'It's perfectly understandable.'

'But that doesn't make it okay,' I said.

'No,' she agreed.

Her hair was cascading over her coat, a fiery crown against the darkness.

'I can't wait to leave,' I confessed.

'You'll miss them,' she said.

'I'll miss Annabelle,' I said. 'Poor kid.'

'She's not really a kid anymore,' Lil corrected me. 'At some point they're going to have to let her grow up.'

'She's strong,' I said, staring at the deadly, black water. Falling into that current, you'd be carried away in a breath. 'Stronger than I am.'

'You've had to deal with a lot,' Lil said, reaching up to touch my cheek. 'It's okay for you to need help sometimes too.'

I felt tears start into my eyes.

'I just don't know,' I said, my voice breaking with emotion, 'if I did the right thing.'

Lil hugged me, and held me, and even though I knew I had to go back and face them, I somehow felt more able to do it with her behind me.

Maybe love was finding unexpected strength in each other, filling up the other's lack. Maybe love was finding new family, family you chose rather than by blood. When I was with Lil, that felt like home… more than my own home in some ways. With Lil, I never felt like an outsider. Being with her was like warming yourself by a blazing bonfire on a wintry night with a sky full of stars: exhilarating, breathtaking, and magical. You truly felt *alive*. By comparison, being with my parents felt like any spark in me was slowly being extinguished. The snuffing effect of a thick, damp towel on fragile embers.

The problem was, they thought I belonged with them. Up until now, I never had a reason to question that.

Now, it felt like there was no going back.

Lil

I held Sam, and the cool stillness of the night wrapped around the two of us. In such a short time, our lives had become completely entwined. Our *spirits*, even. I'd never seen a boy become vulnerable like this before, and have the courage to share the fears of his heart. I'd never felt so in tune with someone that their sorrow truly became mine. As I felt Sam's body move with emotion, tears brimmed in my own eyes. He was so beautiful, the way he cared for his family, but he was carrying more than he should have been. I grieved to see how both he and Annabelle were constrained by Meredith's irrational fear. The way she spoke to me… I wondered if this had happened before, with some of their other friends or church members. I wondered if Reverend Park knew anyone at church well enough to ask for support.

I couldn't tell anyone about this. It wasn't my story to share, and I knew I was out of my depth, but I just needed to be there for Sam. He was holding me tightly, and his crushing embrace felt like the most solid presence I'd ever known. My parents weren't very touchy-feely, with each other or with Darcy and me. It had been a long time since anyone had really *held* me. It felt like I was being re-formed, remade in some way.

At some point, Sam pulled back, and the cloud shifted to reveal a sharp silver moon, literally beaming light onto my face. I'd never seen it so strong. He stared at me as if I was the most beautiful thing he'd ever seen. I drank in his gaze, the rushing river blocking out any noise from the roads or houses we'd left behind.

'I love you, Lil.' He said it again, even though it didn't need to be verbalised; I could read it all over his face.

He traced a finger down my cheek, and a tear glistening in my eye followed its path. He brushed it away with tender wonder.

'You're sad,' he murmured. 'I've made you sad.'

'No,' I said, shaking my head. I raised my palm to his chest. 'You've shared your heart with me. That's precious.'

'Your tears are like pearls,' he said, kissing the top of my cheek, just under my eye. 'Priceless jewels.'

'You sound like you're quoting Shakespeare again,' I said, closing my eyes.

His lips met mine, and it was a timeless, perfect moment. It was better than any movie I'd seen, and more profound than any book I'd read. After all the emotional turmoil of the evening, we walked back hand in hand, unfathomably light-hearted.

'What are you going to say to them?' I asked him, afraid to break the spell.

He lifted his shoulders in a shrug.

'I don't know,' he said. 'But I feel better than I did before.'

I squeezed his hand.

'You know when it's just you and me, out here?' he asked. 'I feel like everything's… right. How it should be, somehow.'

'I feel the same,' I told him.

'Do you think this is crazy?' he asked. 'I mean, we've only known each other a few months.'

I grinned back at him.

'Feels like we were meant to be together,' I said.

'Like Romeo and Juliet?' Sam asked, teasing.

'They die at the end,' I said dryly.

'So like Romeo and Juliet… without the dying part.'

'Something like that.'

Sam

When we finally arrived back outside the house, I could see the living room light was on. I stopped on the pavement, outside the front gate.

'Thanks for walking with me,' I said to Lil, hugging her tightly again.

'Call me later, if you want to,' she said.

I wondered if my dad would be looking out for me, and hesitated before kissing her goodbye. It felt a bit late to be hiding the fact that I'd kissed Lil. Why should I? She was my girlfriend.

I watched as she walked into her house, and turned to face my own front door with a sigh. It still felt unfamiliar, after living in our previous house for most of my childhood. These houses were nice, if a little unoriginal. Classic suburbia. A church minister with a wife and two children, and a homemade wreath to prove we were happy and whole. The familiar anger lurched in my stomach. Did no one see the reality of our lives because we concealed it so well, or because they didn't want to scratch beneath the thin veneer of model family life, afraid of what they might discover?

I closed the door behind me quietly, and stepped into the hallway. Mum was no longer on the stairs; so far, so good. I hung up my coat and kicked my trainers off, then headed straight for the lounge.

My dad was sitting, alone, on the sofa with his head in his hands. He looked up as I came in, and his eyes were bloodshot. I halted in the doorway.

'Where have you been?' he asked hoarsely.

My heart hardened immediately.

'For a walk,' I replied curtly.

Both of us waited in silence for the other to speak first.

'That wasn't very helpful,' he said finally.

I said nothing to reply to that.

'Is Annabelle all right?' I asked, knowing the answer.

He didn't reply either.

'Your mother's gone to bed,' he said.

'Dad—' I said, and my warning tone was enough for him to interrupt straight away.

'She's fine, Sam,' he said, raising his voice to cut me off. 'She just needs a good night's sleep.'

'Dad, the way she spoke to Lil…'

'We need to talk about the fact that you and Lil were alone together, in this house.'

My eyebrows shot up in disbelief.

'Annabelle was here!' I said.

'She was upstairs, being sick, and you were downstairs, taking advantage of time alone with your girlfriend.'

Any rein I was keeping tight onto my anger snapped.

'Taking advantage?' I shouted. 'What exactly do you mean by that?'

'You know what I mean,' he snapped.

It was too much. I'd had the most profound, beautiful evening with the girl I loved with all my heart, and my father just dismissed it as me taking advantage of being alone with her and ignoring my suffering sister.

'I don't understand you,' I said, my voice cracking with emotion. I shook my head. 'Why are you so cold-hearted?'

He flinched as if I'd slapped him.

'I don't understand what you mean.'

'I've fallen in love with the most amazing girl I've ever met, and you seem determined to dismiss it as some kind of sordid affair.'

'You don't know what love is!' He raised his voice this time. He seemed to regret it, then, and rubbed his fingers across his lined forehead. 'You think you do, but you don't.'

'Because I'm young?' I asked. 'I'm nearly eighteen.'

'Exactly.' He gave a hard, cynical laugh. 'What do you know about love?'

'I know that God is love,' I said. It honestly was the first thing that came into my head. 'And I believe that love comes from Him. I've never felt this way about any girl before. Lil means more to me than anyone else. I would die for her.'

He looked up at me with a stunned expression, which quickly morphed into horror.

'How can she mean more to you than your own family?' he asked angrily. 'You barely know her. All this extreme declaration is just… hyperbole. Drama. You've been playing Romeo and now you're acting it out in real life, but guess what? Life is nothing like a Shakespeare play.'

'Because nothing good can ever come of a play,' I said, rolling my eyes.

'It's made up!' he shouted, getting to his feet and gesturing wildly. Ironically, he could give Lord Capulet a run for his money. 'And all this talk of love is just… cotton wool. As soon as the rain moves in, it will just dissolve into nothingness.'

I said nothing, just shook my head.

'You don't believe me?' he continued. 'Try having a sick child, and going back and forth to hospital appointments for sixteen years. Try running a ministry, and juggling responsibilities, and making sure that the roof on the house doesn't leak and there's enough money for groceries at the end of the month. Because starry-eyed declarations don't help you then. They are meaningless.'

The bitterness of his own disappointment winded me. But it was like an important, final piece of the puzzle slotted into place. This was why he was so against relationships. It was nothing to do with me, or Lil really, and everything to do with his own choices.

'I can't speak for your life, and the way things worked out for you,' I said, shaking my head slowly. 'But I don't see the world the way you do. When I say I love Lil, I'm being honest with you about how I feel. You can't take that away from me.'

I turned my back on him to head upstairs to bed, and paused when he started to speak again.

'I'm only trying to save you from the pain of when it ends,' he said.

Lil

I avoided Darcy and paced in my bedroom until Sam called me. He was upset.

'My dad said it's not real,' he said, through tears. 'I can't make him understand how I feel. I've never been able to make him understand how I feel.'

'He loves you,' I reminded him. 'Even if you don't understand each other.'

'He's a minister, but he has no faith in love,' Sam said. 'It makes me so mad.'

'I know,' I whispered.

He sobbed, and I could hear him through the wall, not just through the phone.

'I wish I was with you, so that I could hug you,' I said helplessly.

'My dad was mad enough about us being alone together downstairs!' Sam managed to joke. 'He'd have a heart attack if you were in here with me.'

'I can hear you through the wall, you know,' I said.

'Not enough to hang up, though.'

'No.'

I listened to him breathing.

'I'm putting my hand against the wall where I think you are,' I said.

'*Palm to palm is holy palmer's kiss*,' Sam replied, almost as an automatic reaction.

I smiled.

'Are you doing it too?' I asked him.

'Yes.'

My smile widened.
'I love you,' I said.
'I love you, too,' he said, taking a deep breath.
We didn't end the call.

Sam

Annabelle was humming, making herbal tea in the kitchen, when I stumbled in like a survivor from a wreckage. The kitchen smelled of apples and cinnamon, with a slightly sickly, cloying strength that hit the back of my dry throat.

'Morning,' she said brightly, then did a double take. 'Are you all right?'

'I should be asking you that question,' I said, turning away to grab a bowl to fill with sugary cereal. There's no point being healthy when you feel like a train collision happened over your head. Or on your head. Whatever.

'Sam,' she said sharply, coming right up to me. 'You look awful. What's wrong?'

I looked at her, and it was enough.

'Mum,' she murmured.

I gave a small nod.

'What did she say?' Annabelle asked, reading my face in her uncanny way. 'She said something to you? No?'

I watched as she surmised the horrible truth.

'She said something to Lil, didn't she?' Annabelle brought both her hands up to her hairline and pressed until her fingertips were white. 'She blamed Lil for me being sick… she wanted you to call her straight away.'

'I feel bad that I didn't call her,' I admitted.

'You didn't need to,' Annabelle said firmly, lowering one arm to clasp my forearm. 'I was fine.'

'I didn't know that, though,' I reminded her. 'Not really.'

'Sam, sometimes I need to be allowed to be a little bit ill and go to bed, just like the rest of the world.'

She sighed, and went back to pick up her mug.

'I'll talk to her.'

'What are you going to say?' I asked, panicking that World War Three might break out.

'I'll figure something out,' she said, shrugging.

As I watched her head up the stairs, I heard her speak to Dad. Not ready to face him, I concentrated on filling my cereal bowl and sloshing milk everywhere.

'Sam?' My dad stood in the kitchen doorway.

'Yes?' I took a moment before I looked up.

'I wondered if you'd like your Christmas present early?' he said. 'We bought you some driving lessons with Lil's dad, and he just called to ask if you want to go out this morning as one of his students cancelled.'

My jaw dropped. Finally, some driving lessons! I felt an instant guilt for the negativity I'd been feeling towards my parents.

'That would be amazing,' I said, shoving my bowl to one side and going to give my dad a hug. 'Thanks, Dad.'

Surprised, he patted my shoulders.

'It's okay, son.'

For a moment, I thought he might say something else, but instead he cleared his throat.

'Right, you'd better get ready.'

I'd met Bryan several times, but he never seemed to be at home much. Nor did her mum. I supposed it was the nature of being a driving instructor: always in the car, and through evenings and weekends too. Julia had a stressful job where she often had to work late, although I had no idea what she actually did. She also went to exercise classes and wine bars with her various circles of friends.

Getting behind the wheel of a car was exciting. Dad had shown me a few things, but he had never had as much time to teach me as he'd promised. His free time was more in the day, while I was at school. At least I knew how to start the car and to work the pedals. Bryan took me to a quiet industrial estate, and I was soon trundling around the deserted roads, trying out the gears. Apparently, the test centre was nearby, and there was a coffee shop which seemed surprisingly busy, given the randomness of its location.

'I never knew there was a cafe here,' I said, trying to fill the silence.

'Ah, that's a hidden gem,' Bryan said. 'See those funnels? They've got a wood burner at either end, and moss-covered roofs. Sal calls it a sky garden.'

He laughed.

'You know the owner?' I asked.

Bryan's laugh morphed into a cough.

'Yes,' he said, but he turned to drink some water. 'There are not many options for places to get a coffee and pastry around here.'

His face had turned red, and I shifted my concentration back to the road.

'Are you working today?' he asked.

'Yes, I wondered if we could finish up in town instead of going back home?'

'No problem.'

I daydreamed of being able to drive Lil to work, instead of the other way around. It bothered me that I had so little to offer her. There was still the added complexity of my mum's negative attitude towards her last night. I didn't want to dwell on that. Instead, I pictured her starry eyes when I told her I loved her. And the sound of her repeating it back to me.

Lil

When Sam met me after work, he seemed to be back to normal. He was super excited about having driving lessons, and the strain of last night seemed forgotten. Well, until we pulled up outside the house.

'How's your mum?' I asked.

He shook his head.

'I didn't see her this morning.'

I squeezed his hand.

'I need to write an essay, but you could come and study with me if you like?'

He smiled.

'I'll see if Mum's around and if she wants to talk,' he said. 'I'll text you.'

We stepped out of the car and met for a hug on the pavement. Sam's lips brushed mine, and it was a centring, earthing moment where balance was restored. However wrong the world was, being with Sam made it right again.

He messaged me later to say that they were having a family night, so he'd see me at church. I sighed and went back to my essay. Darcy was sleeping over her friend's house, and my parents were out. It was going to be a depressing Saturday night.

It was probably just as well that it was quiet, though, given that the show was about to start. Our lives were going to be turned upside down for the dress rehearsal and performances. I was eager to do it, but I also felt a premature sadness for it coming to an end. I'd had so much fun, rehearsing with the cast… but mainly, with Sam. He was genuinely talented, too. Confident with his lines, easy with his body language… It all felt so natural. Oddly, I worried that I wouldn't see him so much once the play was over. I had no reason why.

Perhaps the incident with his mum had unsettled me. I hoped that Meredith was feeling better. And I hoped that she had forgiven me.

In church the next morning, Sam met me in the foyer as usual. He hugged me tightly.

'I missed you,' he breathed.

He took my hand and led me to the place where we normally sat. I could see Meredith, sitting with Annabelle, in the front row.

'Is your mum all right?' I asked.

He nodded.

'I think so,' he said. 'Annabelle spoke to her yesterday, and she hadn't been sick again, so Mum didn't need to worry about taking her to hospital or anything.'

'That's good,' I said. It still felt like there was more he wasn't telling me. 'Is she mad at me?'

He looked at me, blushing, and shook his head.

'More at me, for not contacting them,' he said. 'They think I was distracted because of you. Generally, they believe relationships are a distraction.'

He said this as he looked down at our joined hands. I squeezed his hand.

'I don't want to distract you,' I whispered.

'No,' he said, looking up. 'You are a beautiful part of my life. If they don't understand that, it's not my problem.'

The service was about to start, so I had no opportunity to respond. But it troubled me. Weren't we supposed to honour our parents? What about when our parents were unreasonable? Even so, I didn't want to divide Sam from his family. I *envied* the way that he had a family who knew God and were seeking Him together.

What worried me most was that the fracture between Sam and his family had already happened; our relationship was bringing it to the surface. What could I do? What should I do? I no longer felt sure of anything.

Sam

My parents' campaign for me to break up with Lil was well underway, but I was determined not to give in.

I just about endured my father's stern words of disapproval, his logical reasoning about why we were too young, and my mother's irrational point, repeated often, that if Lil hadn't been there, I would have looked after Annabelle properly. This was despite Annabelle's clear declaration that she had been fine, that she had told me not to text them, and that she wanted them to treat her normally. Fat chance of that (I didn't say that, though).

The week of the play, they kept saying how I needed to keep up with my schoolwork, and as much as I reassured them, they didn't listen. They had agreed to watch the play on the final night, Friday. I decided to avoid them as much as possible in the meantime.

It wasn't hard. Lil and I decided to go for walks after school, grab some food on the go, and then return to get ready. The dress rehearsal went well. Lil's parents were coming on the opening night, with Darcy, and they were effusive with praise.

'Sam, you were fantastic!' Julia squashed me into a hug, and then swept up her daughter. I hadn't seen her around that much, so it was reassuring that she was present and affirming to Lil.

I shook Bryan's hand awkwardly and chatted about my next driving lesson.

They gave me a lift home, and I bumped into Dad in the hallway. He saw my stage make up, including the eye liner, and raised an eyebrow.

'Don't,' I said angrily, turning to stomp up the stairs. 'The show went well. Thanks for asking.'

Lil knew something was wrong and tried to ask me about it, but I shut her down.

'I don't want to talk about my parents,' I said. 'I just want to focus on the play.'

She looked uneasy but she didn't push me any further.

The second night went well, and by the final performance, we were high on adrenalin. It was like I downed twenty of those parma violets shots again. I felt terrified because my parents were going to be there, but also recklessly free. They could finally see the version of myself they'd tried to suppress.

'*O brawling love, O loving hate,*' I said, revelling in the audience's laughter and feeding from their energy.

My dad may have doubted the reality of love, but I was sure that most people out there could relate to Romeo's over-the-top expressions. Why else would *Romeo and Juliet* be one of the greatest love stories of all time?

It was while Mercutio gave his '*Queen Mab*' speech that I saw them, sitting quite near the back of the auditorium. Annabelle was smiling. I didn't allow my gaze to linger for long in case it put me off.

At the moment where Lil and I faced each other onstage for the first time, the audience hushed reverently. There was a breathless anticipation in the air as we went through our well-rehearsed sequence, and Lil's eyes sparkled as she said,

'*And palm to palm is holy palmer's kiss.*'

These were no longer Shakespeare's lines; they had become ours. We spoke the words, back and forth to each other, with perfect timing and playful smiles. When I kissed her, I couldn't help waiting a little longer than usual before pulling away. There were a few whoops from the audience and wolf whistles. Lil was blushing but grinned. It could have just been the two of us on that stage.

It all went so smoothly, all the way through the balcony scene, and then up to the marriage scene with Friar Laurence.

'*These violent delights have violent ends*,' he reminded us.

I held Lil's hand, hypnotised by her beauty, and wished it was real, that I could marry her tomorrow, that we could run away where no one could tell us what to do.

The curtain fell for the interval, and I pulled her close and kissed her.

Lil

Sam pressed his mouth to mine and held me like he never wanted to let go. I pulled back, laughing.

'That was very…public!' I said.

'Yeah, save it for the balcony!' one of the crew members said, hauling a piece of scenery past.

'I don't care,' Sam said, grinning from ear to ear. 'I want everyone to know that I love you.'

'Sam, your dad wants to see you!' Miss Carr called over from the wings.

His grin faltered, and I squeezed his hand.

'Go on,' I said. 'You did really well. He'll be proud of you.'

His jaw set and he headed towards the wings with grim determination. I watched for a moment, and then followed in his wake, leaving enough distance that I wouldn't intrude. Reverend Park looked serious. I couldn't hear what he said, but he clapped a hand on Sam's shoulder, patted it, and then walked off. Sam stood, looking stunned.

'What did he say?' I asked, turning him to face me.

He looked pale and shocked.

'They're leaving,' he said. 'They were sat by someone with a bad cough, and Mum didn't want Annabelle to catch anything.'

He was numb with devastation, and I knew his high of excitement was now going to turn into a spectacular crash.

'Come on,' I said, grabbing his hand and pulling him away from the others.

We made our way down the corridor to a dark, empty classroom. I shut the door behind us and left the light off so no one would find us.

'I can't believe it,' he said, shaking his head. He drew his hand up to his mouth, and he looked on the verge of breaking down.

I wrapped my arms around him and held him close, feeling his shoulders start to shake and his breath come in gasps.

'It's okay,' I soothed, clinging onto him tightly.

'It's like I don't *matter!*' he said, and his voice broke my heart.

'They love you,' I said, even though part of me agreed with him. 'They may not always show it very well, but they do love you. I love you, too.'

'I love you so much,' he said, hugging me again. 'I feel like an idiot, crying all the time. I'm supposed to look after you.'

'Says who?' I challenged. 'Sam, you're allowed to have emotions.'

'Not at home I'm not,' he said quietly, shaking his head.

'That's not right,' I said.

His breathing steadied and although his eyes were red, he composed himself.

'I don't want to let this throw me off,' he said. 'We want this to be our best performance.'

'Yes,' I agreed.

And it was. The fight between Tybalt, Mercutio and then Romeo was fiercely believable; Sam's cries of anguish were tainted with his real emotion, that only I knew about. By the time we reached the final scene, where I lay motionless in the tomb, I could hear the spell-bound silence of the audience.

'*O, here/ Will I set up my everlasting rest,/ And shake the yoke of inauspicious stars/ From this world-wearied flesh.*'

I believed him, and everyone else clearly did too, for there was not one sound, not one awkward cough or rustle. As I "woke up" and acted Juliet's horror on realising Romeo was dead, it all felt surprisingly real. Many times I'd read it and thought it was hyperbolic, too much, and for Juliet to quickly grab the first weapon she lands on and kill herself seemed out of the realms of possibility. Now, in this moment, it felt like a part of Sam was genuinely dying, and I wanted to share in his sorrow. I kissed his lips, then gave my final lines.

'*O happy dagger! ...there rust, and let me die.*'

When the Prince gave his speech and ended the play, there was a resounding silence in the auditorium. Then the applause exploded. I sat up, and took Sam's hand, and in a daze, we both stood and joined the rest of the cast in a line onstage. As we bowed, I looked around in astonishment at the heavy applause, and the cheerful whoops of the crew in the wings. The rest of the cast took a step back, and Sam pulled me forwards to take another bow. He looked just as stunned as I did with the reaction. If he was disappointed that his parents weren't there to see it, he hid it well. Like a true professional, he gestured to the lighting box and made sure that the audience applauded them, too. He beckoned Miss Carr to come onstage, and one of the crew gave me a bouquet to give to her. Still, the applause rang out, and we took a final bow all together.

It was euphoric.

I can barely remember the dressing room afterwards, the flurry of hugs and congratulations, the bustle of changing out of costumes and taking off the worst of the make-up. Everyone wanted to speak to Sam and me, and some of them were going out to celebrate.

'You guys coming?' Shannon asked me.

I looked at Sam, and we shared a secret smile.

'No, you go ahead,' I said.

By the time we were ready to leave, the audience were long gone. Miss Carr was thanking the crew, and explaining that the lighting company would collect the rig tomorrow.

'Thank you, Miss,' Sam said, and she flung her arms around him, and then around me, hugging us together at the same time.

'My stars!' she said. 'The perfect star-crossed lovers!'

She was giddy with happiness just like the rest of us.

When we got outside to the car park, where there were only a few cars remaining, we suddenly realised that we'd been planning to go home with Sam's family. But now they had already gone.

'I wonder if Dad remembered,' Sam muttered, checking his phone.

'I could ring my parents,' I said, taking out my phone, but Sam shook his head and grinned at me mischievously.

'We can walk,' he said. 'If we make a few stops along the way… They were the ones who left us in the lurch.'

'It's pretty cold,' I said doubtfully.

Sam wrapped his arms around me in a bear hug.

'I'll keep you warm,' he said.

Sam

It was a perfect December night, clear and sparkling with stars. Lil overcame her misgivings and tucked her arm into mine; after all, we knew this path like the back of our hands. We walked it twice a day. Okay, so never at night… but still. Night time made everything more… interesting.

The play was such an incredible success that not even my parents' disappearance could dent my happiness. I was practically skipping with joy. In the moonlight, I spotted bats flitting between the trees overhead, and I pointed them out to Lil. There was something about the peace of night time that made me come alive. The hustle and bustle of the daytime, the noise of traffic and people, was gone. All that remained was nature, and a world completely self-contained, apart from us. I loved observing it.

'So, were you happy with the play?' Lil asked, knowing the answer.

'Of course!' I said. 'It was just brilliant. *You* were brilliant.'

'I couldn't have done it without you,' she said. 'Imagine if Miss Carr had cast Lewis as Romeo?'

We laughed. Lewis played a great, very over the top Mercutio, but he wouldn't have made a great Romeo.

'I've never done anything like this before,' I said. 'I wish I'd done it sooner.'

'You're still young,' Lil reminded me. 'You've got your whole life ahead of you.'

'And I want to share it with you,' I said, stopping in my tracks and pulling her against me.

Lil looked up at me with her eyes wide.

'Lil,' I said, my throat thickening with emotion. 'I need you to know… you're it for me. You're the only person I ever want to be with.'

'Sam,' she began, but I shook my head.

'I mean it,' I said. 'You know what I thought when we stood in front of Friar Laurence at the end of Act 2? I thought, I wish this was real and I could marry Lil tomorrow.'

She laughed, and then raised a hand to touch my cheek.

'Part of me wishes that too,' she said. 'But I don't want to miss all that the next few years will bring, either. We're going to university, and we're going to learn new things and meet new people… I love you too and I want you to stay part of my life, but it won't be the same as being in the same school, living next door to each other.'

'Do you think that I won't stay true to you?' I asked, feeling even more like Romeo.

'This bud of love, by summer's ripening breath,/May prove a beauteous flower when next we meet,' she quoted, stroking my face.

'Let's make the most of it now,' I said, lowering my lips to hers.

She tasted like honey, and I couldn't get enough of her. I deepened the kiss, and she leaned against me, clutching at the sleeve of my coat.

Like fire and powder, which as they kiss consume.

The stick of dynamite had been lit again, and although the rules I'd set down buzzed around my head like an annoying fly, my instinct took over. I wanted to possess her. I wanted to lose myself in her and become one. I didn't just want to be Sam anymore; I wanted to be Sam-and-Lil forever.

'Sam,' she gasped, turning her face to the side slightly as I trailed kisses down her neck. 'We need to keep walking.'

'Only if you kiss me at regular intervals,' I teased.

She laughed, grabbed my hand, and we ran down the next section of the path together, coming to a low bridge over the canal. Under the bridge, she pressed my back against the wall, and kissed me again. Then I chased her down the next section, until we were both stumbling over the rocky ground and breathless with laughter.

'I've got you!'

I caught her round the waist, and she shrieked, and then we kissed again. It was far more intoxicating than any drug.

'It's still freezing out here,' Lil chided me.

'Wait till you feel my cold hands!' I said, placing them against her warm neck.

She shrieked and then chased me up the small hill, which led to the estate. Grinning, she pulled me in for a kiss, and then suddenly slid her cold hands under my T-shirt onto my middle.

'Revenge is sweet,' she said.

Her hands were cold, but they blazed a fiery trail on my skin. I looked at her, and the desire was thick and palpable between us. Then we were kissing again, more desperately this time. It was late, and we were high on our success, and the sword of my parents was hanging over our heads. Maybe we knew that this was it.

All I knew was that I literally couldn't think straight when she moved her hands and caressed my bare skin.

'Lil,' I moaned, in a sort of blissful agony.

'I want you, Sam,' she whispered, our noses touching, and our breath mingling in the cold air.

Then my phone started ringing.

Lil

The spell was broken instantly. I withdrew my hands and stepped back.

'You'd better get it,' I said to Sam, who was still panting and looking like he wanted to make love to me right here, on this path, under the stars.

He pulled out his phone.

'Hello?' he said, impatiently. 'Yeah, we're walking… How should I know? It's dark… No, no that won't be necessary. See you soon.'

He replaced the phone into his pocket, and ran his hand through his hair distractedly.

'Now Dad remembers about picking us up.'

'I hope he's not mad,' I said, tentatively. I already had the sting of Meredith's anger; I didn't want his too.

'We'd better start walking.'

He took my hand and set off at a brisk pace. His brows were furrowed and I could see he was upset.

'I don't know what I'm going to say to them,' he said. 'It just feels like they won't understand. They don't *want* to understand.'

'Give them the benefit of the doubt,' I said. 'They must feel really torn. They knew how much this meant to you.'

But I couldn't deny that Sam's parents' behaviour was odd, and contrasted greatly with my own family. Of course, my parents didn't have an Annabelle to worry about.

We turned onto the estate, where the streetlights hid the stars with their orange glow, and I wondered as we approached our homes whether I should say something about what had happened before the phone call. Just before I opened my mouth, he said,

'Thanks for being there for me, Lil.'

Before I knew it, we were outside our front doors, and I didn't think it was a good idea to bring it up.

'See you tomorrow?' I said hopefully.

He gave me a brief kiss that showed his mind was on other things.

'Love you,' he said.

I went inside, considerably sobered, and put the kettle on for a cup of tea. *God, what was I doing?* I should never have placed my hands under his T-shirt. It was an act of mercy that his phone had rung.

'How did it go, darling?'

Mum came up to give me a hug, and I sat with her at the kitchen table and told her the highlights.

'What did Sam's parents think?' she asked, excitedly.

I sighed.

'They left at the interval because someone had a cough near where they were sitting,' I explained. 'Sam was gutted.'

Mum winced.

'They've definitely got a difficult situation with Annabelle's condition,' she said. 'But it's a shame they didn't see the whole thing.'

'Sometimes I feel like they don't really care about Sam's feelings,' I blurted.

'Oh, honey,' Mum said, squeezing my hand. 'I'm sure they do.'

'They don't want him to date me,' I said. 'I feel like I'm not good enough for them.'

'Why would they think that?' she asked, genuinely astonished.

I shook my head. Given that Mum wasn't a Christian, I didn't think she'd understand.

'They think we're both too young.' That was the explanation I settled on.

'You're not going to drop out of uni, are you?' Mum asked, looking momentarily concerned.

'Of course not,' I said. She would probably freak out if she knew that Sam was talking about marrying me half an hour ago.

'Well, then,' she said, looking satisfied. 'You'll have to do a long-distance relationship, but if it's the real thing, you'll be fine.'

If this wasn't real, then I had no idea what real love would feel like.

Sam

It was clear why Dad had forgotten to pick us up within seconds of stepping inside my house.

Mum was hysterical, not an entirely unusual event, but this time, Annabelle was equally upset. The living room was a war zone, and Dad was doing a poor impression of Switzerland in the middle.

'You think I'm trying to spoil your fun?' Mum was shrieking, her face a deep shade of red. 'You say that I'm ruining your life? At this rate, you won't *be* alive if you're not more careful.'

'I *am* careful!' Annabelle shouted back, her face streaked with tears. I was shocked at how angry she sounded. 'I've spent my whole life being careful! But tonight was about supporting Sam, and we left.'

My mother gaped at her, then collected herself and pointed at me.

'All right then,' she said, straightening up and using a quiet but deadly tone. 'Sam, you can settle this. Would you have wanted your sister to remain in that auditorium, knowing that someone with a virus was right behind her, coughing their germs into the air?'

My eyes darted to Annabelle, who silently begged me to back her up, and then to my father, who shook his head slightly. I looked at Mum and sighed.

'I would never want Annabelle to be in danger,' I said. 'But it was… hard… that you all left.'

My throat constricted, and I gulped back the emotion. Annabelle saw it, and rushed towards me. She wrapped her arms around me in a tight hug, and I felt her sob.

'I'm sorry,' she said. 'I wanted to stay.'

'Now look what you've done!' my mum said in frustration.

'No, look what *you've* done,' Annabelle said, whipping her face out from my shoulder.

'You've worked yourself up,' Mum said, essentially dismissing my sister's point. 'You're making yourself ill.'

'*You're* making me ill!'

Annabelle was so incensed, she broke free from hugging me and turned her whole body to face Mum.

'I'm beginning to wonder if all this is in your head!' Annabelle shouted. 'Don't go to the shop… don't go to the cinema… You never let me do anything!'

'Oh, so I've made this up, have I?' Mum snapped sarcastically. 'Because of course, I want to spend weeks in hospital and go back and forth to the pharmacy until I'm on first name terms with all the staff. Because of course, I don't want a normal life where I can get a job and support your father and paint pictures and do all the things I enjoy, do I?'

'I'm not stopping you doing any of those things,' Annabelle said, through her tears. 'I never asked to be homeschooled. I can go to Sam's school, and you can get a job.'

'And what happens when you catch the flu? Or measles? Or a sick bug? Can you find me a job where they would give me unlimited time off to attend your appointments? Because funnily enough, I've thought about that, Annabelle. You obviously haven't, because you're young, and the only thing that matters to you is *having fun.*'

She spat the last two words as if they were the worst thing in the world. We all stared at her, waiting for whatever was coming next. My dad cleared his throat, as if to say something, but she ignored him and went for me instead.

'I expect better from you, Sam,' she said, and the words were like daggers to my heart. 'Making your sister feel guilty for looking after her own health, which could be a life or death situation.'

'Meredith.' My father finally spoke.

'Don't you dare support them instead of me,' she warned, pointing her finger at him. 'You know I'm right.'

'There's no need to make Sam feel bad,' he said. 'He's allowed to feel disappointed that we missed his show.'

Hope flared in my chest. Perhaps he was going to say how great the play was, and how much he enjoyed it, even if it was only the first half. But the moment passed, and he said nothing further.

'Seems to me the only reason he did it was so he could impress Lil,' my mum said. 'If she's your girlfriend now, I suppose you got what you wanted.'

Something in me snapped.

'No!' I shouted. 'What I wanted was for my family to show up for me. Just once. And you didn't. I don't blame you, Annabelle.'

'Sam,' my dad said, seemingly incapable of saying more than just our names, in a reproachful tone.

'Surely you could have stayed?' I asked him. 'Mum could have taken Annabelle home, but you could have watched the second half.'

'I…' he trailed off. The idea had clearly not occurred to him. 'I didn't want to leave your mother alone with Annabelle.'

'I don't know why,' Annabelle scoffed.

'Maybe you just didn't like it,' I said bitterly, perhaps in a desperate way fishing for a compliment.

'I thought you put a lot of effort into it,' my dad said.

I frowned. What kind of comment was that?

'He was brilliant!' Annabelle cried. 'Sam, you were amazing.'

I blushed and looked down, unable to cope with my parents' lack of response.

'I'm going to bed,' I said.

Annabelle followed me upstairs, and caught my arm just as I was about to brush my tears away with the back of my sleeve.

'Don't listen to them, Sam,' she whispered.

I nodded, then retreated into my bedroom. I sat on my bed, thought about Lil on the other side of the wall, and buried my head in my hands and wept.

Lil

The next day was Saturday, and I had to de-ice the car window. There were beautiful patterns of frost on the car roof, and although I could see my breath and the cold was bitter, I marvelled at the small details of God's creation. I'd spent time praying last night, repenting of pushing things too far with Sam. I prayed for bigger and better faith, to know God's way was best. The frost seemed like the perfect reminder, that if God could take care of those transient patterns that would melt away by lunchtime, He could be trusted with my life.

I started the engine and sat in the car, shivering and rubbing my hands together before I texted Sam. I wasn't going to ring the doorbell and risk seeing his parents. I also felt a sinking feeling when I remembered what I'd resolved last night: I needed to ask Sam to follow through on his promise, and tell his dad that we got carried away. We needed accountability.

Sam closed the door carefully behind him, like he didn't want to be heard, then walked over to the car. His face looked oddly closed off.

'Hey,' I said, as he climbed into the passenger seat.

'Hey.' He sighed, then gave me a half-smile.

'What happened last night?' I asked, reading the story of his hesitation.

'Mum was upset. Annabelle was upset. So everyone was upset.'

He looked down at his fingernails, which seemed bitten away.

'I'm sorry,' I said, placing a hand over his.

'It's okay,' he said, in a way that shut down the conversation.

I shifted the gear stick and we drove in silence for a few minutes. I felt the pressing sensation of needing to talk about what had happened between us, on the walk home, but I could already guess that I was going to get a stony reception. I prayed a quick 'help me' prayer.

'Sam, I wanted to apologise for… the way I acted on the walk home.' I stumbled over the words, but I had to commit to getting it out there.

'You don't need to apologise,' Sam muttered, shaking his head and looking out of the window.

I felt wrong-footed now.

'I prayed about it, and maybe we should pray together too.'

The tinny sound of my worship CD played a soundtrack to the silence that followed. It was *Blessed Be Your Name* again.

'Sam?' I asked, looking across from the road to check that he heard me.

'I don't think I can say sorry for showing my love for you, Lil,' he said. 'If it made you feel uncomfortable, then I'm sorry, but I never want you to feel a lack of love from me. Because I know what that's like.'

I blinked. This wasn't where I expected the conversation to go at all.

'What do you mean?' I asked, clicking my indicators and turning off the main road.

'Never mind,' he said.

'You know you are showing love for me by respecting our physical boundaries,' I reminded him. 'And we said that we'd tell your dad…'

'I can't,' he said flatly. 'Not right now.'

I pressed my lips together. *What do I say now, God?* I pulled into a parking space and turned off the engine.

'I'm sorry,' he said, turning to face me properly. 'It's not you. I'm just… my head is a mess at the moment. Give me some time to think, okay?'

'Sure,' I said, feeling tears smart in the corner of my eyes.

How could we go from being on top of the world last night to this?

His eyes softened as he looked at me.

'You're beautiful, you know that, don't you?'

He reached out and touched my chin.

'See you later.'

I'd never been so flustered and distracted at work before. Thankfully it was quiet in the library, and I spent most of the time sorting out the children's section after a nursery group had come in yesterday and ransacked it. I had created a Christmas corner with a mini tree and Christmas stories, but that had taken a bashing too, so I tried to focus on recreating my silver tinseltown. But as I arranged books and decorations, my conversation with Sam was playing on repeat in my head. What did he mean about feeling a lack of love? Was he talking about his parents? Did he feel like they didn't love him because they left the show? Was he justified in thinking that, or was it just coming from the bitterness of his disappointment?

I'd wanted so badly to share my journey of repentance with him… I guess I was shocked that he didn't seem to be feeling the same way I did. Perhaps he was too distracted by the emotional carnage to really think about what had happened between us. But that hurt too, because it was all I could think about last night. The idea that Sam hadn't thought about me at all… That was hardly what I wanted, either.

I knew Sam was on his own journey with the Lord, but this was where it was really hard to accept that. And what it might mean for us if we were going in different directions. As much as I loved him,

I knew if he was going in the opposite direction God wanted me to go in, then God had to win. I'd given my life to Him, and I hadn't done it lightly, for just when I felt like it, or for when it was easy to go His way.

God, I don't want to give him up. Please don't ask me to give him up.

In the library's assortment of Christmas books, I managed to find one nativity story. I placed it centrally, in pride of place, and hoped some family would take it home and think about Jesus instead of presents and Santa. But I had to challenge myself: was Jesus really the centre of my life, or was I sidelining Him for Sam?

In the cold light of day, I would give the right answer. Last night in the starlight… The answer was different.

Sam

The cafe was busy with Christmas shoppers and I barely had time to breathe. It was a sweet relief to switch my brain off and simply focus on taking orders, clearing tables and fetching trays from the kitchen. When my boss, Carla, ordered me to take my lunchbreak in the later part of the afternoon, after the rush, I finally sat in a quiet corner with a toasted sandwich and thought about Lil.

She obviously wasn't happy about last night. As I thought about it, I felt my cheeks heat. The moment when she put her hands on my abdomen… I felt the fizz of desire just remembering it. The argument with my parents had doused it. I felt increasingly guilty. I wasn't acting like a Christian boyfriend. If Lil's parents had been less hands-off, they would have the right to grill me about walking her home in the dark instead of just catching a bus or calling for a taxi. Or at least, taking the main road way instead of the canal footpath. Anything could have happened.

If I was honest, I wished it had.

But I'd promised Lil that I'd respect her, and I needed to follow through on my promise. I picked up my phone, thinking I would send her a text, when I saw three missed calls from my dad. My stomach beginning to swirl with dread, I dialled my voicemail.

'Sam, Annabelle's not feeling well. Mum's been on the phone to the doctor. Just thought I'd let you know.'

Then the second message:

'Sam, Annabelle's got a high temperature. We're a bit concerned but we'll keep you updated.'

The final message had only been left twenty minutes ago.

'Sam, we're taking Annabelle to the hospital. Please pray. Can you call me when you finish work?'

I checked my watch: I had another two hours left of my shift. I sent Dad a text to let him know I'd received the messages, and that I hoped Annabelle was okay. He was the second person to ask me to pray today, and I felt sick thinking about it. I wasn't convinced that God wanted to listen to me pray. I was nothing but a hypocrite. *Please let her be okay* I thought.

'Hey Sam,' Carla said, flicking her head towards the growing queue. 'Do you think you could jump back on here?'

I hurriedly put my phone away and stood up. Texting Lil would have to wait.

Lil usually finished work half an hour before me, and she would get a cup of tea and sit in the corner as I finished up. Today, I caught her eyes flicking over to me with nervous frequency. She fiddled with her teaspoon and half-heartedly tried to read her book. Her hair looked luminous in the grey shadows of the cafe; outside was pitch black, and the lighting was dim. The fairy lights glowed around the window, and she leaned towards the snow-sprayed glass. What was she thinking? Did she regret becoming my girlfriend? How could I reassure her that I loved her? How could I be the man she needed me to be?

God, I don't want to screw this up.

'Young love,' Carla joked, giving my shoulder a playful shove.

'Sorry,' I said automatically, realising that I'd dried this plate five times now.

'You can go now, if you like,' she said. 'I cut your break short earlier.'

'Thank you,' I said gratefully, untying my apron.

'Merry Christmas,' Carla said with a grin.

I was already striding towards Lil, who looked up in surprise. I bent down to kiss her cheek.

'Carla said I can go,' I said. 'Are you done?'

Lil nodded and pushed her chair back. I grabbed her coat and held it out for her.

'Don't forget your book.'

I took her free hand in mine and led her towards the exit. Outside, the wind was strong and I had to press the weight of my shoulder against the door to force it fully open. Lil shivered and tucked against me, wrapping her coat more tightly around her. I dropped her hand to put my arm around her shoulder instead.

'Maybe it'll snow,' I said.

'I don't mind once we're home,' Lil replied. 'Don't fancy driving in it, though.'

Being shut up in the humid environment of the cafe all day, I had been fairly oblivious of the weather. Looking up at the dark sky, no stars were visible.

'I've got to call my dad,' I told her, as we hurried towards the car to get out of the cold. 'Annabelle's ill again.'

She nodded and looked concerned as I pressed the call button. We were nearing the car so she unlocked it, the lights flashing in the gloom.

'Sam?' Dad said, answering the call.

'Hi,' I said. 'Are you at the hospital?'

'Yes,' he said. 'I think we'll be sent home soon, though. Annabelle's got a temperature but it's not developed into anything else.'

'Okay,' I said, exhaling in relief. 'That's good.'

I opened the passenger door and climbed in, and Lil started the engine.

'We're just leaving now,' I told him. 'See you later.'

'Everything okay?' Lil asked, her teeth chattering in the icy car.

I turned up the flow of warm air, but it was lukewarm due to the car not heating up yet. I rubbed my hands together.

'I think so,' I said. 'Wow, it's freezing in here.'

'Let's get home,' she said, moving the car out into the road.

The air was starting to heat up by the time we neared our estate, to the point where we were no longer shivering quite so violently, but Lil's face looked white and pinched. Her gloved fingers gripped the steering wheel, and she squinted out at the road ahead. She looked tense and focused, so I didn't want to raise the sticky subject of Last Night. I could barely hear the car radio with the blasting air, but I worried it might distract her if I turned it up. At least Dad had given me good news about Annabelle.

When Lil finally parked outside our houses, I looked across at her and smiled.

'I'm sorry we didn't get a chance to talk properly earlier,' I said. 'Do you want to come in for a bit?'

She smiled back, tentatively, and nodded.

'Sure.'

We stepped onto the pavement, already tinted with frost, and I slung my arm around Lil's shoulders, guiding her to my front door. It was easy to imagine that we'd both finished a day at work and we were now coming home together. It made it so much better, unlocking the door to an empty house, knowing that you weren't going to be entering it alone.

Lil was shifting her weight from foot to foot, shuddering with the cold night air. She sighed in relief as we walked into the hallway, illuminated by the string of fairy lights Annabelle had woven into greenery all along the coving.

'Nice and warm in here,' she said, starting to take off her coat. I helped her out of it and hung it on the hook.

'Come here,' I said, beckoning to her and opening my arms.

She stepped towards me and I held her tightly. After a moment, she responded by tightening her arms around my back.

'I'm sorry,' I murmured. 'You were right about last night. I haven't been thinking straight.'

'It's okay,' she said, her voice muffled by my shoulder.

I kissed her hair, and held her for a few more moments, breathing her in.

'Maybe we should go and cook something for your parents,' she suggested, pulling back. 'We can talk as we prepare it.'

'Yes, boss,' I joked.

We headed into the kitchen, and I switched on the set of fairy lights. It was just like the other night, when Annabelle was sick. I tuned the radio into the Christmas music station, and Lil started setting up a saucepan and grabbing ingredients. It was a sign of how she'd begun to spend more time here that she knew where to look.

'I thought tomato soup might work,' she said.

We set to work, chopping onions and garlic, and I allowed some thinking space while she got the pan going. Once she was stirring the ingredients, I picked up the thread of conversation.

'You were right,' I said. 'I know I'm not being the boyfriend you need right now. I'm sorry.'

'You're going through a lot,' Lil said, setting down the wooden spoon. 'You're allowed to be worried about your sister.'

'Yes, but that doesn't mean that I don't care about you,' I said. 'Or that I don't need to sort out how I treat you.'

I moved closer to touch her cheek reverently.

'You're so willing to serve others,' I said. 'Coming here to cook for my family… I'm so grateful for you.'

'I want to help you any way I can,' she said softly. 'But Sam, you realise that we need to do things God's way. No night-time kissing in places where, let's face it, no one is going to find us.'

'Heart of the law, not the letter,' I said. It was a phrase I'd heard somewhere.

'Exactly.'

Lil put the lid on to simmer the soup, and then started buttering some bread.

'Fancy another cuppa?' I asked, putting the kettle on.

Mariah Carey was playing, and I grabbed Lil's hands and started twirling her around the kitchen.

'*All I Want for Christmas is You*,' we sang, laughing.

I meant it with all my heart.

Lil

We danced in the kitchen, hyper with reconciliation, and when the soup was done, I turned off the hob and gave it a stir. Sam stood behind me, slipping his hands around my waist.

'I love you, Lil,' he said.

I turned in his arms and smiled.

'I love you too, Sam.'

He leaned closer, and our lips met. He tasted of peppermint because he'd pinched a candy cane from the cupboard.

'Ready?' he asked, then hoisted me up onto the worktop. 'You're tall enough to kiss me now.'

I gave him a mock swipe, then kissed him again, with the novelty of being slightly higher up.

'You promised me we could go to Glastonbury Tor after the play,' he reminded me. 'How about tomorrow?'

'You said it was going to snow!' I laughed. Trust Sam to come up with a crazy plan.

'I'll check the forecast in the morning,' he said. 'You're not getting out of it.'

'Why can't your hobby be painting, like your mum?' I whined. 'Then I wouldn't need to freeze.'

'I'll be there to keep you warm,' he said.

The front door burst open, and Sam's family came in, mid-conversation.

'I still think the doctor was wrong,' Meredith was saying. 'She shouldn't have been sent home with a temperature like this.'

'I'm going to bed,' Annabelle groaned.

I had hurriedly slid down from the counter and turned to check the soup, while Sam walked forward to meet them.

'Hey, Mum,' he said. 'We made you some soup.'

'We?' Meredith echoed sharply, and stepped into the doorway of the kitchen.

She'd clearly had a terrible day. Her hair was dishevelled, and she was wearing an oddly combined Christmas jumper with tracksuit bottoms that clashed.

'What are you doing in my kitchen?' she demanded.

I froze in shock, looking at Sam for help. He stood in front of me protectively.

'Lil's our neighbour, Mum,' he said. 'She came to help out.'

'I don't want help!' Meredith snapped. 'What, do you think I can't cook now?'

'N—no!' I stammered, blushing furiously.

'Why does everyone treat me like an idiot?' Meredith asked the room, gesturing into the air.

'Mer, Lil was being kind.' Simon gently clasped her shoulders, and pulled her back away from the doorway. 'You haven't eaten for hours. Why don't you sit down?'

In the distraction, Sam grabbed my hand and led me towards the front door.

'I'm sorry,' he said, passing me my coat. 'When she gets like this, she lashes out at everyone. It's nothing personal.'

Trying not to cry, I nodded and wrapped my scarf around my neck.

'Will you be okay?' I asked him, reaching out to lay my hand on his cheek.

He nodded and kissed my palm.

'We need to take Annabelle's temperature again,' Meredith was saying.

'No we don't,' Simon replied. 'Let her sleep.'

'I'll call you,' Sam whispered.

It was later that night when we chatted, our voices low in our small, boxy bedrooms with the thin wall between us.

'How's your mum?' I asked.

'Very stressed,' he answered. 'She's convinced that Annabelle needs to go back into hospital, and she's paranoid that if it snows, and then Annabelle needs medical care, that she won't be able to get there or something will go wrong.'

I wished I could put my arms around him.

'Did she eat anything?'

'I think Dad managed to get her to have a few mouthfuls,' he said. 'I had some. It was amazing.'

'I didn't mean to overstep,' I said.

'Lil, I invited you in to make some food with me,' he said. 'At no point did you overstep. If Mum was in her right mind, she would see that.'

'How long will it be before she… returns to her usual self?' I asked.

'I don't know.' He sighed. 'It depends what happens with Annabelle, really.'

'How is she?'

'Annabelle? She's gone to bed.'

'We should have prayed for her earlier,' I said, feeling convicted. After all, we'd made time for dancing to Mariah Carey. 'Can I pray now?'

'Sure,' he said.

'Lord, I pray for Annabelle,' I said. 'Please heal her. Please give the doctors wisdom to help her. Please help Meredith to cope and be her strength…'

And I didn't get any further, because Meredith's voice cut across me.

'Is that girl in here with you?'

I listened, my heart in my mouth, as I heard Sam answer.

'Mum, I'm on the phone.'

'Give me that.'

There was a soft thud, and Sam cried out. It sounded like his mum had grabbed his phone off him and tossed it aside, but the call was still connected. Maybe I should have hung up. But I listened, riveted in horror.

'If your sister gets ill, you know it'll be your fault,' Meredith said venomously. 'She came to see your show, because you wanted to be the centre of attention.'

'I just wanted you all to see me,' Sam said miserably. My heart ached.

'See you?' his mum echoed. 'Well, let's get one thing straight. I'm never going to watch another play again. It's not worth this hell we've been put through.'

I heard the creak of a door, and held my breath. There was a ringing silence.

When Sam started sobbing, I hung up, unable to bear it. By then, I was sobbing too.

Lil

I didn't hear from Sam again that night, even though I messaged him to ask if he was okay. I went to sleep with a sick feeling in my stomach, a deep conviction that something was very broken in Meredith, and the situation wasn't right, wasn't fair on Sam.

'Are you all right, love?' Mum asked me in the morning, as I walked like a zombie to get myself some cereal.

'Yeah,' I sighed. 'Just got to get myself ready for church.'

The church building wasn't far away, just a short walk, and Sam usually went there early with his family to help set the service up. When I arrived, though, there was no sign of any of the Parks. I sat alone, in the spot where Sam usually sat next to me, and Mrs Hart, the treasurer, came to join me.

'Have you heard about Annabelle?' she asked. 'Apparently she took a turn for the worse in the night. They rushed her into hospital. Poor family.'

'Oh no!' I said, grabbing my phone and checking for the zillionth time if Sam had messaged. He hadn't.

'I heard Sam stayed at home this morning just in case they needed to call,' she said, clucking her tongue sympathetically.

I felt instantly torn. I wanted to go and be with him… but he hadn't even messaged me. I wasn't sure how he'd feel about me just turning up after what I overheard last night.

Thinking of that, I looked at Mrs Hart. She was a kind, practical soul who faithfully came to every service and mothered everyone. Really, it was important that she knew the full situation. She could make sure that the family got the support they needed.

'Mrs Hart,' I began, hesitantly. 'I wanted to talk to you about the Parks.'

'Yes, dear?' She looked me over with her bright blue eyes. She didn't miss much.

'I'm worried about them. Well, about Sam.'

'Sam?' her eyebrows rose in surprise. 'I thought he was the healthy one.'

'He is,' I said, 'but I worry… With Annabelle's illness, he has to carry a lot. And sometimes… Meredith says things…'

I trailed off, wondering if I was doing the right thing. Mrs Hart pushed her glasses up and furrowed her brow.

'What kind of things?' she asked. Her tone was light, but I could tell that she was listening intently and taking what I said seriously.

'She blamed Sam for Annabelle's illness, because they went to see him in a play,' I told her, the words rushing out. 'She said it had put them through hell and she was never going to see him in a play again.'

Mrs Hart winced.

'That sounds difficult,' she said. 'I wonder if the pressure of Annabelle's condition has… affected Meredith.'

'She never wants to leave her,' I said. 'When they went to the church Christmas dinner, Sam and I were in the house with Annabelle. She was sick once, but she didn't want us to call them. She went to bed and we kept an eye on her. But when they came home, Meredith was furious.'

'I had a feeling that she was struggling that night,' Mrs Hart said, nodding. 'You know, as a parent, it isn't easy to let go. Especially with what they've been through. But I don't really know them very well yet.'

'I know,' I said. 'I felt like I was just starting to get to know them. Now I'm worried they're going to forbid Sam from seeing me.'

'The joys of young love,' Mrs Hart said wryly. 'Well, remember that you *are* young. You've got your whole lives ahead of you.'

'When did you get married?' I asked her.

She grinned.

'I was nineteen, and Winston was twenty. Don't go getting any ideas, though!' she said, giving me a mock frown. 'Neither of us were going to university or anything like that. We were both working full time. Things were different then.'

'I know,' I sighed. 'Sometimes I worry that we won't be able to cope with a long-distance relationship over three years.'

'Well, it's a test,' she said, shrugging. 'If you're really meant to be together, if it's the Lord's will, then somehow you'll get through it, and be stronger as a result. But don't force things too soon. What's that verse? *Do not awaken love before its time.*'

'I think Sam's dad would have that tattooed on our eyeballs. If he believed in tattoos.'

She giggled, then squeezed my hand.

'They're a good family,' she said. 'Don't worry too much about Sam. I'll see what I can do to help.'

'Thank you,' I said.

I tried to focus on the service, on the songs and the last-minute talk by one of the other leaders, but I kept double-checking my phone for Sam. Nothing. I was feeling increasingly uneasy. Was he actually okay? Why didn't he even text me to tell me what was going on?

In the end, I cracked first and texted him, saying I heard about Annabelle, and could I bring him anything. He texted back: *Waiting for my parents to call. I'll be ok thanks.*

I knew it was nothing personal, but it stung to be shut out. Especially when I wanted to be the person who made things better for him. I wanted to hold him, to comfort him and pray with him. It hurt that he wouldn't let me in to share the hard times as well as the good. It made me question whether him saying that he loved me was real.

From the time that I'd first met him, Sam had been a conflicted boy. He seemed to be constantly grappling with what he wanted, versus what he thought he should do, and how he thought he should behave. Or rather, how his father thought he should behave. I had hoped that doing the play would help him to open up that side of himself that he so often seemed to shut down. Miss Raine was right: he really did understand Romeo.

But when something happened, like his sister going to hospital, or his mum spouting poisonous words, then he just seemed to retreat, withdraw back into himself. Like he was afraid or ashamed of his emotion.

I wanted to tell him that it was all right, that we could cry together, but I knew that deep inside, there was a wound in Sam that I couldn't heal.

Only God could.

Sam

I sat watching the rain lash against the window, a constant spatter of sound. The day was bleeding by, washed out sunlight barely breaking through the thick grey cloud. It could be nine a.m., or it could be three p.m. I was stuck in a timeless waiting zone.

Last night already seemed worlds away. Mum's sharp words had broken my skin like a serrated knife, but these were old scars that reopened easily. Annabelle getting sick soon morphed into familiar chaos: phone calls, packing bags, and the screech of car tyres. I'd been left alone, which was understandable—I'd be in the way in hospital, and I was planning to leave home in a few months' time. Guilt blossomed in my chest as I felt the straining desire to be free. An uninterrupted night's sleep, no demands pressed upon me, and the carefree decision of which pizza to cook for dinner.

I waited for my parents to call.

I knew I could have gone to church, or asked Lil to come over, but also… I couldn't. How could I go along and sing the hymns while my heart was echoing *Why*? How could I taste Lil's sweetness when my family were in crisis and needed me to be alert and ready for them?

The thing that hurt most, what I couldn't avoid, was that my mum's words were true. I did want to be the centre of attention, for once, and it was down to me, insisting on them coming, that my sister was now in hospital. Potentially fighting for her life. Yes, Annabelle seemed less fragile now than when she was younger, but it was still frightening how quickly she could deteriorate. My beautiful, caring sister, who was the only person in my family to praise my performance. It made me feel like I was fooling myself.

My limbs were stiff and my throat was dry. I walked, almost staggered, to the kitchen to get some water. I was putting myself through a self-proclaimed fast. Given that I had no ability to pray, my actions would have to suffice. I didn't deserve to eat and enjoy food, anyway.

I had just drained the glass when my phone went off. I answered it eagerly.

'Dad?'

'Hey, Sam,' he said, sounding tired. There was background noise of multiple conversations.

'How is she?'

'She's on a drip, and she's stable.'

I exhaled, not even aware I'd been holding my breath.

'That's good.'

'I think we'll be staying in until tomorrow,' he said. 'Are you all right?'

'Yeah, I'm fine.'

'Did you go to church?'

I considered lying, but then he'd ask someone and just find out anyway.

'No.'

'Have you eaten anything?'

I didn't answer.

'Sam, you need to look after yourself,' Dad said, an edge of reprimand in his tone. That edge was always present. 'I've got enough to worry about without you too.'

'I just… wanted to be ready to help,' I said. Part of me wanted to cry, but I held it in.

'I appreciate that, son,' he said. 'Honestly, there's nothing you can do. Except pray, of course. Listen, why don't you go for a walk with Lil? Might take your mind off things.'

I blinked. Dad was suggesting that I should spend time with Lil?

'Okay,' I said, waiting for a catch.

'Keep active, you know?'

I heard my mum's voice murmuring something indistinguishable.

'I think the doctor's coming—I'd better go. Speak soon.'

He rang off, and I stared at the phone in my hand for a moment. At least Annabelle was alright. I opened the cupboard under the sink and pulled out a flask. It was time to text Lil.

Lil

The weather was disgusting. I drove along the winding, country road, my wipers going at their fastest pace, and Sam was humming along to the music in the passenger seat. He seemed oblivious. His fingers tapped a rhythm on his knees, and he kept opening up my plastic tub of sweets in the glove compartment, then snapping the lid back on. The nervous energy was palpable.

'So Annabelle is doing okay?' I asked.

'I think so.' He nodded. 'She'll be in overnight. See what they say tomorrow.'

I drove, thinking about all of the things that I wanted us to talk about, but I didn't dare to mention what I overheard on the call yesterday. It was all off-limits. The thermometer on the dashboard said two degrees Celsius. The rain had the consistency of sleet now, and there wasn't much daylight left in the afternoon. Still, when Sam had suggested Glastonbury Tor, I hadn't the heart to turn him down. I wanted to see him so badly.

We finally arrived, and I stared at the grim scene outside of the safety of the car.

'Are you sure you want to do this?' I asked him.

'Course!' He unclicked his seatbelt. 'Where's your sense of adventure?'

The car park, unsurprisingly, was deserted. As soon as I stepped outside, I pulled my jacket tighter around me, with my hood up. I grabbed my wellies from the boot and pulled them on, throwing my trainers inside.

The Tor stood, a lone icon on the hill, and it wasn't going to be a very long or difficult walk to get to it. But with the adverse weather, it felt like a mission. The wind was driving the sleet into my face, leaving cold trails over my cheeks. Sam took my hand and led us at an energetic pace. I guessed he'd been cooped up all day and now he was desperate to explore. I didn't understand his love of the outdoors, especially in times like this, but I was determined to go along with whatever he wanted. What was a bit of discomfort? A slightly cold shower?

Sam was undaunted. I huffed and puffed up the steeper part of the hill, while he seemed to find it all easy. Usually, there would be a panoramic view, but the moisture had formed a hazy mist, and it was nearly twilight. There weren't going to be any pretty sunset colours or any stars visible in this.

'Guess there's not much of a view today,' Sam said, surveying the scene. He looked at me and grinned apologetically. 'You okay?'

'Can we head back now?' I asked, nodding, but my teeth were chattering.

'Sure,' he said, rubbing my hand between his. 'I can warm you up.'

We stumbled back to the car, the light fading fast, and the ground was uneven. All of me felt drenched, right down to my underwear. I was going to need a nice hot bath after this.

'I brought some tea for you,' he said.

'I think I'm going to need more than tea,' I huffed.

I changed back into my shoes, and got behind the wheel with my soaking coat and clothes. My hair was frizzing over my face and my hands were shaking as I turned the key in the ignition to get the warm air flowing.

'Here you go.' Sam passed me the flask.

I tried to control the juddering of my shoulders as I brought it to my lips. It was wonderfully hot.

'Careful you don't burn yourself,' he said, brushing my hair back out of my face.

I handed it back to him, and he drank a few swigs himself, then put it in the footwell.

'Let's warm you up a bit,' he said, rubbing his hands up and down my shoulders.

'Let's just get back,' I said.

The inside of the car window was misting up, so I had the wipers going and used the car cloth to clear it up. The thermometer now said it was freezing.

'That sleet's turned to snow,' Sam commented.

We could only see what the car headlights illuminated.

'It won't stick, given how wet everything is,' I said.

Still, I didn't want to be driving in a blizzard. I put the car in gear and then drove off, willing the air to warm up inside the car. At the moment it felt like air con.

'Will you ever forgive me for making you do this?' Sam asked mischievously.

'Never,' I said, but I grinned as I said it.

Sam

I was high from adventure and Haribo. As we made our way back, I kept bursting into laughter. We'd walked to Glastonbury Tor on one of the worst days of the year. It was preposterous, and I loved it.

Lil stopped shaking as much once the warm air kicked in, but we were both soaked through.

'All I want is a nice, hot bath,' she said longingly.

I couldn't get that image out of my head.

I knew it was reckless, but when we pulled up outside the house, I invited her in.

'I don't want to be alone,' I said. It was true.

I locked the door behind us and took her hand.

'How about a hot shower?' I asked. 'Together?'

She raised an eyebrow suspiciously.

'We'll keep our clothes on,' I added. 'They're soaking anyway.'

'What will I put on afterwards?' she asked.

'I'll lend you some of my clothes.'

She laughed, and I hung our coats up on the bannister, then led her upstairs. It felt strange, my house being empty, and the bathroom with my mother's book on the windowsill and a new bottle of shampoo left on the side.

'Sam, this is *weird*,' Lil said, laughing awkwardly.

'It doesn't have to be,' I said, pushing my doubts to the side.

I turned on the faucet quickly, before I could change my mind. My hand was shaking. The stream of water gushed out, and soon steam was rising.

'Look.' I took off my socks, and stepped under the shower. 'Ah, it's so warm. Come on!'

Blushing and giggling, Lil took off her socks and then took my outstretched hand, stepping in too. She closed her eyes and tilted her face up, and her hair was flattened and hung in a glistening curtain over her drenched sweater. I pulled her close to me, so we could both be under the water, and I ran my fingers over her cheekbones.

'I love you,' I whispered.

She opened her eyes and looked at me, water streaming down her face, and my breath caught in my throat. Suddenly we were kissing, our mouths meeting with the water gushing around us, and I was so tempted to run my hands all over her body, and peel off every item of clothing that stood in the way of us being completely bare with each other. I moved, and bumped into the faucet, so I turned it off. We stood there, dripping wet, and panting.

'I'll get you a towel,' I said, conscious of how aroused I was and wondering whether she'd noticed.

I grabbed one off the rail, and handed it to her, burying my own face into the other.

'You stay in here,' I said. 'Dry yourself off and I'll pass you some clothes through the doorway.'

I walked across the hallway to my bedroom, and started taking my layers off with a sense of surreality. Lil was just in the shower with me! She was gorgeous. She was undressing right now…

I tried to push that thought away and concentrated on pulling my wet clothes off. I quickly found some joggers and a T-shirt, and spares for Lil. I hurried to the bathroom door.

'Here you go,' I said.

She opened the door and took them from me, her arms long and bare with the towel wrapped around her. She had nothing on underneath it, I was pretty sure. I blushed and looked away.

'Thanks,' she said.

I waited outside the door, shifting from one foot to the other, until she was ready.

'Don't laugh,' she said, opening the door.

She was wearing my joggers and T-shirt, which were ridiculously loose on her and oversized, but at the same time, her womanly figure was even more evident than usual. I realised that she no longer had a bra or underwear to wear.

'You're staring,' she said, a slight smile playing upon her lips.

'Sorry,' I said automatically. 'We should… hang up those wet clothes.'

It was difficult to form sentences. She giggled and picked up her clothes from the floor.

'Where shall I hang them?'

I took her to my room, and gave her some hangers, watching her hook them over my curtain rail. Every time she stretched up to reach, the T-shirt pulled against her. She knew the effect she was having on me.

'Cat got your tongue?' she said flirtatiously, walking up to me.

I licked my lips.

'You look stunning,' I said.

She arched her eyebrow and put her arms around my neck, pressing herself against me. I suppressed a moan.

'Kiss me, then,' she murmured.

It was all the invitation I needed.

Away from the running water and steam of the shower, our mouths met again, and she tasted of rain.

'I love you, Sam.'

I would never get tired of hearing her say it.

Lil

Outside it was pitch black, and in Sam's room, the light was dim. He kissed me hungrily, and after the hours we'd spent apart, with me constantly worrying about him, I felt a sweet relief that he still loved me. After being freezing cold in the driving rain and sleet, Sam's clothes were soft against my skin, and his hands smoothed over my back with warmth in his touch… Well, more like fire.

I didn't know where this was going to lead, and I knew it would have to stop, but I was enjoying the sensation too much. The closeness, our bodies pressed together, tasting each other in the bliss of utter privacy. This time, we weren't cramped in a treehouse or on a public footpath, or in a car with the gear stick jamming into us every time we tried to move. It felt… untethered.

'Sam,' I murmured. 'You should probably check your phone.'

He pulled back, his eyes refocusing on my face. I could see the battle between his desire and his obligation, the latter gradually sharpening the haze of the former.

'Okay.'

He looked around and realised he'd left it in the bathroom. While he went to get it, I tried to compose myself. I needed to leave before something happened. Well, something else, anyway. My hair was dripping wet and I'd towel-dried it, but I needed a hairdryer. I wrung it out and grabbed my clothes off the hangers, bundling them up. On the landing, Sam appeared in the bathroom doorway, looking pale.

'My dad's on his way home,' he said. 'They decided only Mum was going to stay in the hospital.'

'I'd better go,' I said, feeling a lick of fear that we might be discovered. But then, I was the one who suggested he should be accountable to his dad. I was such a hypocrite.

I hurried down the stairs, carrying my wet clothes, and hearing the unmistakable reminder of what I'd made Sam agree. I slipped my trainers on, and lifted my coat from the bannister.

'I think you should talk to your dad,' I said, facing him.

'What do you want me to say?' he asked, a defensive tone edging into his voice.

'Just… be honest with him.'

His expression was pained. He didn't say anything, so I turned and opened the front door.

'I hope Annabelle's doing alright,' I said, then I closed the door behind me.

Back in my own house, I flung my wet clothes in the tumble dryer, then ran upstairs to change before my parents saw me. But I kept Sam's T-shirt by my pillow. It smelled of laundry detergent, but there was also something of him. I wasn't going to give it back.

Sam

My dad arrived about five minutes after Lil had left. The first thing he did when he came inside was hug me. I was shocked. My parents weren't touchy-feely usually. When he drew back, there were actual tears in his eyes.

'I want you to know that I love you,' he said hoarsely. 'I'm sorry there's been so much pressure on you.'

I blinked. My parents had never apologised to me about pressure. It was so much of a norm that I didn't even think they noticed it.

'Have you had something to eat?' he asked. 'I could make some bacon sandwiches if you like?'

I nodded.

'That'd be great.'

He smiled and headed into the kitchen, placing the frying pan on the hob and retrieving ingredients from the fridge.

'Did you see Lil?' he asked, focusing on laying strips of bacon in the pan.

It was the perfect opening, but I couldn't do it. I couldn't tell him the truth.

'Yes, we went for a walk,' I said, hating my own cowardice.

'Bit wet, isn't it?' Dad laughed, and looked out of the window into the darkness. 'I think the snow might stick overnight. It was one of the reasons Mum wanted me to stay in the hospital, but Mrs Hart pointed out that you'd been on your own and probably needed some moral support.'

'Mrs Hart?'

'Yes.' He turned around to face me, the bacon starting to sizzle. 'She phoned me to see how Annabelle was doing, and you. When I thought about it, I hadn't spoken to you much and I felt I ought to come home.'

I felt a completely irrational pang of annoyance. Lil and I had finally been alone together, and then everything had been spoiled by my dad coming back, just because Mrs Hart had asked how I was doing.

'What's the matter?' Dad asked

'Nothing,' I said, schooling my expression.

We ate the sandwiches, then Dad went up to bed. He was exhausted. I was left to pace my bedroom with restless energy. If the weather hadn't been so bad, I would have put on my coat again and gone out for a walk. That's what I should have done. But I was tired of trying to make the right choice all the time.

Lil

In the morning, even though it wasn't light outside when my alarm went off, I could see the white gleam of snow under the streetlight. The temperature had stayed low, and the snow had begun to stick. The roads still looked all right, and it wasn't snowing anymore, but there were warnings all over the weather app. More snow forecast.

I checked that my school was still open—sadly, it was—and then dressed in my uniform. I hadn't heard from Sam since I left his house yesterday, but I assumed he'd be calling for me to walk to school.

I decided to wear wellies. There were only a few days left of term, so what were they going to do?

'I hate snow,' my dad said, as we ate breakfast in the kitchen. 'I might have to cancel lessons.'

'The main roads will be all right,' I said.

'Yes, but I've got to drive right up to people's houses,' he said. 'The cul-de-sacs don't get gritted.'

There was a knock at the door. I sprang up to answer it. Sam stood, and all the memories of what happened yesterday (the shower!!!) filled the silence as he looked at me tentatively. I smiled, and grabbed my coat.

'Bye, Dad!'

We set off. As soon as we got onto the footpath, away from the main road, the snow was crunchier under our feet. The frost touched all of the leaves on the verge, and the sky was a light shade of grey, almost white.

'How's Annabelle?' I asked.

'She slept better last night,' he said. 'Mum texted Dad, and he left this morning to go back to the hospital.'

'It was nice that he came home to see you,' I said.

Now Sam, now is the time when you need to say that things went too far and you spoke to him…

Sam didn't respond, beyond the barest of shrugs. We walked on, and I felt conflicted over what to bring up next. The list of taboo topics was growing.

'He only came because Mrs Hart called him,' Sam said finally.

I looked over in surprise, and felt my cheeks turn pink.

'She was worried about you,' I said. 'Well, I was worried about you, and I was speaking to her in church—'

'Wait, you spoke to Mrs Hart?' Sam interrupted. His tone was unusually sharp.

'She was the one who told me about Annabelle,' I said. 'You didn't text me, remember?'

'Some things need to be kept within the family,' he said, and his words sliced my heart.

We walked in silence, and I struggled to hold the tears back. Maybe I had misjudged the situation. I didn't realise it was going to make him angry.

We came off the canal, and onto the last stretch of road leading to school.

'Look, what you need to appreciate is that my sister's illness is something we've lived with ever since she was born,' he said. 'There were busybodies in our last church, who thought we should have done this or that differently, but they didn't understand. My parents are doing the best they can. I'm practically leaving home anyway, so you don't need to worry about me.'

'I do, though,' I said, tears spilling down my cheeks. 'Especially when I heard what your mother said to you the other night.'

He paled and stiffened.

'That was private,' he said.

'I couldn't help it!' I cried. 'The call was still on.'

'You should have hung up, then.'

'I did!'

I swiped my hand under my nose.

'She needs help, Sam,' I said. 'Counselling, support, or something. I know you don't want to hear it, but she's a ticking time bomb and it's only a matter of time before she lashes out and isolates your whole family from the people who are trying to help you.'

'Just because she said a few things to offend you—'

'This isn't about me, Sam!'

'Really?' he asked. 'Are you sure it's not you trying to get the Christian family you've always wanted through me, and you don't like that my parents are reserved, and like to keep things between us without outsiders interfering?'

'Is that what I am to you, an outsider?' I asked in disbelief. 'What was yesterday about then? Inviting me in to take a *shower* with you? Is that how you normally treat outsiders?'

Guilt flashed across his expression.

'I bet you didn't tell your father about that,' I said, hoping that he would contradict me. But he didn't. 'Did you tell him about any of it?'

'No.' Sam shook his head.

'Why not?' I demanded.

Sam lifted his shoulders.

'Because I know I would do it again this afternoon, if I could get away with it.'

We looked at each other, my eyes wet but his were dry.

'I'm tired of pretending,' he said.

'I'm not asking you to pretend—'

'You are, though,' he cut in. 'You've got this idea in your head of Sam, the perfect Christian boyfriend. And that's not who I am, Lil.'

'I don't know where all this is coming from,' I said, feeling like he'd taken a baseball bat to every single ornament on my Christmas tree.

'I have so many struggles I've never shared with you,' Sam said.

'Then tell me,' I pleaded. 'Let me in.'

'What, so you can go to my father and tell him how sinful I am?' he asked.

It was like he had slapped me. I took a step back.

'No, just because I love you and I want to help you—'

'I don't want to be fixed, Lil,' he said. 'And it's not your job to do that.'

I shook my head, tears falling down my face again.

'Well, that's it, then,' I said. 'I don't think we should see each other anymore.'

Pain flashed in his eyes, but he didn't argue.

'You deserve a good Christian boyfriend,' he said. 'I hope you find one.'

We went our separate ways at the school gate, walking off to different corridors, and I couldn't think about all the people who were going to talk to me about how brilliant the play was, and how perfectly Sam and I played Romeo and Juliet, or the R.E. lessons where we'd now be sitting on different tables, or the bus journeys I was going to take instead of walking. I just wanted to lock myself away and cry. Miss Carr took one look at me and sent me home. By lunchtime, the snow started to fall again. This time, it fell heavily and there were several inches on the ground. They decided to close school for the Christmas holidays early, and I stayed within the four walls of my house for the hardest Christmas I'd ever known, trying not to think about the boy who was just a few feet away on the other side of the wall.

Sam

Every day, I started typing a message to Lil. I never pressed send. I missed her so much, and I hated being apart from her, but it just felt like we'd reached an impasse. She needed me to be someone I wasn't. I was no good for her.

It was a strange Christmas. Annabelle came home from hospital, and both she and Mum were so wrung out, they spent a lot of time in bed. Christmas Day was quiet. Dad went to church to run the service, but the rest of us stayed at home.

It wasn't until New Year, when Annabelle was well enough to watch movies on the sofa, that she asked me if Lil was coming over.

'We broke up,' I told her. I managed to say it without crying, but when her mouth opened in shock, I struggled to keep my emotions in check.

'What?' she asked, horrified. 'When did this happen? Why?'

She was loud enough that Mum poked her head around the door.

'What's wrong, love?' she asked.

'Sam's broken up with Lil,' Annabelle announced. 'Did you know?'

'No.' Mum looked at me. She didn't seem instantly happy about it, which is what I expected. 'You didn't mention anything.'

No one asked me anything, that was why. I shrugged. Non verbal communication was the best way to go when you felt like sobbing.

'Or was it Lil breaking up with you?' Annabelle asked, in that unique sisterly way of sliding the knife under your ribs and twisting it. It couldn't have been any more painful than what I was feeling.

'It was a mutual decision,' I said in a strangled voice, then got to my feet. 'And no, I don't want to talk about it.'

I escaped to my room where I could fall apart without being disturbed. Or so I thought. Annabelle knocked on the door and opened it a crack.

'Sam?' she said softly.

I didn't answer. She pushed the door open further, saw me on the bed, and came to sit next to me. I wiped my eyes.

'You love her, don't you?' she said.

'Yes, but it's not enough,' I said, running my fingers through my hair. 'I'm a mess, Annabelle. I can't offer her anything. She's better off without me.'

'I think that's a lie you're telling yourself so that you don't have to deal with things that are painful,' she said, putting her arm around me. 'We all have mess, Sam. Any relationship between two humans is going to involve mess.'

'Some messes are worse than others,' I said.

She rubbed my shoulder comfortingly.

'You know when we were younger, and one of us hurt the other, Mum and Dad used to make us apologise and forgive each other?'

I smiled through my tears and nodded at the memory of many forced apologies and professions of (not very genuine) forgiveness.

'Well, I don't know what's happened between you two, but can't you just say sorry and forgive each other? Work through it?'

'You know Mum and Dad don't want us to be together,' I reminded her. 'We're going to university. I don't know how to navigate all that.'

Annabelle's eyes narrowed.

'Those aren't insurmountable problems,' she said. 'If you were certain that she was the one for you, then you would get through those challenges.'

'It's not that she's not the one for me,' I said. 'It's that I'm not the one for her.'

'Did she say that?'

'Not exactly… but that's pretty much what she meant.'

I thought for the hundredth time about our final, infuriating conversation.

'You don't sound sure,' Annabelle said.

'You weren't there, okay?' I snapped. 'I'm nearly eighteen; I need to be allowed to make my own decisions.'

'You're seriously telling *me* that?' She arched her eyebrow. 'I'll be lucky if I get to leave home before I'm thirty.'

'How about you come and live with me, then?' I joked.

'The problem is, you can't cook.'

We both smiled.

'I appreciate your support,' I said.

She squeezed my shoulder.

'I'm here for you,' she said. 'I have zero experience with relationships but I will always be in your corner if you need me.'

'Thanks, sis.'

After she left, I felt a hollow sensation of guilt. What would Annabelle say if she saw everything that had happened between Lil and me? Kissing in the nightclub, in the car together, Lil's hands on my stomach on the footpath at night, and the two of us under this very roof, in the shower together? What kind of example was I setting? I sure as heck wouldn't want *her* to be doing any of those things with some guy. In fact, I would punch his lights out if I got my hands on him.

But I felt so conflicted, because I was being honest when I said to Lil I wasn't really sorry. I would have done it again if I had the opportunity. That was what scared me so much about my sin. It felt so… inevitable. My passions were just too strong to resist.

If Lil had started undressing, what would I have done? Part of me wished that I was the noble hero, who would cover his eyes and gently refuse her. Who cared more about her dignity and purity than his own selfish desire. But I knew I was not that guy. I would have taken anything she offered me, as long as she was willing. And that troubled me even more, because I knew even if she offered it willingly, she would one hundred per cent regret it afterwards. Sure, I could argue in a court of law that it was consensual, but deep down I would know the truth. Lil's purity was precious, and something I should protect, not exploit. I couldn't trust myself to do that, and so I had no business being in a relationship with her.

But it meant breaking both our hearts.

Spring

Lil

Given that we lived next door to each other, it was surprisingly easy to avoid Sam. School was absorbing, both inside and outside of its four walls, and he had his friendship group from Biology, while I spent my time with the girls. I didn't socialise much. I kept my Saturday job, but I was studying a lot at home. I still went to church, but he wasn't always there. I knew from my dad that he sometimes booked a driving lesson on a Sunday morning, and I sat on the other side of the room so I wouldn't have to speak to him. There were times when I felt his eyes on me. There were times when I looked at him, too. But eye contact was difficult. There was too much between us: too much recognition, and too much pain.

Darcy still went over to see Annabelle on a regular basis, and I would pounce on her every time to ask how Sam was.

'Just text him and ask him yourself,' she said, rolling her eyes.

'I can't.'

'He does exactly the same thing, you realise,' she continued. 'He asks me the same questions every time without fail: how's Lil? Are her studies okay? Anything else going on? I take that to mean, *does she have another boyfriend yet?*'

'What did you say?' I asked, my heart hammering in my chest.

'I said *you should ask her yourself* and *I think it's unlikely she has another boyfriend when she stays at home studying all the time, and when she's not studying she's watching cheesy romantic movies and crying over you.*'

'You did not seriously say that?' My jaw dropped.

'Words to that effect.' She waved her hand callously, then opened up the cupboard and pulled out a lollipop.

'Darcy!'

'Look, your pining thing is a bit depressing,' she said. 'If you want to be together, just be together! Why's it got to be so complicated?'

I sighed.

'It just is.'

'Is this something to do with God that I wouldn't understand?' she said dryly.

'Well…' I took a deep breath. 'I want to put God first. I'm not sure Sam feels the same way. We can't really be together if we want different things in life.'

'I thought he was a Christian too. His dad's the vicar guy, isn't he?'

'Pastor,' I corrected. 'That doesn't mean that Sam is automatically a Christian, Darce. It's something you have to make a personal decision about.'

'Only if you know about it,' she said, removing her lollipop to make this pronouncement.

I stared at her.

'What?' she asked, catching my expression. 'I know that you started going to church and all that stuff, but I've never been. Mum and Dad never told me anything about it. So how am I supposed to make a decision when I don't know what I'm making a decision about?'

I sent up a quick prayer and then focused on my sister.

'I can explain it to you, if you like,' I said. 'We could maybe do some Bible study together.'

'Okay,' she said. She stuck the lollipop back in her mouth to check her phone. 'I'm going over Stacey's tomorrow night so maybe the afternoon could work? And I can come to church with you on Sunday, too. It's kind of sad that you go on your own.'

She left me in the kitchen, staring after her in amazement.

God, I don't know what You're doing, but I trust You.

Sam

I turned eighteen in February. It had been an icy two months, and there was fresh snowfall on my birthday. At first, it was just a light covering over the ground, sticking mainly on the grass but not the road. While we were in R.E., Sarah pointed at the window. Thick flakes were pelting down from a pewter sky.

We were sent home. In the moment of elation, I grinned at Lil, and she smiled back before turning to speak to her friends. I reminded myself of where we stood. We weren't messaging each other and we weren't really speaking, either. It was for the best. That's what I was trying to tell myself, anyway.

I walked out of the school grounds, but when I reached the main road, Lil was waiting at the bus stop alone. I hesitated. She looked so beautiful, with her long red hair, and her scarf arranged in that way that made her seem stylish and aloof. Out of my league.

She looked up and saw me. I watched her eyes widen with recognition… and pain. It brought a sharp pang into my stomach to see it.

How many times had I put on my favourite music, laid back on my bed, and thought about what I would say to her if I had the opportunity? How many fictional conversations had I invented, in a parallel universe where we were together again?

Perhaps it was selfish, but it was my birthday. I walked towards her.

'Hey,' I said.

She didn't reply, just raised her eyebrows questioningly. *Why are you talking to me?*

'Where are your friends?' I asked.

'They already left,' she said. 'I missed the bus.'

'Only takes forty minutes to walk,' I said.

'There will be another bus before too long,' she said, checking her phone with a frown, dusting the snow from it.

I looked up the street. The bus stop was deserted, and there were barely any cars on the road.

'You sure about that?' I asked.

Her eyes met mine, the golden brown colour I'd missed. I pleaded with her silently. *Come with me.*

She turned her head to look up the road. The falling snow made it hard to see much; the end of the street was lost in a white-grey haze. Murky.

I brushed flakes from my face, spreading wetness onto my cheeks. Lil shook her hair, dusted with snow, and then started walking alongside me.

'Isn't it your birthday?' she said.

I felt excited that she'd remembered.

We followed the familiar path, now transformed by the layers of white. We were both subdued by the memory of the last time we walked here together. Now we were physically with each other, but separated by all of the things that had come between us. Mainly, me. I was the problem.

'Are you doing anything to celebrate?' Lil asked.

'Getting a tattoo.' I managed to say it with a straight face... for about one second. Her shocked expression made me guffaw with laughter. She smiled reluctantly when she realised, but her heart wasn't in it.

'Only joking,' I said. 'We're going out for dinner.'

I wished she was coming too, and from what I caught of her expression, she did too. She looked away, and I stopped walking.

'Lil,' I said.

'Don't, Sam!' she said, continuing to walk.

She sounded close to tears. I hated that I made her cry, but I also wanted to know that she still cared. Clearly, she did.

I caught up with her.

'So, we can't talk about anything?' I pressed. 'You're upset.'

'I've been upset for two months, Sam,' she said, her tone sharp. 'You know why.'

'It's not easy for me either,' I said, feeling annoyed. I had honestly tried to do what was best for her.

'Why don't you come to church anymore?' she asked. She was finally looking straight at me. Now it was my turn to look away.

'You know why,' I said, repeating her own words.

'I don't understand,' she said.

'I can't pretend anymore,' I said. 'I'm not who everyone thinks I am.'

'You can be honest,' she said.

'No, I can't,' I said, my fingers pulling through my hair in frustration. 'You don't know what it's like being the pastor's son.'

'No, I don't!' Lil said, her cheeks flushing with anger. 'Instead, I've had to go to church on my own for years. Darcy's coming with me now—she says she feels *sorry* for me. You have a Christian family and you grew up with everything I didn't. But now you're pushing me away, and pushing God away, and where does it lead, Sam? Where are you going to end up?'

'I don't know,' I said, losing the will to fight.

We continued to follow the canal, the snow creating a vacuum of silence. Lil didn't like who I was becoming… who I was. Let's face it, I didn't like myself either. She was right: I was privileged, and I had taken it all for granted.

We reached the bridge that led back to the residential streets. It was where we kissed, the night of the play when we walked home. Lil paused, and looked at me.

'I don't understand why you can't just be honest, sort all of this out, and then we could be together,' she said. 'I've missed you.'

Her face crumpled and she started to cry. My insides churned with guilt and sorrow.

'Come here,' I said, opening my arms to her.

We hugged, and I smelled her hair, dusted with snowflakes. I wished I could tell her that it was all fine, that we could be together. But I couldn't lie anymore.

'I don't know where I am with God, and I can't be the man that you deserve,' I told her. 'Even now, I can't trust myself not to do something stupid like kiss you.'

She pulled back, so that her face was inches from mine. Tears had reddened her eyes and wet her cheeks, along with the melting snowflakes. I could see in her expression that if I kissed her, she would kiss me back.

'I can't do it, Lil. I mustn't,' I whispered.

She lowered her eyes, but I saw her longing and disappointment.

'Let's go home,' she said.

Sam

When we reached our front doors, my resolve wavered. Perhaps we should kiss goodbye… to bring some sort of closure…

'Enjoy your birthday,' Lil said, giving me a final, lingering look before she went inside.

I stood, helpless on the pavement, wishing that things could be different. I wanted to believe that I could change, that I could 'sort things out', as Lil had said, and that she would wait for me. I knew it wasn't fair to expect that from her.

My nose was cold and my fingers were stinging, even through my gloves. I wiped the snow from my face and trudged inside, heading straight for my room without speaking to anyone. I stared at the wall which separated me from Lil. What was she doing right now? Was she sitting there, feeling as lost and forlorn as I was?

The hours passed, and the sky darkened. I didn't bother turning on the light. I could hear voices downstairs, and my mum texted me to ask when I'd be home. She obviously hadn't realised I was here. It was horribly familiar, the feeling of being overlooked. The only person who had seen me was Lil, and now I was cut off from her. And even with her, I hadn't been totally honest and transparent.

Finally, my dad opened my bedroom door and found me.

'There you are!' he said in surprise, flicking the light switch on. 'Are you going to change out of your uniform for the meal?'

'I don't want to go,' I said.

He frowned.

'What's the matter?'

I didn't answer. There was no point. He wouldn't listen, anyway.

'You can't keep doing this, Sam,' he said, shaking his head. 'Locking yourself away, sitting in the dark, crying over a girl. You're leaving home in a few months' time. I need to know that you can look after yourself.'

'I can't just turn my emotions off like you,' I said, dropping my head onto my arms to hide my tears.

'You have a choice, Sam,' Dad said. 'You can let yourself be controlled by your emotions, and then you'll be up and down like a yoyo. Or, you can take control. Even if you feel terrible, put on a brave face. Your mother and Annabelle are waiting to go out for a meal with you, to celebrate your birthday. Think about how hurt they'll be if you refuse to come.'

It was a familiar narrative, reminding me of my own selfishness. I knew he was right, but I hated how he made me feel.

'We'll be waiting downstairs,' he said.

Once he'd gone, I rubbed my hands over my face. I took a deep breath. Then I stood up and pulled out a shirt to wear, with my Romeo jeans. Romeo was going to have to die (again). I downed the glass of water by my bed and rearranged my mussed-up hair. It was time to grow up.

Summer

Lil

After our last exam, we were all going out to celebrate. It was a sweIteringly hot day right at the end of June. We had two months of freedom ahead of us before we started at university in September.

In many ways, the last six months had been a marathon, a pure test of endurance for me. I had studied, worked, and tried not to think about Sam. Part of me couldn't wait to go to uni and have a new start. Part of me didn't want to let go.

I wore a white cotton dress and shared a taxi with the girls. We were at a club with patio doors, open onto a yard area. Practically everyone from our yeargroup was there. I scanned the crowd for Sam; he hadn't arrived yet. I accepted a glass of white wine from Shannon and we toasted the end of exams. I made small talk with Clare's boyfriend, Tom, and his mate Chris. Still, I knew the exact moment when Sam entered the room. My cheeks began turning red, even though I wasn't looking at him. I could feel him staring at me.

I'd seen him, of course. We'd sat through R.E. lessons, separated now by three desks. I'd lined up with him to enter the exam hall. He had occasionally asked me how I was. What could I say to that? Every time I said "fine", he looked disappointed. How else could I respond?

Actually, Sam, I'm hoping that you'll sweep me off my feet. That you'll want me back enough to change. That you'll be who I thought you were.

He could probably read all that from my eyes anyway.

Perhaps it was inevitable, that as the evening progressed, we drifted towards each other like moths to a flame. The last traces of sunlight were disappearing, and merging into a twilight with a few eager stars.

'That's Venus.'

I turned, and Sam was there, looking up at the sky.

'You shouldn't sneak up on people,' I said, but inwardly, I sighed with relief.

Everyone was in various stages of drunkenness. I'd seen Sam holding beer bottles, and I could smell it faintly on his breath, but he seemed his usual self.

'Are you here with anyone?' he asked. His tone was light, but I could tell he cared.

'You know I'm not.'

'That guy seemed interested in you.'

He nodded towards Chris, who was talking to Tom and occasionally looking back over in my direction.

'Well, I'm not interested in him.'

Sam stepped closer, still behind me, and his fingers lightly touched my elbow. How did he still have such an effect on me? I tried to hold myself rigid, so that I wouldn't fall backwards and sink into his arms.

'How are you getting home?' he asked, his voice sending tingles of sensation down the back of my neck.

I twisted round to look at him. The smell of alcohol was definitely stronger now that I was facing him, and in the background I could see the Xbox crew. Cole was brandishing a massive pitcher full of something... Beer, maybe? They were shouting over the music and I knew that Sam would go back to them if I pushed him away. I made a split second decision.

'Why don't you get the last bus with me?' I asked. 'We can leave now.'

His eyes lit up.

'Okay,' he said.

I grabbed my jacket and we headed towards the patio doors, ready to brave the dancing crowd. It was impossibly jam packed. Sensing my hesitation, Sam took my hand and began to weave a path through the club. I squeezed my way around sweaty bodies, the cloying smell of booze making me claustrophobic. I made up my mind that I was not going to bother with the clubbing programme of Freshers' Week when I started uni. I didn't belong here, in this world. I'd come out tonight because I felt I should. Celebrating exams was a rite of passage. Well, not for me.

When we stepped outside, the cool air jolted us back to reality. Sam seemed to sober up, rubbing his hands over his face. I took a step forward to assess the right way to the bus stop, and a drunk guy reached out for me.

'Nice dress, darlin',' he drawled.

Sam suddenly stepped in front of me.

'Back off,' he said. 'She's with me.'

He was tall and alert, and the other guy shrank back quickly. Sam put his arm around me and steered me in the opposite direction. We walked towards the bus stop together. I sighed, and leaned into him. I'd missed this so much. His jacket smelled of his cologne, and I breathed it in like a drug.

We didn't talk much, on the bus. It was as if we'd both agreed not to bring up any of the awkward barriers between us. I rested my head on Sam's shoulder. He'd broadened out a bit, even in six months. I knew he'd started running, because I'd caught glimpses of him heading off down the street, not that I was watching. Much.

The bus did a shorter route at night, so we had to walk from a different stop. The sky was now fully dark, painted with a tapestry of stars, and all the noise of the club and the town was now gone. I understood what Sam meant, when he'd told me before about feeling he could breathe again when he was out at night. The pavements were empty, the houses were in shadow, and I was drinking in every moment alone with Sam. His arm was still around me, and we didn't want the spell to break.

When we reached the front doors, we hovered reluctantly. There was so much mixed up in the air between us: the pain of the past, the hum of attraction, and the sense of belonging I felt with him. I'd never felt it with anyone else. After the crowded club, with a hundred people my age, here we were: two kindred spirits who loved stargazing.

'We should say goodnight,' he said, lowering his arm and turning to face me.

'*I shall forget, to have thee still stand there,/ Remembering how I love thy company*,' I murmured. Old habits die hard.

'*And I'll still stay, to have thee still forget,/ Forgetting any other home but this*,' he said, automatically.

We both smiled, and then he reached out to touch my cheek. The next moment, we were kissing, and I wouldn't be able to tell you who made the first move. Like being underwater, we were desperate for oxygen and life from each other.

It was bittersweet. He tasted like beer, not like himself.

'I'm sorry,' I said breathlessly, pulling back.

'I'm not,' he said.

'You will be tomorrow.'

We stared at each other, moonlight giving our faces a silvery glow.

'I'm going away tomorrow,' he said.

'Oh,' I said, nodding.

'We've got a family holiday,' he explained. 'First time in years. We're going to Cornwall.'

'Sounds lovely,' I said, my heart yearning already for the inevitable separation.

'When we get back,' he continued, 'I'm going for a summer internship, staying with my uncle. I thought it might not be a good idea to hang around here all summer when… Well, you know.'

I wanted to cry, so I just nodded.

'You're working, right?' he asked.

'Yes,' I said, clearing my throat. 'I got a temp job.'

'I'll see you,' he said, stepping away towards his house.

I had no idea when that would be, and it was killing me.

Christmas

Sam

At the end of my first term of uni, I caught the train home. To my surprise, Mum picked me up from the station. No one else was in the car. She wrapped her arms around me in an unexpected hug.

'I've missed you,' she said.

I wished I could say the same, but honestly… it had been a relief to leave. But I didn't say that out loud.

'I thought you could drive us home,' Mum said, opening the passenger door.

She had put 'L' plates on the car. I'd had a stint of driving lessons with Bryan, but with being away over the summer, I never got round to taking my test.

'Okay,' I agreed, taking the keys.

Once I had gone through the first few roundabouts, I settled into driving. Mum seemed more relaxed than usual, too.

'Where's Annabelle?' I asked.

'She's at home,' Mum answered. 'She's working on a project. She's doing an Open University course and she might start something at the local college next year.'

I felt guilty that I hadn't really been in touch with my sister. I resolved to text her more often.

'That sounds great,' I said.

'Well, I accepted that we had hit the limit of what I could teach her,' Mum said. 'It was time for her to move onto something new. And it's freed me up to do things like this.'

She gestured to the dashboard.

'I thought I could take you out every day for some driving practice,' she said. 'That way, we can spend some time together too.'

I couldn't help raising my eyebrows in surprise. I was grateful, definitely grateful, for the opportunity to drive. It was just… not like my mother.

'Thanks,' I said. 'That would be great.'

'I know I haven't made enough time for you in the past,' she said, as if reading my thoughts. 'I'm sorry.'

'It's okay, Mum,' I said, although I felt like I was spinning out in a zero-gravity zone.

'I want to hear all about your first term,' she said, smiling.

I told her about my lectures, my friends, and my attempts at cooking. By the time I finished, we were pulling into our street.

'Now, this is going to be a bit tricky,' Mum said. 'You'll have to parallel park.'

As I drew up alongside cars parked outside our house, I saw a flash of red hair. Lil and her sister were getting into Julia's car.

'Oh good, you can take their space,' Mum said, waving at them.

I sat there awkwardly, holding the wheel, and watched as Lil started the car up and then pulled out into the road. She barely looked at me.

I pulled into the parking space and shut off the engine. Mum was looking at me.

'Everything okay?' she asked.

'Yes,' I lied. 'It's great to be home.'

Lil

On Christmas Eve, I was alone in the house as my parents had gone shopping and Darcy was working in a department store. The doorbell rang and I was surprised to see Meredith, holding a box of biscuits.

'Hi,' I said. 'Sorry, Mum's not home…'

'It's you I wanted to see, actually,' she said. 'Can I come in?'

I nodded, stunned, and stepped backwards to let her in. She walked through to the kitchen, placing the biscuits down on the table, and sliding into a chair. I chose a chair opposite her. My heart rate had picked up nervously and I was thinking about Sam. Was she here because I'd done something wrong? I'd been away at university, so that didn't seem very likely.

'I wanted to apologise,' she said.

I stared at her. This was Meredith, and she was wearing a Christmas jumper with a smart skirt. No changes there. But her face was different, somehow. A little softer.

'Last Christmas, I was not in control of my emotions,' she said. 'When Annabelle was ill, I reacted in a selfish and ugly way. I was very rude to you, and I would like to ask for your forgiveness.'

Her eyes were shining with tears, and I immediately felt my own well up. I reached over and took her hand.

'You were under a lot of strain,' I said. 'I'm sorry for getting in the way.'

'You weren't in the way.' She shook her head. 'We were thinking, wrongly, that we needed to deal with everything ourselves. That we didn't need help. I recognise now how foolish we were.'

I tried not to sob out loud. Here was Sam's mother, apologising to me. And yet, I hadn't seen Sam for months. It felt like a year too late, but I didn't want to be uncharitable to a woman making herself vulnerable before me, especially when she was the same age as my parents.

'I forgive you,' I said. Somehow, as I spoke the words, I meant them, even though I had not felt particularly compassionate to Meredith in the last year.

'Thank you,' she murmured. She looked at me and hesitated. 'You haven't been in touch with Sam, have you?'

I shook my head, and the tears started to silently fall. How could it have been a whole year, and yet the grief for our broken relationship was still as raw as ever? I buried my face in my hands, ashamed of my emotion, but to my surprise, Meredith crouched on the floor beside me and put her arms around me.

'Is it my fault that you broke up?' she asked. 'Is there anything I can do to put it right?'

'No,' I said, pulling back and shaking my head.

She looked at me with concern in her eyes.

'I'm praying for him,' she said. 'I can't control his decisions, and I understand why he wants to make his own way in life, but I'm praying that he comes back to the Lord.'

'How is he?' I asked, wiping my cheeks.

'Enjoying uni,' she said, with a wry smile. 'Perhaps a bit too much. I don't think he goes to church. He's been getting parts in different plays, and rehearsing every weekend.'

She sighed.

'You know yourself, he doesn't often come along to services, even when he's at home.'

I nodded. I'd been at a few services since coming home for the Christmas break, and Sam hadn't been there.

'I'm hoping he'll come tomorrow,' she said. 'Christmas Day and everything.'

She climbed back into her chair.

'What about you? How are you enjoying uni?'

'It's great.' I smiled and nodded. 'The Christian Union is fantastic. I've found a good church to settle into, and I've found a group of girls from the same church to live with next year.'

'Any boys?' she asked, with a hint of humour in her tone, but I could tell she was interested in the answer.

'No.' I shook my head.

She could tell from my certainty the reason why: no one came close to Sam. She looked at me with sympathetic understanding, then patted my arm.

'If it's the Lord's will, He'll bring you back together,' she said. 'You're young. Just keep seeking Him.'

After she left, I went upstairs to my bedroom and dropped to my knees.

Lord, why have You done this? Why is my heart still broken? What am I supposed to do with these feelings that won't go away?

In the end, I sat at my desk and took a Christmas card out of the box. I wrote a sprawling letter to Sam, filling up both sides of the card.

Dear Sam,

I miss you. I know it's been a year and we've both moved on… but to be honest, I haven't. Every time I go for a walk, I think of you and all the mornings when we walked to school together. If it's dark, I remember the last night of the play. I know I did so many things that were wrong, and I'm sorry. But can we remember the good times? Can we have some form of peace with what happened between us, because I still feel so sad and broken about it?

I never wanted you to feel that you were not good enough for me. If anything, I didn't feel good enough for you. You are warm, kind and caring. You know how to make me smile. You give the best hugs. I remember doing our R.E.

homework in the treehouse together, and laugh. I couldn't have done that with anyone else.

Your mum came to see me today. She apologised for what happened last year, and I feel awful because of the way I shared your private, family business with Mrs Hart. I'm sorry for that. But truthfully, I'm more concerned with what she said about you not going to church and trying to find your own path. Sam, whatever burden you're carrying, bring it to Jesus. He doesn't want you to bear it alone. I don't know what your struggles are, your doubts or your fears, but I know that Jesus can handle them. I feel partly responsible for your decision to withdraw from church—perhaps it's due to my blatant hypocrisy. I am so sorry for how badly I've represented our Saviour. I can say to you now that I know He is trustworthy. He hears our prayers. Did you hear that Darcy started coming to church? It's amazing what God is doing in her life.

Sorry if I'm rambling, and it seems very random for me to write you this card. Feel free to ignore everything I've said, apart from the stuff about God.

Love, Lil

I sealed the card in the envelope, and wrote Sam's name on the front. I had no idea if I was going to give it to him or not, but I felt better for writing it.

Sam

It was odd being home again. I was loving the freedom of student life, going out at all times and no one berating me. At home, everyone acted as usual, as if I'd never left, but I didn't feel that I fitted anymore. Well, I'd felt that for some time.

Church was the big battleground. I felt my family's disapproval every time I didn't go. Dad had asked me about churches in Plymouth and I'd given casual answers. I'd filled my time with other things. The student drama scene was brilliant, and I'd landed a lead role in a production of *Pygmalion,* and then other roles followed after that. I was excited to follow my passion, alongside my studies.

On Christmas Day, I went to the service. Fair enough: if Jesus was born, and I did believe that, it was worth celebrating. Not all the consumerist rubbish about buying more stuff we didn't need. I knew I'd see Lil, but I wasn't prepared for how it felt the moment I spotted her. She was sitting next to Darcy, her hair as long and red as ever, and my heart literally ached. I was sitting on the other side, but there were more than just rows of chairs between us. The chasm of who I should be, and the reality of who I was.

Most of the time, it was easy to push the niggles of my conscience aside and silence them with well reasoned arguments. When I saw Lil, I longed for connection with her again, but also to recapture the fervour she had when she sang, and when she prayed. Well, perhaps capture it for the first time myself. I was increasingly convinced that I had never had faith like Lil. If I was brutally honest, I wanted it. But I was also afraid of what it would mean for my life. Would I turn into my parents? I loved them but… There were issues.

That was putting it mildly.

I was distracted throughout the carols and my dad's address, thinking about whether I should go up to her at the end, and what I should say. It had been a year since we broke up. Surely we could start being friends again now? If I couldn't be Lil's boyfriend, at least I could have a piece of her still in my life somehow, even if it was just the odd text and the odd meet-up when we were both home.

The thought—fear—crossed my mind that she might have a new boyfriend, but I dismissed this. Annabelle was best friends with Darcy, and she would tell me straight away if something like that happened. She knew that there had been no one else for me since Lil.

During the final hymn, Lil looked over and caught me staring at her. Instead of diverting my gaze, as I usually would have done, I smiled at her. After a moment's hesitation, she smiled back.

As soon as the final prayer was finished, I made a beeline for her, almost tripping over three old ladies and their handbags, and nearly spilling someone's coffee which they'd (ill-advisedly) left on the floor. She stood up to face me, wearing a russet coloured dress that enhanced her hair beautifully. She was breathtaking. No other girl at uni had caught my attention like this. I was beginning to think that no one else ever would.

'Hey,' I said, feeling my cheeks glow. 'Merry Christmas.'

'Merry Christmas,' she said, smiling.

We gazed at each other, and her eyes said so much. I could see hope and fear mixed in her expression.

'How's uni?' I asked.

'Good, thanks,' she said, nodding. 'How about you?'

'Yeah, I'm loving it.'

Now I sounded like I was a walking advert for McDonalds. Come on! Why couldn't I think of anything decent to say? It was just so hard in this busy room, full of other people's conversations…

'Do you want to walk home together?' I blurted out. 'We could… catch up?'

She hesitated and looked at Darcy.

'Don't mind me!' Darcy said, with a cheeky grin. 'I'll go in your parents' car.'

Lil looked at me and smiled again.

'Okay.'

As we walked to the church doors, I caught Mrs Hart's eye. She gave me a wink. I blushed even more, feeling my whole face heat up. Did I always get this embarrassed? I was nearly nineteen. Surely I was supposed to be getting more, not less mature?

We managed to get onto the path without anyone committing a *faux pas* ('Are you two back together, then?' etc), and the streets were quiet and still in that calm, Christmas morning way. I felt myself breathe more deeply.

'It's been a while since we've walked together,' Lil said.

I wondered if she was thinking of our walk back from the bus stop, when we'd kissed in the summer, or when we'd walked back from school in the snow. I was so conscious of her nearness. We weren't touching, but I knew exactly where her hand was at all times. Not that I was allowed to hold it.

'Yes,' I said.

After a pause, we both started speaking at the same time.

'Sorry,' I laughed. 'I said, do you walk much in Exeter?'

'I do,' she said. 'There's a great path that follows the river… It's one of my favourite places.'

'What were you saying?' I asked.

'I said I've missed it.'

She looked across at me and my heartbeat quickened. She meant she missed *me*, I was sure of it. I stopped dead in my tracks and faced her.

'I've missed you, too.'

'That's not what I said,' she protested, with a laugh, but I noticed a tear sparkling in her eye.

It undid me.

'Lil,' I murmured, stepping closer to her.

'Stop it, Sam!' she said, holding her hand out in front of her to block me. I froze. 'We can't keep doing this. No contact for six months, and then take a walk, kiss… and then you disappear again.'

'Lil, you know where I am,' I said, stung. 'I'm an hour away from you when we're at uni, and I'm *next door* to you when we're home. You've got my number.'

'Well maybe I should delete it, then!' she said.

My heart dropped at the thought of it. I was already effectively cut off from her, but this would make it even worse.

'Why would you do that?' I asked.

'Because I don't want to just be some sad, desperate girl who you think is always going to be waiting around for you to grow up.'

It was like talons scraping across my heart.

'This was never about me 'growing up',' I protested.

'Well, it is from where I'm standing,' she said. 'You're running away from your problems instead of facing them.'

'I'm not the one who wants to delete your number.'

'You may as well, if you're never going to contact me.'

'I thought we agreed—'

'You think I agreed to *this*?' she said, her voice higher pitched and louder. 'The last time I saw you, you kissed me—'

'I think that was a mutual decision,' I said, interrupting her this time.

'—and then you disappeared,' she finished.

'I told you where I was going—'

'That doesn't make it any better!' she shouted.

Her lip was quivering now. I was hypnotised by it. I wanted to get closer to her and take her in my arms but I was too scared of how she would react.

'I wish everything was different,' I said. 'But nothing's changed.'

We stared at each other. I had missed her, so much it was like a semi-permanent ache in my stomach, but I knew I couldn't offer her the happy-ever-after she wanted. Christian boyfriend Sam was MIA.

'Maybe we should be friends again,' I said. 'Then I don't disappear, we still have contact… I mean, we're not going to be at home that often anyway.'

'Sam, with the way I feel…' Lil said. 'I don't think I can be just friends with you.'

Another knife to my heart.

'Not even friends?'

She shook her head.

'I can't even be with you for five minutes like this without wanting to…'

'Yes?' I prompted, although I knew exactly what she meant. I just wanted to hear her say it.

'Stop it,' she scolded.

'You're beautiful when you're angry,' I said.

'You've been practising your chat-up lines, I see,' she said, lifting her chin. A challenge.

'There's no one else, Lil,' I said flatly.

'Really?' she asked, her face instantly softening.

I nodded.

She started crying, then. I followed my instinct and wrapped my arms around her, pulling her close against my chest. I wanted to cry, too, but I wanted to be strong for her. I willed myself not to give in and press my lips to hers. It was like trying to separate two magnets, drawn inevitably together.

'It's Christmas Day,' she said, pulling back. 'I need to get home.'

We walked back, still not holding hands, but my mind was whirring through all the possibilities, all the lives where we could be together, like Romeo and Juliet in a parallel universe where Romeo never killed Tybalt.

All too soon, we arrived by our front doors.

'One last hug,' she said, stepping up to me and holding me again. She smelled of blackberries. I think it was her favourite perfume. I breathed her in while I could.

With one lingering look, she turned to go inside her house. I didn't realise she was saying goodbye.

When I texted her, later that night, because I couldn't stop thinking about her, the message wouldn't send. I realised she had blocked my number.

Lil

It was agonising, but I knew I had to do it. I had to give him up, because I was always going to give in to him. I couldn't trust my feelings.

God, please bring him back to me.

It was only when I was on the train back to uni, and I came across a Christmas card that I'd been using as a bookmark, that I remembered the card I had written for Sam. As I'd packed to return, I knew it had not been on my desk. I had no idea where it had gone.

Maybe God didn't want me to give it to him, I reasoned. Maybe it was just to help me process things a little better.

It was time to trust God with my future: with Sam or without him.

Christmas

One year later

Lil

My first year at uni had passed quickly, in a blur of finding a church, settling into the Christian Union, making friends and studying. It was the first term of my second year where time just seemed to slow down and d-r-a-g by. I thought the hardest part (starting) was behind me, but actually, this was much more challenging. I was no longer living on campus, but in a student house. Whilst I was living with friends, they all seemed to have much busier social lives than me. I often found myself alone in the evenings, in the dark, eating reheated leftovers and watching TV. And still—still!—I thought about Sam.

It was ridiculous. I was twenty years old, and I couldn't get over my seventeen-year-old crush. I kept seeing him everywhere—after all, Plymouth was only an hour away. He might come for a visit one weekend to… Well, I had no valid reason why he would come to Exeter other than to see me. Part of me hoped that he would… but it was unlikely.

Not only was I hallucinating on a regular basis, but I also kept comparing all the other guys to him. I'd been asked out by a few different guys, from church and the CU, and I'd had a coffee date with one and a walk along the river with another. Mum had phoned me up and asked for an update on my love life, and all I could say was "there was no spark". This was the problem with having a technicolour romance—everything else seemed black and white.

I was fed up. I wanted to be grateful for this stage of my life; didn't everyone always say that their college days were the "best days of their lives"? Honestly, though, I was counting the days till

I went home for Christmas. And maybe a big part of that was because of the possibility of seeing Sam.

I used to study in the library, and I had to get some assignments finished before the end of term. It was late afternoon, and I knew if I didn't leave soon, I'd be cycling home in the dark. Our house was some way out of the city centre. Even then, the rent was still really expensive.

I took my pile of books back to the shelf, and caught the eye of the library assistant, who was replacing textbooks. It seemed so long ago that I was working in the library, and then I'd go to Sam's cafe to wait for him to finish…

Why did December seem to hold memories with such firm hands compared to the other months of the year?

Trying to shake off the inevitable melancholy that accompanied my reminiscing, I grabbed my coat, scarf and rucksack, then headed out into the street. I unlocked my bike and its helmet, clipping it on. I was waiting at a set of traffic lights when a car drew up beside me. *Last Christmas* was playing loudly on the radio.

I cycled back, hid in my bedroom and sobbed. We had said we loved each other. I deleted his number a year ago. Was there going to be a time when this felt less painful, less raw? When this was all going to make sense?

Was an overrated, overplayed song from the eighties always going to reduce me to tears?

God, I need some comfort that I won't always be alone.

I decided I needed a quiet night, so I put on my pjs and buried myself under the duvet with my weathered copy of *Persuasion*. Years of pining, but with an eventual happy ending? Jane Austen had me covered.

My phone buzzed with a new message. I grabbed it, with the completely irrational hope that it might be Sam. *You blocked him, remember?*

Mum: Do you fancy coming home a bit earlier so we can have a spa day? I won a voucher in a raffle at the gala but it has to be used before Christmas.

My heart lifted. I texted back YESSS! and then raised my eyes to the ceiling. *Thank you God.*

Lil

When I came home for Christmas, the first thing I did was to take a silver shoebox down from my shelf. Darcy called it my 'Sam shrine'. Inside it was the *Romeo and Juliet* book he gave me, pictures from the play and a programme, and a few other random photos. I hadn't told her about the T-shirt and joggers that were still bundled up at the back of my drawer either. Perhaps it was obsessive that I still kept them. Getting the box down gave me the odd sensation of simultaneous relief and pain. Everyone always said not to pick a scab… but it's irresistible.

Part of me hoped that crying a few tears, then putting the box away and pulling myself together, would result in no more meltdowns this Christmas. It was ripping the plaster off. I didn't want melancholy to mark my time with Mum and Darcy at the spa.

My mum was the opposite of Meredith Park. She was always out, always rushing from one thing to another, and always glamorous. I never saw her without lipstick.

She worked in management for a designer clothing brand based in Somerset, and often travelled for business or networking events. Both she and my dad worked hard, rarely taking time off, so I definitely wasn't going to pass up her invitation.

As we lounged around together in white bathrobes and slippers, I reflected that my mum was slim, beautiful, and successful in her career. And yet, I knew without Christ, it was all empty. She had that restless drive that nothing was ever enough to completely satisfy her.

Darcy had actually continued to go to Cross Street Baptist, even when I was away at uni. She went with Annabelle. I was encouraged that she seemed to be taking it seriously, and we had done some Bible studies together where she had asked questions. I knew she was similar to Mum: image-conscious and wanting to impress others. I hoped she would see through that, and pursue better things.

'So,' Mum said, and I knew she was going to ask about boys. 'It didn't work out with Richard.'

'His name was Richmond, actually,' I said, rolling my eyes.

'What does he study? Chemistry?' Mum won the award for answering her own questions. 'Shame that there was a lack of chemistry between you, eh?'

She laughed at her own joke.

'There's no point Lil going out with anyone when she's still in love with Sam,' Darcy said.

I side-eyed her.

'Don't deny it. You've still got that box of stuff from him, haven't you?' she asked.

'It was a very nice edition of *Romeo and Juliet*,' I said defensively.

'When's he home, Darce?' Mum asked.

Darcy was round at the Parks' enough to be in the know about Sam's comings and goings. I knew he'd gone backpacking across Europe in the summer, which was why I hadn't seen him.

'Couple of days' time,' she said.

'Are you going to see him?' Mum asked me, with her characteristic directness.

'Possibly,' I said. 'I mean, I might bump into him.'

Mum shook her head and tutted.

'If you feel that strongly for him, you need to have a proper conversation where you set out what you want,' she said. 'That's what I did with your father.'

Mum would probably not really understand the dynamics between Sam and me, but it was a far cry from the dynamic between her and my dad, that was for sure. She told him what to do; he agreed.

'His parents don't want us to date,' I said, trying to shut the conversation down.

'That's not true,' she said immediately, with such certainty that I looked across in surprise. 'I can't speak for Simon, but Meredith told me she was really sorry that you two broke up.'

'When did she say that?' I asked.

I remembered Meredith's apology a year ago, but when had she spoken to my mum?

'She's mentioned it a few times now,' Mum said casually, with a wave of her hand.

'Since when do you speak to Meredith?' I said.

'We have a cuppa together all the time,' Mum said. 'Especially with Darcy and Annabelle being joined at the hip.'

I looked at Darcy, and she nodded. I leaned back and sighed. Why couldn't she have come to this realisation two years ago?

'So, are you going to see him, then?' Mum pressed. She never let anything go.

'I might,' I said finally.

It would have been nice to think about something else, but Sam's face dominated my mind. I couldn't stop wondering what he was doing now, and whether he was thinking of me.

Sam

The music at the party was loud. I'd had a few beers, but not enough that the noise didn't affect me anymore. I'd been there before and I did not want a hangover again. There were a bunch of people here I knew, mainly from the Drama Society, but also a lot of strangers. There was a girl on the sofa next to me, who seemed to be inching closer to me every minute, and I didn't even know her name. She had long, bleached blond hair, and false eyelashes that looked painful. Her perfume was the cloying type that stuck in your throat.

'Hey Sam, 'sup?' Dex, who played Puck in *A Midsummer Night's Dream* this summer, leaned over the girl to give me a high five.

'You can sit here,' the girl said, sitting on my lap and grinning at me suggestively, then patting the space for Dex beside her.

I was annoyed, but I did nothing. I tried to focus on speaking to Dex, hoping that if I ignored her, she'd go away.

'We're doing auditions tomorrow for *Miss Saigon*,' he said. 'Are you coming?'

'I don't know,' I hedged.

So far I'd mostly stuck to Shakespeare. Fewer scantily clad girls, swearing and troubling storylines about brothels. I imagined my dad's face at the opening scene… I also wondered what Lil would think if she saw me cavorting with other girls on stage.

But then, I was the one with a girl I didn't know sat in my lap.

'Come on!' said Dex. 'It'll be a blast!'

The song changed, and the achingly familiar chords of *Last Christmas* rang out from the speakers. I scrambled to my feet, almost dropping the girl onto the floor in the process.

'Sorry,' I said. 'I have to go.'

I pushed past people singing and dancing in the lounge, past people snogging in the hallway, and stepped out into the cool night air. I took a deep breath.

The very next day, you gave it away.

I could still hear the song playing, and I couldn't suppress the memories of dancing with Lil in my kitchen, of telling her I loved her. Now, I was only at most an hour's drive away from her, but it felt like a million miles. We'd broken up because I knew I wasn't the boyfriend she deserved, but where was I now? I didn't know who I was anymore.

I started walking home. It was an hour across the city, but I didn't care. I wanted to find peace. I just wished I knew how.

Sam

It was frighteningly easy to drift away from God, to kid myself that I didn't need church, that I could worship 'in my own way'. What that translated to was worshipping my own will. I wanted to call the shots, and I didn't want to question whether I was making good decisions or not.

The thing with God is, He knows how to get your attention.

The day after the party, there hadn't been any snow, but the wind was biting and there were patches of black ice on the ground. I was cycling, as I had done many times before, through the busy centre of the city, and I stood up to give extra power as the road went uphill. My chain slipped, and I overbalanced, falling onto the road where a double decker bus was looming towards me. The driver slammed on the brakes, and a guy ran over to help me. He lifted the bike off me and then crouched down beside me.

'Are you hurt?' he asked.

Amazingly, I wasn't. The bus had stopped in time; just ahead of me was a sheen of ice which had been narrowly avoided by both the bus and me. I was stunned, and a bit sore, but I hadn't broken any bones. He helped me to my feet.

'I'm Paul, and I'm studying medicine,' he said, introducing himself. 'That was a bit of a close call! Can I walk you back to your house? I think that chain needs replacing. I've got a friend who's really into bikes, if you want me to call him?'

He was fresh-faced and confident, and cracked jokes as we walked along the street. I was in a bit of a daze. If the driver hadn't seen me, I would have been steamrollered. My life, snuffed out just like that. It was deeply sobering, the wake-up call I needed.

What exactly was I doing with my life?

Yes, I was having fun, living the student life. But I hadn't found any meaning or purpose. It was all an endless round of partying and pleasure, but completely hollow. Like a film set where you discover there's no food in the kitchen cupboards and behind the door is a dirty, concrete floor with cables and cardboard boxes.

Feeding the pigs is just that: feeding the pigs.

The words came into my head out of nowhere, and I remembered Lil. Thinking about her still gave me physical pain, and I must have winced, because Paul asked if I was alright.

'Yes, it's nothing,' I said.

But really, it was everything.

'Look, there's a kiosk just up here. Can I get you a hot drink? You look like you're in shock.'

Paul made me sit down on a bench, left the bike leaning against it with me, and then brought me a cup of hot chocolate.

'Drink this, and you'll feel better,' he said.

I was overwhelmed that this stranger was doing so much for me.

'You're like the Good Samaritan,' I said, without really thinking about it.

'You know that story?' Paul cocked his head in interest.

'My dad's a pastor,' I said, sipping the drink. Maybe it was the shock, or maybe it was the burning desire to be real with someone, but I continued, 'I think I'm living the Prodigal Son at the moment.'

Paul looked at me for a moment, compassion in his eyes. In that moment, I knew he was a Christian.

'We've all been there, mate,' he said. He took a deep breath. 'I know I don't know you, and you'll probably think this is weird, but I saw that accident and it was like witnessing a miracle. I don't know how you are alive! But to me, that means God saved you. And He must have a reason.'

'Why would God want to save *me*?' I asked. 'I've spent the past two years running away from Him.'

'Well, I think He's telling you to stop running, before something worse happens to you,' Paul said. 'Remember Jonah and the giant fish?'

'I guess we're short on whales in Plymouth,' I joked.

'You asked why God would want to save you,' he continued. 'You're a pastor's son, so you must have heard this before. It's *grace*.'

'My dad did talk about grace,' I said. 'But he also laid down a lot of rules at home. So it felt like he was really saying: God saves you if you're good enough. And I was never good enough.'

I felt my throat choke up. It had been a while since I'd cried over anything. I sipped my drink to hide it. Paul was looking at me with a serious expression.

'It's not about being good enough,' he said. 'You're right, you'll never be good enough. But Jesus was good enough for you.'

We talked together, and my heart was churning with all the emotion of a near-death experience and the thought, the *possibility*, that God might actually love me. That I didn't have to pretend to be someone else, but that I could be me... well, a transformed version of myself that was becoming more like Jesus.

Once I'd finished my drink, we continued to walk back to my house. In my room, Paul asked if I had a Bible. I pulled out the holdall from under my bed. My Bible had stayed stowed away in it, and I hadn't bothered removing it every time I packed to go home. It just had never been taken out of the bag.

With the turbulence of guilt and shame, I picked up the dog-eared hardcover, with the spine cracked and weathered and the pages folded and chewed up. Something fell out onto the floor. A white envelope with *Sam* written across it. In Lil's handwriting.

I stared at it, then picked it up. How long had it been there, hidden in my Bible? How on earth did it get there? I hadn't seen her since last Christmas. Come to think of it, I hadn't opened my Bible since then.

'What is that?' Paul asked. 'A Christmas card?'

'It's from Lil,' I said, murmuring her name like a prayer, even though he didn't even know her. 'We used to be together, but…'

I trailed off. There was no easy way to summarise what had happened with the most beautiful girl I'd ever met, and the only girl I'd ever loved. That was still the case. No girl had even come close to making me feel the emotion that Lil evoked in me. She was the one girl who made me feel truly alive. And I'd lost her.

'How about I give you some privacy to read that while I call my friend who can fix your bike?' Paul suggested.

He went downstairs to the kitchen, and I opened the envelope with shaking hands.

I read the card and wept.

It was as if God was speaking directly to me. It wasn't about me not being good enough. I needed to bring my burdens to Jesus and ask Him to take them for me. I just felt so unworthy, so weighed down by all my wrong decisions and my secret sins.

When Paul came back, he was understandably surprised to find me an emotional wreck. I gave him the card to read, as I had no words. He opened up my Bible and read me some Scriptures, words of invitation for the broken. He read out the whole of Psalm 51, and I continued to weep. His friend Nathan arrived, and he was a Christian too. They both spoke to me about the love of God with such passion. When I was more composed, Nathan fixed my bike, and then Paul invited me to go with them to a Christmas outreach meeting that evening, organised by the Christian Union. I went (I had no reason not to, by this point), and the room was packed with students. We sang a bunch of carols and then a local minister stood up to give a talk.

'I was planning on speaking about shepherds, angels and a baby in the manger tonight,' he said. 'But I felt the Lord give me a different message. I want to speak to you tonight about the Prodigal Son.'

I couldn't believe it. I looked in wonder at Paul and Nathan, and they looked equally stunned. The whole message went straight to my heart, in a soul-cutting way I had never experienced before. At the end, the preacher made a final appeal.

'I don't know who needs to hear this tonight, but if you're feeding the pigs, please wake up and come home to the Father who loves you, who's never stopped loving you.'

When he asked anyone who had responded to the message to stand, I leapt up out of my chair like I'd been electrocuted. Tears streamed down my face. It was like Jesus was saying to me *I've been here all along, waiting for you.*

Paul and Nathan prayed for me, and my heart finally felt released from its prison.

It wasn't about finding out who I was; it was all about finding the One who made me, coming back to the relationship that fixed everything broken.

God had called me back to Him, and this time, I was going to listen.

Lil

Mum, Darcy and I were all going to the Parks' house for some Christmas wreath-making. I'd seen Annabelle produce amazing creations before, but I wasn't prepared for the Parks' house being full of people. That would never have happened a year ago.

Darcy rang the bell and then walked straight in. She spent a lot of time over there, so it was practically her second home. I hung back on the doorstep, feeling uncertain. I hadn't been in this house since… Well, I didn't want to think back to that time.

'Come on,' Mum said, ushering me from behind.

I stepped inside, and the familiar smell of cinnamon, mixed with something sweet, wafted from the kitchen.

The house was decorated with beautiful greenery and fairy lights, and their kitchen table was laden with home made mince pies, shortbread, and fig rolls. Simon was ladling out mulled wine, and his forehead had lost its furrowed look. Meredith, wearing a Christmas jumper and *jeans* (I had never seen her wear them before), brushed past him and stopped to kiss his cheek. Their tender gaze felt private, and I looked away. It was how Sam used to look at me.

Moving into the lounge, I gasped. The sofas had been pushed back, and there were trestle tables running down the middle of the room, with a huge sheet on the floor. The tables were covered with greenery and Annabelle was standing, confidently explaining how to make a wreath, and demonstrating. She caught my eye and smiled. She definitely looked older now, and more on a par with Darcy. She was still pale, but seemed more comfortable in her own skin.

Darcy beckoned me over, so I took my place next to her, and started to follow Annabelle's instructions. Mrs Hart was there too, and a few other church folk, so we chatted about how uni was going and caught up on church news. I threaded some greenery around the wreath ring and then started weaving ivy in and out.

'It's all about layering,' Annabelle said. 'Just keep building it up and then you can make artistic touches at the end.'

'I've used about a ton of this wire,' Darcy said.

'I've got some holly, but you'll need gloves to handle it,' Annabelle said.

I managed to place some sprigs of holly and berries around the wreath.

'I'm going to get my phone to take a picture,' I told Darcy.

I stepped into the hallway to find my coat, as my phone was in my pocket, and I overheard Mum talking to Meredith in the kitchen.

'...I thought it was odd,' Mum was saying. 'But then, it could be anything.'

'Maybe you should book a special date,' Meredith said. 'Since we started doing that, things have been so much better.'

'Maybe you're right,' Mum said.

I hoped my parents weren't having some sort of marriage crisis. I returned to the lounge to snap my work of art, and tried not to stare longingly at the family photos of Sam dotted around the room.

'He'll be home for Christmas,' Darcy said, cutting into my thoughts with annoying precision.

'So?' I said.

She rolled her eyes, then held up her wreath.

'What do you think?'

'Lovely,' I said. 'Now we just need to figure out where to put them.'

'Do you fancy getting me another mince pie?' she asked.

I headed back for the kitchen, and thankfully Mum's conversation seemed to have moved on.

'What have you been studying, Lil?' Simon asked, as I hovered over the buffet.

'I've been doing Shakespeare this term,' I said.

He smiled.

'I think Sam's goal is to play every Shakespearean hero by the time he graduates,' he said.

'He's still acting?' I asked, unable to resist fishing for information.

'Yes, he seems very passionate about it,' Simon said.

He used to be passionate about me. I pushed that thought away and concentrated on choosing a mince pie.

'Personally, I hate the idea of dressing up in a costume and standing on a stage in front of an audience,' Simon continued.

'It's not that different to preaching,' I pointed out.

He laughed.

'I hope I don't break into '*To be or not to be*' next Sunday.'

I smiled.

'Will Sam be back?' I asked, hoping I didn't look too desperate.

'Yes.' He nodded. After a pause, he said, 'I don't know if he'll be there, though.'

He looked sad, and resigned. I didn't want to cry (again), so I nodded, not trusting my voice.

'It's been great to have Darcy,' he said, changing the subject.

'She seems to have really settled in,' I said. 'Thanks for looking after her so much.'

'She's part of our family,' he said, shrugging as if it was nothing. 'It's been so good for Annabelle to have a friend her own age. We feel very blessed to have moved next door to you… All of you.'

I swallowed the lump in my throat. Last year, Meredith apologised. Now Simon was saying that he welcomed us into his family. Why was all this happening so long after Sam and I had broken up, and when there was so little hope of us getting back together?

'Thank you,' I said, making a swift exit with my plate of mince pies. I set them down before Darcy and then grabbed my wreath. 'I'm going back next door,' I told her, and left before she could question me.

At home, I hung up the wreath and sat down on the sofa, my head in my hands. Surely, at some point, I would run out of tears for this boy?

Part of me also felt inexplicably angry that while some kind of healing had happened between Meredith, Simon and Annabelle, Sam was presumably still wounded and broken from the dysfunctional interactions I'd witnessed two years ago. I felt angry on his behalf, that he was still on the outside, and for what he had to go through. I'd had to watch it.

Why was everything so messed up? *God, why can't you fix this situation?*

The wreath hung on the door, the feathery red cedar against the sharpness of the holly. If I wanted a thorn-free life, I wasn't going to get one this side of heaven.

My grace is sufficient for you.

I felt like I was clinging on by a thread, but I had to keep trusting. After winter, spring would follow. I just had to wait for this long, long season to end.

Sam

I was still reeling when I went home for Christmas a few days after the accident. I had a group text chat with Nathan and Paul, and they were regularly pinging me messages of encouragement and helpful Bible verses. I'd told them more about Lil, because of the card, and asked them what I should do.

'If she blocked your number, it doesn't seem right to ask your sister for it, or to use your sister as a go-between,' Nathan said. 'If you see her, maybe you should suggest going for coffee and you can tell her how you read the card and what happened. I'm sure she'd like to know about it.'

'But she may have a new boyfriend now,' Paul pointed out. 'I think you should make it clear that you're not expecting anything from her.'

Annabelle hadn't mentioned anything to me, so I hoped that Lil was still single. Even so, we were still in different cities, and studying, and we hadn't been in contact for a year. We'd had that argument last Christmas, when she'd blocked me, so it wasn't the best place to pick things up from. How could I suddenly crash back into her life?

I grabbed the first opportunity, when I was home, to speak to Annabelle.

'I need to tell you something,' I said.

We sat on her bed and I told her about the accident, about meeting Paul and Nathan, about Lil's card, and about the mission meeting. Tears streamed down her cheeks and she hugged me.

'I've been praying for you,' she said. 'I'm so happy you've given your life to the Lord.'

'Can you tell me about Lil?' I asked. 'I'm hoping to see her, but I don't know if she will want to talk to me.'

'She's still the same as ever,' Annabelle said, with a smile. 'She's been on some dates, Darcy said, but nothing serious. She told Darcy and me to avoid boys because they're idiots. So yeah, don't expect a warm reception.'

'She's right,' I said, swiping my hand over my face. 'I've been worse than an idiot to her.'

'Can I make a suggestion?' Annabelle said. 'You said she wrote you a card. Why don't you write her one back? Then, if she doesn't want to talk to you, you could give it to her and it's her choice then if she wants to read it or not. Plus, it'd be kind of sweet and romantic.'

I sighed. Writing it all down was going to be hard. I didn't know if I could do it, but Annabelle was right. Lil may not want to speak to me, and then I'd never get the chance to tell her how she changed my life. How God used her to bring me back to Him.

'Okay.'

Lil

The Sunday before Christmas, I had a thick cold. My voice was croaky and I was definitely going to have to mime along to the carols if I went to church.

'Are you coming?' Darcy asked.

She made a face when she saw me in my old joggers and faded uni sweatshirt.

'I feel rough,' I said, hoarsely.

'It's the special carol service,' she pointed out. 'You can't miss it!'

The kids were going to be doing a nativity, and there would be mince pies after the service.

'Alright,' I groaned, following her downstairs.

'You don't want to put on something nicer?' Darcy said. 'Sam's going to be there.'

'Unlikely,' I said. 'He only came on Christmas Day last year.'

'Annabelle told me he's coming,' she said. 'And he wants to see you.'

'What if I don't want to see him?' I said, pulling my coat on.

'I thought you might say that,' Darcy said with a sigh. 'I was hoping we could all sit together.'

'Darce, you know I'm trying to stay away from him!'

'And you have… for a whole year!'

I glared at her.

'Look, it's not my business I know,' she said, 'but Annabelle said that he had an accident a few days ago. He nearly died.'

'What?'

It felt like my heart dropped to the floor. How, after a year of no messages, no conversations, nothing at all, could my feelings just reappear, as if they'd never disappeared? Well, maybe they had never disappeared.

'What happened?' I asked, in a panicked voice. 'Is he alright?'

'He's fine,' Darcy reassured me. 'You'll have to ask him for the details. But Annabelle said he's coming to church again and he's got right with God again.'

'Are you serious?' I asked. I wanted to laugh. It just sounded so incredible.

'I wanted it to be a surprise for you,' she said. 'But you're being a grump.'

'I haven't even got any make-up on!' I wailed, looking in the hallway mirror.

'Sam's not going to care about that,' she said. I knew she was right; he'd always said he preferred me without it. Well, he was going to see me at my worst, that was for sure.

'Do you want to walk?' Darcy asked.

'Nah, let's drive.'

I grabbed the keys with fresh enthusiasm.

The church was packed, and I ended up parking what felt like a mile away anyway. We rushed in, and Sam and Annabelle were waiting for us in the foyer. When I saw him, it honestly felt like everything else disappeared. He was the same tall, athletic boy with piercing blue eyes I'd always loved, but straight away I could tell there was something different about him. The way he stood, his shoulders relaxed and his hands in his pockets… He looked at peace with himself, somehow. Like he didn't have a care in the world. And when he saw me, his face split into the widest grin.

'Hey,' he said.

'Hey,' I replied.

It was the world's biggest understatement.

'Come on lovebirds,' Darcy said, corralling us towards the door. 'We're late!'

I blushed, and shot her daggers through my eyes, while Sam indicated for me to go first through the door.

'We saved four seats at the back,' he said, leaning closer to tell me, and the hum of his voice made the skin of my neck tingle as if he'd touched it.

Keep it together, Lil.

As I scanned the back rows, full of proud parents and grandparents, he stood behind me and gently grazed my elbow, turning me in the right direction.

'Just over by the sound desk.'

I longed in that moment to be a Jane Austen heroine and swoon into his waiting arms, but they were about to start the carols and the grannies were tutting at me already. Murmuring apologies, I pushed my way past ladies with very large handbags until I finally collapsed into the right seat, with Sam next to me. They had pushed the rows more tightly together to accommodate extra visitors, and we were rammed like sardines. To avoid touching the total stranger on my right side, I was shoulder to shoulder with Sam. I felt my whole face turning red, and even more so when I felt his eyes on me. Once I dared to meet his gaze, and he smiled at me again with dazzling brilliance. I'd missed his smile.

We went through the service, singing and laughing at the kids' rendition of Mary and Joseph's dilemma, and when I needed a tissue for my blocked up nose, Sam passed me the box from the sound desk. He smelled of bergamot and nutmeg and my mind was just going haywire. Our legs were a hair's breadth apart, and an electrical current was live in the air between us. His hand rested on his thigh, and I remembered how it felt to hold his hand in mine. It was like experiencing a wave of homesickness.

Was what Darcy said true? Had Sam changed? Was God giving him back to me? I couldn't deny that my body was craving him, but I knew that my desires were not exactly trustworthy.

I'd felt so proud of myself this year, blocking Sam and resisting the temptation of boys. I'd been on a few dates, but I'd been very well behaved. The most I'd done was hold someone's hand. But even then, it had felt wrong. Where I'd been congratulating myself for conquering desire and achieving self control, sitting next to Sam in such close proximity was definitely making me realise that I just hadn't really been genuinely tempted by any of those boys. I hadn't clicked with any of them, and they hadn't made me light up. Now, next to Sam, I felt I was about to spontaneously combust.

From what I could tell, he was having trouble concentrating too. He shifted in his seat as often as I did, and kept looking sideways at me. Never had a carol service been so torturous.

When it was finally over—literally the second after his father dismissed the congregation—Sam whispered in my ear,

'You want to go and grab a coffee together? Away from here?'

I nodded. wide eyed. I had lost the power of speech.

'Did you bring the car?' he asked.

'Yes, she did,' Darcy said, giving me a playful shove by leaning across Sam. 'Have fun!'

Blushing furiously (again), I followed Sam past Darcy and Annabelle (who both made thumbs up signs at me in the most unsubtle way), out of our cramped row of people and into the fresh air of the vestry.

'You okay?' Sam asked, his eyes searching mine. 'I don't want you to feel under pressure to go anywhere with me. But… I would love to talk to you.'

I nodded, wondering at the way he was speaking to me. It was like he'd suddenly grown up. We weren't teenagers anymore. Well, I was twenty, and his birthday was in February.

'Yes,' I said, realising he was waiting for some kind of verbal reassurance. 'Let's go.'

We walked down the church steps, and I led him down the street, wrapping my scarf tightly around my neck. The sky was grey, but there was no snow, just stinging cold air.

'How are you?' he said. 'You look like you're ill.'

'Just a cold,' I said.

'I mean, I didn't mean that you look bad,' he said hastily. 'You don't. You look beautiful. Am I allowed to say that?'

He looked at me worriedly, and I blushed and laughed.

'I haven't got a boyfriend, if that's what you mean,' I said. 'And I don't need one, either.'

I lay it down as a gauntlet. The truth was, I was a bit annoyed at myself for how easily I'd swooned at him. I couldn't let him think it was okay to break my heart and then swan back into my life and become my boyfriend again, with or without some kind of spiritual transformation.

'I know,' he said, looking abashed.

'This past year, although it's been hard and lonely at times, has been marvellously uncomplicated by romance, or failed romance I should say.'

'I think you made the right decision,' he said, clearing his throat. 'Although I was disappointed that I couldn't message you. I understand why you blocked me. You were being wise. I was being an idiot.'

I raised my eyebrow at this admission. We turned the corner, and arrived at my car.

Once we were seated, I turned to face him before I started the engine.

'Darcy told me you had an accident,' I said. 'What happened?'

'The chain came off my bike, and I fell in front of a bus.'

I gasped in shock. He smiled, and there were tears in his eyes.

'God saved me,' he said. 'It was a miracle. And He sent two Christians to help me.'

He told me about Paul and Nathan, and then reached over and took my hand.

'Then I found the card you wrote me. I had never seen it before. I read it, and it was like God was speaking straight to my heart.'

Both of us had tears running down our cheeks at this point.

'I wanted to thank you,' he said. 'Because if you hadn't written that card, I don't know if I would have gone with the guys to the mission meeting, and then I would never have heard the message which was exactly what I needed to hear.'

He told me about the Prodigal Son, and about responding, and I wrapped my arms around him and we sobbed together. *God heard my prayers! God used my card!* I was overwhelmed.

'I don't even know how the card got inside your Bible!' I exclaimed. 'I never gave it to you!'

'Perhaps an angel put it there,' he said, smiling.

I pulled out a pack of tissues from the glove compartment and blew my nose.

'I look like a complete mess,' I said. 'I wish you'd given me some warning that you were going to emotionally wreck me.'

'I'm sorry,' he said immediately.

'Don't be stupid,' I said, grinning. 'Now, are we actually going to get coffee, or was that just a euphemism?'

'Let's go to Sal's,' he said. 'Your dad always took me there when I had my driving lessons.'

'The one by the test centre, right?' I checked. 'He told me you passed.'

'First time,' he grinned smugly. 'I don't have a car yet. I'm waiting to see where I'm going for my placement next year.'

'What are your options?' I asked. I vaguely remembered looking at the course details with him when he applied.

'Costa Rica,' he said. 'Spain. Or Dartmoor.'

I giggled.

'Dartmoor seems like a consolation prize compared to the other options.'

But underneath, I was thinking *Costa Rica! That's so far!* If God was restoring Sam and bringing him back into my life, it seemed cruel that he was about to live abroad for a whole year.

Sam eyed me, as if he could read my thoughts. I started the car and pulled away.

'Dartmoor's close to Exeter, where you are,' he said.

My heart thudded in my chest whilst I tried to ignore it. *Don't get your hopes up.*

'It's creepy to follow people around, you know,' I said.

He laughed.

'Fair point.'

I turned out of the side street onto the main road.

'Lil, I owe you a massive apology. I had this big speech all planned out, but I just want to say it now, and say it simply. I treated you in the worst possible way, and I tried to run away from God, so I ran from you too. Please forgive me.'

I looked over at him, and his face was completely sincere. It was funny to think that a year ago, his mum said those same words to me. I had forgiven her readily enough. Would I be able to forgive Sam?

I sighed.

'Sam, I was just as much in the wrong as you,' I said. 'I made a lot of mistakes. I need your forgiveness too.'

'That's very humble and gracious of you,' he said, 'but you must allow me to take full responsibility. I ignored your spiritual antennae, when you didn't want to go to the Sixth Form social. I pushed you way beyond the boundaries you were comfortable with. I told you I didn't want you to be my girlfriend, but then I couldn't keep my hands off you. I failed to stick to the accountability you requested, and I didn't repent of the sinful way I'd behaved. You deserved so, so much better. I wouldn't blame you if you never wanted to speak to me again.'

'Does this mean that you *have* now repented?' I asked. I hoped so, because the idea of cutting him off again was too painful to imagine.

'Yes,' he said. 'I told Paul and Nathan all about it. I've got a feeling they're going to be really good friends.'

Wow, he must have been really honest with them. I tried to get my head around this new, open version of Sam. I think I liked it.

The test centre was coming up, and I indicated to turn right.

'Oh, wait,' Sam said. 'I think you missed the turning. Never mind, take the next one and we can drive round the back way.'

He directed me along the industrial estate, which was a bit of a maze, and we pulled up alongside the kerb near the delivery bay for the coffee shop.

'Lil,' Sam said, and his tone of voice caught my attention. 'Is that your—'

I followed the direction of his gaze. By the back entrance to the cafe, a woman I'd never met was in my father's arms.

Sam

'Dad!'

Lil cried out in a strangled voice, opening the car door and stumbling onto the pavement.

Bryan and Sal jumped apart, and I quickly got out of the car as Lil headed towards them.

'What are you doing?' she said.

Her dad flinched like he'd been struck. Sal looked down, avoiding eye contact with us, wiping her hands on her apron.

'How long has this been going on?' she asked, her tone thickened by her cold and more muted now as she stood in front of them. I caught up with her and stood behind her.

Her dad didn't respond. He looked frozen, like a rabbit caught in headlights.

'It's nearly Christmas!' Lil said, and her voice broke with emotion.

Instinctively I reached out to steady her and placed my hands on her upper arms. Immediately she folded into my arms, sobbing. It was an agonising sound to hear. Sal quietly slipped back inside the cafe.

'Can you take me home, Sam?' Lil said, pulling back slightly. She looked at her father with disgust and disappointment.

Bryan still said nothing. I helped Lil into the passenger seat of her car, then took the keys and went round the driver's side. As I drove, she was on her phone.

'I'm telling Annabelle to keep Darcy with her,' she said. 'And I'm telling Mum that we're on our way, but we're bringing bad news.'

When she was done, she threw her phone down and leaned against the window, tears rolling down her cheeks.

'I can't believe it,' she said. 'How could he be so selfish?'

I was struggling to process this turn of events. I'd barely told her what I wanted to share, and now this train wreck was happening right before my eyes. It had been my idea to go to Sal's. God obviously wanted this affair to come to light, and He wanted me to be there for Lil. My mind was reeling.

'I'm so sorry, Lil,' I said.

She continued to cry, pulling out tissues from the glove compartment again. I noticed Bryan's car in the rearview mirror—it was so distinctive as a driving instructor's car. He was following us back to the house. I wondered what scenes were going to unravel.

We pulled up outside, and Lil's father wasn't far behind us. I had no idea what he was thinking. I avoided looking at him because it was just too awkward. I walked around to open Lil's door, and she strode forward into the house.

'What is it?' Julia rushed forward, putting her arms around Lil. 'What's happened?'

She looked at me questioningly, then at Bryan, who came through the doorway last.

'You need to sit down,' Lil said, brushing away her tears and ushering her mum towards the living room.

Her mum, eyes wildly moving between all of us, trying to pick up clues as to what the matter was, found her way to the sofa. I hovered in the hallway, not sure what to do. Bryan pressed his lips together tightly and went into the lounge. Lil stood and pointed at him, her hand shaking slightly.

'You need to tell Mum about what I just saw,' she said.

She walked out of the room and closed the door behind her.

'What can I do?' I asked her.

'Let's go in the kitchen,' she said, raking her fingers through her hair. 'I don't know what he's going to say, but Mum may want to hear my side of it, and I want to be there for her…'

Her voice disappeared into a sob. I put my arm around her and led her into the kitchen and closed the door.

'This is going to destroy her world,' Lil said, her eyes filled with pain. 'But she needs to know.'

'You've been very brave,' I said. I thought she was magnificent, so level headed and clear-thinking in the worst of situations. She'd even thought about her sister.

'I'll put the kettle on,' Lil said, needing her hands to be busy.

She pulled out some mugs and started filling the kettle. I was grateful for the noise, because I was trying not to listen to what was happening in the lounge… but also listening out for it at the same time. By the time she'd finished the tea, she looked at me.

'Do you think I should go in there?'

'I think you should wait until they call you in,' I said.

She nodded, and picked up a mug. We sat at the kitchen table, and twenty-four hours ago I could have never predicted this situation.

But I was here for Lil when she needed me, and that was all that mattered.

Lil

My world as I knew it was falling apart. I couldn't comprehend what my dad had done, and how it was now going to tear up our family unit.

How was I going to tell Darcy?

I had no idea how my mum was reacting. I couldn't hear anything from the lounge. Fresh tears kept starting in my eyes as I thought about Christmas, and how all our plans were now ruined. I didn't know how I was going to look my dad in the eye again. At a loss, I prayed broken prayers silently. *God, please give me a sign that You're here with me, that You'll get us through this mess.*

'Do you remember when we studied Calvin?' Sam said.

I nodded.

'God doesn't make mistakes,' he said. 'Maybe He led us to discover your dad today to save your mum from finding out some other way.'

'Even if the way she's finding out is better, it doesn't change the fact that this situation is your worst nightmare.'

He looked at me sympathetically. We'd only been in each other's company for a few hours, and yet I couldn't deny that his presence was comforting. Something else God had given me; I hadn't found my father out on my own. How would I have driven home after that?

The lounge door opened, and my dad walked out and headed up the stairs. I pushed my chair back and darted into the lounge. My mum was sitting on the sofa, cupping her face in her hands. Her eyes were dry.

'Mum!' I said, sitting down beside her and putting my arms around her. 'Did he tell you?'

She nodded, her eyes glazed over in shock.

'What did you say?'

'I said what any self-respecting woman would say,' she replied, turning to face me. 'I told him to pack his bags and leave.'

I nodded and tried to suppress a sob. I was supposed to be comforting her. She wrapped her arms around me and squeezed.

'Lil,' she said, pulling back to hold my gaze. 'We're going to be fine. You, me and Darcy.'

'We need to tell her,' I said, sniffing.

'I can go and get her, if you like?' Sam stood in the doorway, tentatively.

'Yes, Sam. Thank you,' my mum said calmly.

It was excruciating. When she told Darcy, and my sister started sobbing like me, that finally released her own emotion. The three of us cried together.

At some point my dad came downstairs, and then finally spoke to us.

'I'm sorry,' he said. His eyes were glassy with unshed tears. 'I'm going to stay at my mum's.'

My mum nodded, and wiped her face with a tissue.

'Don't bother calling me,' Darcy said venomously. 'I never want to see you again.'

I squeezed her hand. There was no point telling her not to say things she might regret later, because I felt the same way.

Dad looked down at the floor and nodded. He truly looked pathetic. Maybe one day I would feel a sense of compassion or forgiveness towards him… but not in this moment. Not right now.

Once he had gone, and closed the door behind him, the reality sank in. It was just us, the three of us, now. What did you do when you discovered such a brutal betrayal? You couldn't just turn on the TV.

'I'm going to make some phone calls,' Mum said, standing up and making her way to the door.

I rubbed Darcy's shoulders. She was still sniffing.

'What do we do now, Lil?' she asked.

'Let's make Mum some tea,' I said.

In the kitchen, she tapped on her phone.

'You don't mind if I tell Annabelle, do you?' she asked.

'Well, Sam knows.'

Thinking of him, my heart ached. He had seemed different, and yet wonderfully familiar. I wished he was in the room right now so I could fall into his arms again.

'What happened with you and Sam?' Darcy asked.

Typical: not even the dramatic events of the afternoon could put off my sister's nosiness.

'He told me about his accident,' I said, choosing more mugs from the cupboard and setting them down. 'It really does sound like a miracle. Some guys, who are Christians, helped him, and they took him to a mission. He responded to the message, and he says he's come back to God.'

'Wow,' Darcy said. 'You sound like you're about to say 'But', though.'

'I'm not,' I said, pouring hot water in the mugs. 'I just… need to be careful when Sam's involved. I was so in love with him before—'

'You've never *stopped* being in love with him,' Darcy said. 'Anyone who saw the play was convinced in about five seconds.'

'That was years ago, now, Darce,' I said, removing the teabags. 'We broke up soon after that, and then I didn't speak to him for so long.'

'Lil, the way he looks at you, I can tell he's never stopped loving you either,' she said.

I couldn't suppress my smile at that.

'Really?'

'Do you have eyes?' she exclaimed. 'Listen, I know you broke up because of God stuff, and having different paths and all that, but I don't see why you can't give him another chance.'

'I need to know that he's serious,' I replied, finding the milk from the fridge and pouring it.

'About you or about God?' she asked.

'Both.'

Sam

It was torture, knowing what Lil was going through in the house next door, and being stuck this side of the wall.

After telling Darcy she needed to go home, I left them to it. Families need privacy, I'd told that to Lil often enough. But now I was experiencing something of what she'd gone through when Annabelle was sick. Desperation to do something, anything, to help. Wanting to know that the other person was okay. I thought back to my long silences and felt ashamed. I checked my phone compulsively to see if she messaged, but she hadn't.

I needed to give her space, but it was so frustrating. I'd written the card for her and never had the chance to give it to her. I had no idea how she was really feeling towards me, and whether she could forgive me, really forgive me, for the past—enough to want to try again.

My mum had served up a roast dinner, but I could barely eat. After the meal I went upstairs and shut myself in my room to pray. *God, I don't know what to do. Please help her and look after her. Do we have a future? I don't know what I'm supposed to do anymore.*

My dad came up and knocked on the door.

'How are you doing?' he asked, sitting down in my desk chair. 'Did something happen with Lil?'

I nodded. I told him about my accident, about reading the card, and the mission meeting. He was astounded. It was the most emotional I'd ever seen him; there were actually tears in his eyes.

'I can't believe it,' he murmured.

I explained how I wanted to tell Lil all about it, but how our conversation had been cut short by what we had seen.

'I feel like it's my fault that she found out, but then I think it's a good thing that it happened, to stop it going on in secret for longer…' I said, wringing my hands, '…but then I feel guilty because she's going through so much pain. I wish I could take it away, that I could be there for her, but we haven't spoken in such a long time, and I don't think she trusts me anymore.'

He pulled the chair close to the bed and laid his hand on my shoulder.

'Do you love her, son?'

I nodded, my eyes filling with tears.

'Then you need to offer her whatever she most needs right now. Be a friend to her. Don't expect anything else until she's ready.'

I looked down at my hands.

'When we were going out, I didn't honour her,' I confessed. 'I broke the boundaries we set and I also failed to take the steps we'd put in place, which was to tell you. I was a coward.'

'You're young,' Dad said, with a sigh. 'You made mistakes. What matters is that you do things differently next time.'

'What if she never gives me another chance?' I asked, my voice breaking with emotion.

'That's her decision, and you can't control that,' he said. 'You do need to trust the Lord with the situation.'

He stood up to leave.

'Your mother and I were thinking that we should invite them to come here for Christmas dinner. Would you be okay with that?'

I stared at him in shock.

'I would love that,' I said.

He nodded.

'For what it's worth, we think she is a wonderful young lady and we're sorry we weren't more encouraging… before.'

He left and closed the door, and I cried some more. *Please God, bring good out of this messy situation. Please mend the brokenness and heal the pain.*

Please, give me another chance with Lil.

Lil

Darcy and I slept in Mum's bed to keep her company. We clung together and pushed through what felt like fog. Mealtimes were erratic and Mum didn't go into work the next day. The office was shutting down for Christmas anyway.

Sam had messaged me about going for a walk, and I hadn't replied. Darcy caught me staring at my phone.

'Is it Sam?' she asked.

'What's going on between the two of you?' Mum asked me.

'Up until yesterday, nothing,' I said. 'But he found a Christmas card I wrote to him last year… I still don't know how he got it.'

'Oh, that's probably the one I found,' Mum said. 'I went to get the Christmas card box from your room, and as I was getting some cards out, the one for Sam fell out. I was popping some Christmas cake round to Meredith anyway, so I took it over and gave it to her. I'm sorry, I should have asked you first.'

'It's okay,' I said. 'It turned out to be just what he needed to hear when he opened it. God knew the right time.'

'You girls inspire me with your faith,' Mum said. 'I've often wished I had faith like yours.'

'You can,' Darcy said simply. 'Just ask God. It's a gift.'

'Hmm,' Mum said, not convinced. She turned to me. 'So, are you going to see Sam today?'

'I could,' I admitted. 'But what about you?'

'I don't want you girls feeling you've got to stay at home with me all day,' Mum said. 'I've got some things I need to sort out.'

'I might go over Annabelle's to watch a Christmas movie,' Darcy said.

'Good,' Mum said. 'Lil, go and call for Sam. I need a bit of head space.'

Still feeling numb, I pulled on an old pair of jeans and a jumper. I considered wearing Sam's old T-shirt but in the end, I wasn't brave enough. I felt myself blush as I thought about the Shower Day. If I saw Sam again, were we just going to go down that old road again?

I looked at my pale face in the mirror. My hair had darker streaks in it—Sam used to call it gingerbread. Did he still find me attractive? Darcy seemed to think so. The service seemed to suggest it too.

I groaned. I wanted him to find me attractive, but I didn't want us both to lose our heads again. How on earth were we supposed to navigate this?

'Are you ready?' Darcy called.

As I'll ever be.

I trailed behind her as she rang the doorbell and marched straight into the Parks' house.

'Hey.' Sam appeared, looking gorgeous in a long, knitted jumper and jeans. He'd only managed to grow more good-looking in the past two years.

'Hey,' I murmured, feeling my voice disappear.

He stepped out, shut the door behind him, and held his arms out.

'Can I hug you?' he asked.

I nodded and allowed him to wrap his arm around me. A sob caught in my throat. Being with someone outside the family, I could just be myself and express my grief without having to worry about holding others up. Sam held me tightly, and I buried my face in his chest. He smelled so familiar, and safe.

'It's okay,' he said, stroking my back. 'You can cry as much as you want.'

We stood there, holding each other, and time stood still. I could hear his heartbeat. I wondered if the neighbours were twitching their curtains, and pulled back once I felt more composed.

'Thanks, Sam,' I said.

'Still fancy a walk?' he asked.

'Sure.'

We went along the canal, an easy peace between us. We walked side by side, not holding hands, but when he held his palm out to help me over a stile, I didn't let go of it afterwards. I linked my arm through his, and leaned my head on his shoulder.

'I've missed this,' I breathed.

'Me too,' he said.

We had two years to catch up on. We asked each other questions, and laughed at old memories. We didn't ignore the pain of the breakup and our separation.

'There were so many times when I just wanted to call you,' he said. 'But I knew I couldn't. It was so hard.'

'I just wanted you to come back to church,' I said. 'But you had to figure stuff out on your own.'

'I wished I'd figured it out sooner,' he said, looking at me wistfully.

'But then, what would we have done?' I asked. 'Even now, we've still got the rest of our courses to complete. You might end up in Costa Rica.'

'I am absolutely happy to turn that down if it means that I get to see you more often.'

I stopped, and faced him, searching to see if he was genuine.

'Are you serious?' I asked.

He nodded.

'I can't let you give that up for me,' I said, shaking my head.

'Why?' he asked. 'It's my choice.'

'But, things may not even work out between us, and then you will have lost that opportunity forever.'

'It's a risk I'm willing to take,' he said, taking one of my hands into his own. 'But Lil, it's up to you whether you want to take a risk with me. I don't expect you to trust me right here, right now. I'm just asking you to consider giving me a second chance.'

I looked at him, and no part of me wanted to refuse him, but I made myself slow down.

'How do I know that things will be different this time?' I asked him.

'I told my dad,' he said. 'So I finally came clean. I know it's two years too late.'

'What did you tell him?' My eyebrows shot up. I really hoped he hadn't mentioned the shower.

'I didn't go into too much detail,' he said.

'Phew,' I breathed out a sigh.

'He said I should just be a friend to you, without expecting anything more,' he continued. 'And he said that they think you're amazing. So I think it's fair to say we have their blessing this time.'

'Wow,' I said. That was a seismic shift if ever there was one.

'What are you thinking?' he asked after a moment.

'I'm thinking I need time to process all of this,' I said, turning back and starting to walk again. 'I don't want to have to make any decisions right now.'

'It's okay,' he said. 'I just want you to know that I'm here, waiting, and I'll be waiting for you and only you.'

Sam

If the time we'd spent apart was an iceberg between us, it was slowly thawing.

I'd done my best to reassure Lil that I wasn't planning to disappear, that I wanted to start again with her, but I was happy to leave her to think it over and simply enjoy the moments we had together.

The winter air was crisp and the sunlight was unusually brilliant. Lil kept her arm tucked into mine, and it felt like we fitted back together with a satisfying, if inaudible, click.

When we arrived back, I invited her inside. She checked her phone and her mum had gone into town.

'I hope she's okay,' she said, frowning.

'Do you think she'll go to find Sal?' I asked.

Lil's eyes widened slightly.

'I don't think so,' she said slowly, but she didn't seem certain.

'How far away do your grandparents live?'

'Towards Bristol,' she said. 'So she's not going to bump into him.'

Yet, I thought. The problem was, his business was based here, and he never seemed to take much time off. He wasn't going to disappear into thin air, and they were going to need to talk and work out their next steps.

Lil hovered on the pavement.

'I could take you to town, if you'd like to find her?' I suggested.

Her face brightened.

'That would be great, if you don't mind.'

I checked with my parents, then we got into the car. This would be the second time I had driven Lil, and I already loved having her in the passenger seat next to me. She smelled of oranges, and she wore a bright scarf with red, gold and green thread.

It was a bit of a wild goose chase, but I didn't care. Lil was texting her mum, trying to pin down where she was, and every car park was busy as it was so close to Christmas. In the end, Lil directed me to the supermarket, and we walked up and down, checking each aisle.

'Perhaps I missed her,' Lil groaned, pressing her fingers to her temples.

'It's okay,' I said, taking her hands in mine gently. 'Is there anything you'd like to get while we're here? Some food for tonight?'

She shook her head sadly, looking close to tears.

'Can we go home?' she asked.

'Of course.'

She looked so forlorn, I put my arm around her to guide her to the exit. She nestled into me and I just wanted her to feel better, to feel safe. Would she let me be there for her? I'd made so many mistakes that I knew I didn't deserve her trust, but I hoped I could win it back.

'You want to listen to some Christmas radio?' I asked her, once we were back in the car.

She nodded, and when I found a station, Michael Buble was playing. I caught her eye and smiled. She gave a small smile in return.

For so long, I had tried not to think about her. I had focused on what a negative influence I was on her. Now, if I could make the smallest difference to bring her some happiness, I would do it.

When we arrived back, Lil had to unlock her front door. Her mum wasn't there.

'Let me make you some lunch,' I suggested.

Putting a Christmas playlist on, I pulled together some scrambled egg on toast, and it was a relief to see her eat something.

'Have you learned to cook then?' she asked.

'I'm not sure scrambled egg counts,' I said with a laugh.

'Dad used to make it on his day off,' she said, then rubbed her forehead with her fingertips. 'I don't know why I'm talking about him as if he's dead.'

'It's going to be hard adjusting,' I said.

The current song ended and the chords of *Last Christmas* began.

'Come on, time for a dance," I said, pulling her to her feet.

She giggled as I swung her arms and danced exaggeratedly around the kitchen floor. By the time the verse started, we were both thinking about our memories of this song. I calmed down my movements, and she began to move in time with me. The atmosphere changed. I held her gaze, and where I was holding her hands at a slight distance, she stepped closer. Then her eyes filled with tears and she wrapped her arms around my neck, leaning into my shoulder. We swayed together, and I clasped her tightly, dropping my face to smell her hair against my chest.

'Don't you ever wish the last two years had never happened?' she asked. 'That we could somehow travel back in time to your kitchen and all of this pain would go away?'

I gently drew back so she would be forced to look at me.

'I know what you mean,' I said, 'but I also know that God has a plan, and a purpose for the way things have turned out, even if it's painful.'

Her tears threatened to spill over.

'I cried a lot over you, Sam,' she said, and it broke my heart.

'I cried a lot over you too,' I told her. It was true.

I hugged her tightly, and she buried her face in my shoulder. We were clinging to each other with the desperation of sailors on a lifeboat.

'I'm so grateful for the card you wrote,' I said. 'That and all the prayers which have been prayed for me. Without them, I might not be here now.'

She drew back to look at me and raised her hand to my face.

'I'm so glad you are here right now,' she said.

We had stopped moving to the music by this point, and Lil was leaning in closer. I tried not to move, because I wanted her to set the boundaries of what she was comfortable with, but I longed for her to kiss me from the depths of my being. At some point I closed my eyes, and the moment her lips brushed mine was a sweet relief.

Now I just had to make sure we didn't drown.

Lil

It may have been the fact that I was fighting so many emotions—of anger, pain and fear due to what had happened with my dad—that I couldn't fight my feelings for Sam as well. Or it may have been the fact that I felt like I was falling apart, and he was here, he was strong and he was holding me up. Either way, my lips found their way to his, in a dance that we'd done before. It was like muscle memory. His scent was so familiar, and his arms were so warm… I'd spent so many nights alone, the blackness of loneliness caving in on my heart, and it felt like it would be worth it if I was finally given Sam as my reward.

I'd met a lot of guys at uni, through my course, church and the Christian Union. None of them had drawn me the same way as Sam. With him, I couldn't bear being in the same room without finding my way to his side. Those R.E. lessons had been torturous. Between us there was a raw, charged energy that never seemed to fade. If our eyes met, my stomach flipped. And neither of us could ever forget what had passed between us. For better or worse, those memories were formed and revived every time we met.

Now, when I kissed him, it was like a pencil sketch turning into a full colour animation. We both came to life. I could push aside the consuming sadness for my father's betrayal by the immediate feel of Sam's mouth upon mine, the heat of his body, and the smell of his skin.

I'd missed him so much.

If the past two years had been filled in on my calendar with shades of grey, this moment was pure incandescence. Quite simply, Sam illuminated me. And like a moth to that flame, I craved him.

I clung to him, desperate for the moment to last forever. I wanted him to *want* me.

'Are you okay?' he whispered, breaking his mouth away and trying to assess my expression.

I nodded.

'Better than okay,' I replied, my eyes dropping to his mouth again. 'I've thought about this a lot.'

'I've tried *not* to think about it,' he confessed. 'It would drive me mad otherwise.'

'Did you kiss other girls to try to forget me?' I asked.

It was something I was desperate to know, but in some ways I was afraid to hear his answer.

'If I did, it didn't work,' he said firmly, then his eyes softened. 'I'm sorry for the things I did, Lil. I wrote you a card, actually.'

He went back into the hallway to retrieve it from his bag, and handed it to me.

'I've been waiting for the right moment to give it to you.'

I opened it up, and it was a card with a candle on the front, and John 8:12 *I am the light of the world.*

Dear Lil,

I'm a year late in responding to your card, but maybe it's a good thing that I only just read it. I wouldn't have been ready for it otherwise.

I've been running away from God. Like Jonah, it hasn't led me anywhere good. I had an accident and God used it to get my attention. In His grace, I realised what a destructive path I was going down. It's time to stop running.

Everything you said about coming to Jesus, and giving Him my burdens... I've finally done that for the first time. I feel this amazing, indescribable peace. I know that's what you wanted for me, and I want to thank you for your beautiful words, which ended up being read in just the right moment. God's timing is perfect.

I read the card and started to cry, my left hand reaching up to cover my mouth. I was completely overwhelmed that he read my card at just the right moment. It just seemed both incredibly impossible and poetically beautiful. For him to apologise to me, in writing, was so profound. It was finally an acknowledgement of how things had gone wrong between us, and I felt hopeful that I could now lay it to rest. I knew I was forgiven, and now it seemed that Sam finally knew the reality of grace too.

Sam gently took the card out of my hand, and held both of my hands within his.

'Lil, please can you forgive me?'

'You asked me that already,' I pointed out, sniffing.

'Yes, but then… stuff happened,' he said, inclining his head. 'So I wanted to have this conversation properly.'

I looked into his blue eyes, and it finally felt like there were no more areas gated and barred to me. He was being whole-hearted and laying himself bare. I'd waited for two years for this moment.

'Of course,' I said, my face breaking into a smile.

He grinned, and drew my right arm out to the side in a dancing position.

'Then let's dance.'

The song playing now was *Have Yourself a Merry Little Christmas*. It felt timeless, and as we swayed together in the darkening afternoon, close and cosy in the kitchen, all our troubles really did feel as if they were miles away.

We were barely twenty, but we'd been on this road for two, weary years. Now, we'd finally found common ground again. It seemed that Sam's brokenness had finally started to heal, although it would be a winding journey. But my pain was just beginning.

Sam

On Christmas Eve, Lil and I were both kept busy by our families. Julia was apparently doing some investigation work into the affair with Sal, and was going to the cafe to 'civilly' speak to her. Lil was accompanying her. Mum had a list of Christmas jobs for me to help with, and we roped in Annabelle and Darcy, too. Now that Lil's family were coming for Christmas dinner, Mum had extra preparations to make, although I kept telling her there was no need to go all fancy.

'They're going through a rough time, and I want to make Christmas special for them,' was her response.

Dad, as usual, was busy with church stuff, and it was only after dinner that I was able to text Lil to suggest a walk so that we could catch up. She met me outside, her woollen coat buttoned all the way to her chin, and a cute bobble hat on her head.

'Hey,' I said, holding out my hand to take hers.

She ignored it and wrapped her arms around my neck in a hug.

'I'm so glad to see you,' she said. 'I've got so much to tell you.'

From what Julia had managed to piece together, Bryan had been a regular at Sal's cafe for years. Sal had recently gone through a divorce. Bryan had offered a listening ear, and at some point that had turned into something more. Both Bryan and Sal claimed that they never wanted to hurt anybody.

'What was Sal like?' I asked. We were walking along the streets, admiring the different Christmas lights in people's front windows.

'She was actually very sorry,' Lil said. 'I wanted to hate her, but I just couldn't.'

'What did your mum say to her?'

Lil gave a dry laugh.

'Mum went all cold steel on her. She's used to doing it in her job. She was very business-like, didn't cry or anything. Sal was the one who was emotional, apologising. Mum was like a private investigator, collecting facts and then thanked Sal for her time, and then we left.'

'Is your mum okay?' I asked with a frown.

Lil sighed and shook her head.

'She's ploughing her time and energy into gathering as much information as possible. Then I think she's going to see Dad after Christmas and give him both barrels.'

'Have you spoken to your dad?'

'No,' she said flatly. 'I don't want to, either.'

I tried to reconcile the Bryan I knew from driving lessons with this newly revealed version of Bryan, the adulterer. It was hard to accept. In my mind, I supposed that I'd always viewed people like that as being drastically different, as standing out somehow. The reality was, they were people just like everyone else.

If I faced the truth, I knew all too well what it was like to hide sin away and present a respectable exterior.

'What are you thinking about?' Lil asked, eying my face curiously.

'Just the fact that it's easy to hide things,' I said. 'You don't know from looking at someone what's really going on with them, behind the scenes.'

'Yes, but in some ways, this shows that you can't hide forever,' Lil argued. 'Your sin finds you out.'

We turned the corner, and there was a house absolutely covered with lights, the garden crammed with inflatable snowmen and 'Santa stop here' signs.

'Wow,' Lil said. 'No hiding this place!'

'It's probably visible from space,' I said, and we both laughed.

As we walked on, my thoughts were uncomfortable. How had Bryan's affair started? Was it an innocent friendship with Sal? Small conversations which turned into bigger, more in depth chats? At what point had he started to conceal it from his wife? As much of a novice as I was about relationships, I felt instinctively that secrecy was a red flag. You couldn't hide things and expect the relationship to work.

At what point was I going to start telling Lil my secrets? Opening up about my past, so that we had nothing between us anymore?

'You seem far away,' Lil commented, squeezing my hand.

'Just thinking,' I said.

It was Christmas. She deserved to be happy, not burdened with more heaviness. I resolved to focus on celebrating and being there for her. That conversation was for another day.

Lil

Christmas morning felt strange with only three of us in the house. As much as Mum put on a brave face, and both Darcy and I pretended not to notice Dad's absence, there was a strange echoey emptiness we couldn't escape. We exchanged presents, and then Darcy and I needed to get ready for church. She went upstairs and I went in the kitchen to put my mug in the dishwasher.

'Your father just messaged.' Mum stood in the doorway, holding up her phone.

'What did he say?' I asked.

'Read it,' she said, pushing the phone towards me. I took it and scanned it.

I miss you all this morning. Please know that I love you and I'm sorry if I have ruined your Christmas. You deserve to be happy. I'd love to call later if you'd like to chat.

I looked up and saw tears in her eyes.

'Don't reply,' I said, handing her phone back. 'He doesn't deserve a reply right now.'

She nodded sadly. I wrapped my arms around her and held her close, and felt her thin shoulders shake with a sob. I had no idea how to navigate this. They had been married for twenty-five years, and now it was all disappearing like a puff of smoke. Saying sorry was not going to be enough to make it right. But I also worried, as I stood there rubbing my mum's back, that maybe I was saying the wrong thing. Maybe I should be encouraging her to speak to Dad.

'Mum, I don't want you to be here on your own this morning,' I said, sounding a lot more certain and in control than I felt. 'I'd love it if you came to church with us. If you don't feel up to it, I'll stay home with you.'

'I don't want you to miss it,' she said, pulling back and composing herself. 'I'll come.'

'Great.'

I dashed up the stairs and found Darcy in her room, crying.

'Not you, too,' I said, going over to hug her. I sat down on the bed next to her. 'Listen, Mum's just agreed to come to church.'

'Really?' Darcy said, brightening.

'Yes,' I said. 'Let's focus on getting ready.'

It was the first time my mum had crossed the threshold of the church doors. Everyone welcomed her, coming over to wish us a merry Christmas and introduce themselves. We sat in a row together: Mum sandwiched between me and Darcy, Sam by my side, and Annabelle next to Darcy. Meredith sat next to Annabelle, and hugged my mum when she saw her. It felt surreal. Last year was so different. I thanked God for this miraculous change, even though it had come about with unexpected pain. I felt tears spring into my eyes when we sang '*Light and life to all He brings/ Risen with healing in His wings.*' How badly we needed His light and life right now! How much I was feeling the reality of the darkness all around. As I thought about the battles Annabelle faced with her health, Meredith with her mental wellness, Sam with his prodigal phase, and Mum with her broken marriage, I cried for God's healing, even if I had no idea what that would look like.

Simon gave his address, focusing on John 1:

In him was life, and that life was the light of all mankind. The light shines in the darkness, and the darkness has not overcome it. Friends, we are living in dark times. But we can celebrate. Why? Because Jesus Christ came down into our darkness, bringing light and life. His light cannot be extinguished. And if He lives in you, then you have His light, and it cannot be put out. You are shining the light of

Christ wherever you go. You are the carriers of this great hope. God did not leave us alone in the darkness of sin and shame. He brought light.'

I wasn't sure how much my mum understood, or what she thought of it all, but it was a message she needed to hear. I needed to hear it, too. What was I going to gain from keeping my dad shut out in the darkness? Was I trying to punish him? What would it achieve? Surely God wanted me to bring him into the light, not exclude him from it? Was I willing to live the gospel when it meant offering forgiveness to those who had hurt me, to those I didn't believe deserved it? Was I willing to let God change my heart, and show me how much I didn't deserve His grace, but I'd received it anyway?

My head full of these thoughts, we went over to the Parks' for Christmas dinner, and Meredith absolutely excelled herself in making us feel welcome. It was another sign of how God could work in people's lives. She allowed my mum to help her in the kitchen, and they were deep in conversation every time I passed by. Darcy and Annabelle were thick as thieves, and Simon relaxed in an armchair with a new book. Sam and I sat together on the sofa, both quiet with our thoughts. He put his arm around me, and I leaned my head on his shoulder.

'It was good that your mum came this morning,' he said, tracing his finger in a circle on my upper arm.

'Yes,' I said. 'I think my dad might ring her later.'

'Will she talk to him?' he asked.

'I don't know,' I answered.

This morning I was so sure of myself, and now nothing felt certain anymore.

Sam

Although I felt so sad for Lil's family and their situation, it was wonderful to have them all with us for Christmas. Our families had never felt closer. Later on, Julia wanted to go home to call Bryan, and asked Darcy if she wanted to join her. Darcy looked at Lil.

'Go,' Lil said. 'Maybe Sam and I can go for a walk.'

I leapt to my feet and we grabbed our coats. It was a crisp, cold Christmas Day, and frost was already beginning to form on the ground in shadow. It was twilight, and a stretch of purple cloud loomed over the horizon, a streak of washed out sky above it. A few gulps of air and already I felt fresh again. Lil's eyes were focused on the ground, like she barely noticed anything.

'Are you okay?' I asked, squeezing her hand.

She lifted up her head.

'What am I going to do if he comes back?'

The question resounded into the silence. I barely heard a bird call.

'I'm thinking that you wouldn't want to cut him off for ever,' I said. 'That you'd want to speak to him again at some point?'

'I don't want to live with him. I don't want Mum to take him back.'

Her voice was hard, but I knew how brittle she was underneath.

'You know, you're not going to be at home that much anyway,' I pointed out. 'You're in your second year studying. Two more terms and then you've got your final year. Presumably after that, you're going to get a job and move out.'

'That's what I'd always planned,' she said, 'but now, everything's up in the air. I feel bad enough as it is for going back to uni when the holiday ends. I'm leaving Mum and Darce to deal with everything alone. And Darcy's got her exams in June, then she'll be off to uni in September. What if Mum can't cope on her own?'

'So you don't want to leave your mum on her own, but you don't want your dad to move back in either?'

I kind of got Lil's logic, but it was hard to see a way forward.

'I don't know,' she said, sighing. 'I don't know anything anymore.'

I wanted to reassure her of my love for her, but it seemed too premature. I hadn't said those words to her for two years, and she'd have every right to question whether I meant them. Would it be enough, that I was there for her now?

It was a quiet walk, out round the back of the houses and taking the footpath that skirted the edge of the woods. We didn't see anyone else, and the daylight was fading quickly. A sudden fear gripped my heart: what if we went back to uni, in our separate places, and then Lil drifted away from me? What if she met someone who was more impressive? I wished that we had more time together, but it was going to be all too brief.

'If he just moves back in, it'll be like he never did anything wrong,' Lil said, obviously verbalising what had preoccupied her thoughts.

'Remember that *'in the course of justice none of us / Should see salvation.'*

'Is that the Bible?' Lil asked, her brow raised suspiciously.

'No, it's Shakespeare,' I said, blushing. '*The Merchant of Venice.* I was in a production.'

Before she could ask any more questions, I carried on.

'But it reminds me of James 2:13 *'mercy triumphs over judgement.'*

'I know I should agree with you right now, but I don't want to,' Lil said.

Her hair was rich and beautiful, framing her face, and I lifted my hand to cup her cheek.

'Give it time,' I said, dropping my gaze to her lips.

The wind teased her hair, brushing it against the back of my hand, and the storm in her eyes was softened as she looked at me.

'Kiss me, Sam.'

I dipped my head and brushed her lips with mine, a tentative beginning. She linked her hands together behind my neck, pulling me closer. She kissed me longer, with more need, and she murmured,

'I could get lost in this forever.'

I knew exactly what she meant, but I didn't just want to be a means of her escaping the reality of her broken family. For once, I'd been there at the right time for her. But what about when she didn't need me anymore?

Two years ago, I never questioned myself like this. There was no need to overthink everything. Why was life so complicated now?

I felt like I was edging past a landmine that at any point could blow up.

Lil

The usual Christmas haze of Boxing Day, and the weird limbo up until New Year, were fogged up with the murky sadness of Dad not being with us, but the conflicting emotions I felt towards him. Mum and Darcy were talking about going to visit my grandparents, and seeing Dad, on New Year's Day. It made me feel cross just hearing them discuss it.

'Just make sure he knows in advance, so you don't turn up and find him with Sal like I did,' I said, crashing mugs about in the kitchen.

Mum and Darcy exchanged a look.

'He's ended it with her,' Darcy said.

'So he says,' I scoffed. 'Until the next time.'

'People make mistakes,' Darcy said, in a firmer tone than usual. He was really convincing them.

'If it had been you that day, instead of me,' I said, setting down my teaspoon on the worktop, 'then I guarantee you would not be saying that now.'

'Don't fight,' Mum pleaded. 'Darcy, leave Lil to make her own mind up.'

'It doesn't matter what I think!' I shouted, making her flinch. 'If you take him back, it's irrelevant. It's you who's going to get hurt, and I don't want to watch that happen.'

'If Dad hurts Mum, that hurts all of us,' Darcy pointed out.

'I'm not giving him the power to hurt me again,' I said darkly, pouring hot water into the mugs.

'You can't pretend he's not your father,' Darcy said, raising her voice.

'Watch me.'

I grabbed my coat and walked out, too frustrated to stay indoors. I paced along the front path, texting Sam. It only took a minute before he came out of his front door, shrugging on his coat.

'You want a walk?' he asked.

I nodded and set off impatiently, with him rushing to catch up.

'What's wrong?' he asked, frowning with concern.

'They want to spend New Year with him. It's been literally a week since our world imploded because of his infidelity, and now they want to toast in the New Year and sing Auld Lang Syne!'

I blinked back tears and pushed my hair back out of my face. Emotion was so annoying sometimes.

'Hey,' Sam said, catching my hand and forcing me to stop.

'I can't stand it, Sam,' I said, my voice catching. 'I can't pretend we didn't see what we saw. How can they just ignore it?'

'Lil.' He drew me into his arms and hugged me tightly. I started to sob.

'Those promises they made when they said their vows,' I said, pulling back with tears running down my face, 'he's broken them. You can't just *carry on*.'

Sam said nothing, but kept his arms around me until I was ready to walk on. Once we'd resumed our path, he said,

'I had a text today from the Xbox crew. They're going out for New Year's Eve and they've invited us to join them.'

'Really?' I asked. I hadn't been in touch with any of those guys—they were Sam's friends, really—but the idea of New Year alone at home was a bit pathetic.

'What do you think?' he asked.

'Sure,' I agreed.

In the end, Mum and Darcy left on New Year's Eve in the afternoon, so it lessened the pain that I was going out somewhere and had a reason to dress up. I scavenged through my wardrobe and found the black dress I wore to the Sixth Form social when I went with Sam. I hesitated for a millisecond before plucking it off the hanger.

I piled my hair up onto my head and pinned it, and used liquid eyeliner to accentuate my eyes. So what if my parents were going to drink wine and watch Jools Holland? I was going out, and I was determined to have fun.

At seven, Sam knocked on the door. I studied his reaction when I opened it, and I wasn't disappointed. His eyes travelled all the way down to my feet and then back up to my face.

'Wow,' he said.

'Come in a sec,' I said. 'I just need to find my shoes.'

He stepped into the hallway, closing the door behind him and shutting out the icy air. I slipped on my fancy wool coat, then stepped into my heels. I adjusted the back strap, and then straightened up. I saw Sam swallow.

'You look smart,' I said, walking up to him and straightening his collar.

He was wearing a charcoal grey shirt that made his eyes look darker. I ran my hands up to his neck, then leaned in to smell his cologne. I brushed my lips against his jaw.

'You smell amazing,' I said.

He swallowed again, and his fingertips reached for my waist, underneath my open coat. As soon as he touched me, I claimed his mouth with mine. I could feel every nerve ending of mine in contact with his body.

'How do you taste so good?' he murmured. I grinned against his mouth. 'We're never going to get there, at this rate.'

He gently extracted himself and exhaled deeply.

'I've got to be in a fit state to drive, remember?' he teased.

We walked out to the car, and I could feel his eyes on me, irresistibly drawn. The electric charge between us was palpable. I sat in the passenger seat, my dress riding up my thighs, and he blinked and gave his head a little shake before starting the engine.

We were meeting the guys at a pub with class Christmas hits blaring. It was definitely a nicer atmosphere than the Sixth Form social, and we enjoyed catching up and picked up easily with them. Sam wasn't drinking, so I had a glass of wine. Nothing fancy.

When *Last Christmas* started up, I grabbed Sam's hands.

'It's our song!' I yelled, pulling him to the dancefloor.

We danced to the familiar track, and I felt the giddy happiness of being back with Sam, the one who'd broken my heart two years ago. If we were back together now, for good, then maybe it was all worth it.

When it got to the phrase about the man 'with a fire in his heart', Sam pulled me against him and kissed me. It felt like Romeo was back. I relished the way that he held me so tightly, the way his body felt against mine, and the way he tasted. We'd been here before, but it had been so long. We'd both been in a desert, starved of physical affection, and now we were in a tropical storm.

'Come on,' I whispered in his ear, and we grabbed our coats to sneak away to the car.

Each kiss, stolen on the way, was like a bolt of lightning.

Sam

The air was sharp enough to catch in your throat. Avoiding the patches of ice on the ground, we dodged and ran through the car park as if we were still dancing together. Every few steps were punctuated with kisses. Lil's red hair streamed behind her, a flaming beacon.

The car was iced with frost. Inside, we shivered while I started up the engine and the hot air fan. The inside of the screen was misted with condensation.

Lil's phone started beeping.

'It's Mum,' she said, and answered the video call.

'Hey!'

It sounded like Darcy, and there were other voices in the background.

'Is Mum okay?' Lil asked, leaning forward in her seat.

'Yes,' Darcy said. 'Here she is.'

I presumed that she was panning the camera around the room. I didn't want to be rude and look over Lil's shoulder, so I focused on rubbing my hands together for warmth.

'We miss you,' Darcy said. 'You should have come.'

'I'm fine where I am,' Lil replied, a defensive edge in her voice.

'Is Sam there?' Darcy asked. 'Hi Sam!'

'Hi Darcy,' I said, as Lil tilted the phone towards me.

I could see Lil's parents in the background, talking. Lil was frowning at the screen.

'Happy New Year,' Darcy said. 'Enjoy your evening.'

Lil said goodbye and then put her phone down in her lap. I could tell she was annoyed, and a bit unsettled.

'Are you okay?' I asked, laying my hand on her knee.

'Yeah,' she said flatly. 'I just don't understand how Mum can sit there with a glass of wine and celebrate New Year with him in the room.'

'You don't know what they've been talking about,' I said. 'They may have had a difficult conversation, but they're putting on a brave face for Darcy's sake and your grandparents.'

'She shouldn't have to put on a brave face,' Lil said emphatically. 'She's perfectly justified in going to bed and crying all night. That's what I would do.'

It sounded like she was speaking from experience. I thought with pain of all those nights of misery she had gone through in the last two years, some of which would have been my fault. I'd had times when I'd missed her so much that I'd sat on my bed staring at the wall, knowing she was on the other side of it. So close, and yet so far. The times when I'd seen her in school and not been able to get close to her, seen the shine of her hair but not been able to touch it, seen her face downcast and not been able to cheer her up.

'I thought I was doing the right thing by staying away from you,' I said.

The car was finally starting to warm up now, and I turned the heat down a notch.

'Because you were having doubts?' Lil asked.

'Partly,' I said. 'I knew I couldn't be the person that you needed me to be and I thought you were better off without me.'

'So how about now?' Lil asked, a challenge in her voice. 'Are you the person I need right now? Because I don't want you to suddenly disappear again.'

'I'm not going to disappear,' I said as firmly as I could.

We drove back home in silence, and when I parked up, I switched off the engine.

'Do you want to come in?' Lil asked.

I felt my gut twist… it probably wasn't a good idea… but I didn't want to leave her like this.

'Sure,' I said.

I followed her into the dark house. She went to the kitchen and put the kettle on, more out of habit than anything else, and twisted her hands together while we waited for it to boil. I clasped my hands over hers, to still them, and waited for her to look up and meet my gaze. When she did, her eyes were sparkling with tears. I wrapped my arms around her and held her tightly. She sobbed into my shoulder. Only the fairy lights were on, not the main overhead ones, and the dim lighting accentuated the intimacy of being here, in this moment, alone together.

'In a strange way, it's like it's worse for me than for Mum,' she said, pulling back slightly. 'She knew Dad wasn't perfect. But in some ways, I guess I thought… Well, he's not the person I thought he was.'

I stiffened slightly as she said these words. She noticed, and pulled back further.

'What?' she asked. 'What's wrong?'

I debated how to answer.

'I'm worried that you'd say the same thing about me,' I said finally.

'Is this like our conversation we had before about Sam the Terrible Sinner?' she teased, raising an eyebrow.

'We both know that it's not a joke,' I said, in a more reprimanding tone.

'It's like playing Truth or Dare,' she said, her face lighting up with excitement. 'Only it's both the Truth and the Dare. I *dare* you to tell me the truth: what's your worst sin?'

'I don't think you can easily measure sins out like rice in the supermarket,' I said, sidestepping the question.

She tilted her head and assessed me.

'So what about this, then: what's the worst lie you've ever told?'

Steam filled the air from the kettle, and she leaned against the worktop, waiting for me to answer.

'It wasn't one I ever spoke out loud,' I said. 'But I lived it. I knew the right words to say, the right way to act in public. But I knew it wasn't real in my heart.'

'Are you talking about being a Christian?' she asked.

'Yes,' I said. 'It was always assumed and I think I joined in because I didn't know what else to do. I didn't feel I could really tell my family what I actually thought, given my dad's position.'

'But that's different now?' she asked, making no move towards the teacups. Perhaps the tea was forgotten now.

'Yes,' I said. It sounded lame. 'I know it's only been a week but I feel so different, like I don't have to pretend anymore… It's why I want to be honest with you, Lil, because you deserve that.'

She said nothing but looked at me expectantly. The kitchen was silent now the kettle had finished boiling I could hear the tap dripping slightly. I took a deep breath.

'For the last few years I've struggled with porn,' I confessed, watching her eyes shift and widen. 'I never told anyone, and I felt so ashamed, and it's why I knew I wasn't any good for you. I wasn't surprised when I took things too far with you, pushed the boundaries, because I know how rubbish my self-control is. I know that when you feed wrong desires, it's like putting more fuel on a fire until it's a raging inferno. It's never satisfied.'

I'd finally managed to say it. I was equally relieved and terrified to see how Lil would react.

'So at first you wouldn't go out with me, and you made a fuss about what we could and couldn't do, even though you were doing all this behind closed doors, in secret?' she said, raising an eyebrow.

'Yes,' I said, 'and I'm sorry.'

'I get that,' she said, looking me straight in the eye. 'You're human, Sam, and I even understand why that could be an issue for you because I think it is for a lot of guys. But it does feel like you deceived me. You were living a double life and I *knew* that something was wrong. There were times when you were so distant and you didn't contact me.'

Guilt twisted in my stomach. Of course she noticed. I'd already caused her pain, even though I'd tried to hide my struggles from her.

'I wish you'd have opened up and not made me feel like I wasn't good enough for your family,' she said, folding her arms.

'I never said that,' I said straight away. I was desperate for her not to put the barriers back up, the hostility which had broken down over the last few days.

'Well, I think that was what your parents thought initially,' she said.

'They don't think it anymore,' I told her.

'I know my own worth,' she said, lifting her chin. 'I don't need your parents to affirm it, but I think it's going to be difficult to be together if they're always wishing I was someone else, or even wishing that *you* were someone else.'

She eyed me sympathetically.

'The question is, do you know your worth, Sam? Have you embraced who you are and how God's made you? If you're still on the run from yourself, then you won't be able to stay still in one place to be with me.'

This was beginning to sound like a break-up speech, and we'd only just got back together. *Please God, no!*

'I do want to be with you, Lil,' I said, stepping closer to try to hold out my hands to her. 'I know I'm weak and I know I need help, but what God's done in my heart is real.'

Would she believe me? I could barely breathe as I stared into her eyes, willing her to give me a chance. Her expression wasn't completely hardened towards me, but there was a new sense of reservation that reminded me of when I'd sat next to her in church.

'When my dad made promises to my mum on their wedding day,' she said, 'he fully intended to keep them. For whatever reason, he didn't. I don't doubt your sincerity, Sam, but how can I trust that you've really overcome these problems? That we won't end up back where we started?'

'I don't know,' I said helplessly, dropping my hands to my sides.

She looked at me and I thought about how beautiful her eyes were, shining golden in this light, and about how it felt to kiss her and take her face in my hands, run my finger down her cheek, and how it would feel if I lost her forever. Tears started in my eyes.

'Okay,' she said, straightening up. 'This is what we'll do. In a few days, we'll go back to uni and I don't want us to text or call each other.'

My heart sank.

'We can write,' she continued, 'the old fashioned way. You can tell me about how things are going, and you have to be honest or there's no point. If you're really serious about me, you'll do it.'

So it wasn't an ending… more like a break… a test.

'All right,' I agreed. I couldn't really refuse.

It was so hard, now that I just got her back, to let go again.

'Listen,' I said. 'Be honest. If you're not interested in me anymore, I'll understand. I'd rather you told me now than in six months' time after I've written a folio's worth of letters for you.'

She gave a wry smile.

'I'm not rejecting you, Sam,' she said, finally taking my hand and squeezing it. 'I'm just putting some boundaries in place to protect myself. After what my dad did, I have to. Please can you understand?'

'Has what I told you changed your opinion of me?' I asked, afraid of how she might respond.

'It's helped me understand you better,' she said. 'And if you're truly willing to be real with me, then that's a privilege that I don't want to take lightly.'

'Do you forgive me for lying to you?' I asked her.

'Yes,' she said, 'although that doesn't erase the hurt. And it doesn't mean that I can instantly trust you again.'

'I love you, Lil,' I said, and I couldn't help the tears from falling. 'I've never stopped loving you.'

She stepped even closer, and put her arms around my neck. She smelt of oranges.

'I love you too Sam,' she said, and I felt her whole body sigh. 'Please know that I'm not saying that you're not good enough for me. I may not struggle with the same things as you, but I have plenty of struggles too. I know I'm supposed to forgive my dad but I have no idea where I'm going to find the heart to do that.'

I held her against me, breathing her in and letting my tears drop silently onto her silken hair. We stayed there for a long moment.

'You'll find it,' I managed to speak, 'at the same place where you and I both find forgiveness. The cross.'

She pulled back enough to look at me. Both of our eyes glimmered in the light with emotion. She looked down, and nodded. I wanted to kiss her, but it wasn't fair to claim that after the disclosure I'd just made. In the tired, fragile state we were both in, who knew where it might lead? Reluctantly, I let my arms drop and moved away.

'I don't like the idea of leaving you on your own here,' I said.

'I'm fine,' she said firmly, looking up again. 'It's better than you staying, and then something happens that we both regret.'

'So we're back to being on separate sides of the wall,' I said sadly.

'That's the way it should be for now,' Lil said.

We heard the sound of fireworks, and I looked at my watch. Midnight.

'Happy new year,' I said.

'Happy new year, Sam.'

I looked at her, feeling a wave of hopelessness. She wasn't mine. We'd shared so much together, and suffered being apart, but she was still out of reach.

What if I wrote to her, and she never wrote back? Worse still, what if she wrote to tell me she'd met someone at church, or the Christian Union, who'd never struggled with lust and seemed much more reliable and worthy than me?

Lil looked at me, as if she could tell what I was thinking.

'Do you remember last year when you told me there was no one else?' she asked. I nodded. 'I'm going to say it to you now. There's no one else, Sam.'

'Yet.' I couldn't allow myself to believe it, to hope.

She shook her head.

'Sounds like you need to trust me, then,' she said.

'I don't want you to be restricted or held back by me,' I said.

'Then do me a favour,' she said. 'Pray about us and whether we should be together.'

'Do I need to wait for your name to be written in the sky?' I joked.

'We're already star crossed lovers,' Lil said, with a slight smile. 'Now we just have to figure out an ending where we both survive.'

'And where we can be together?' I added hopefully.

'*This bud of love, by summer's ripening breath,/ May prove a beauteous flower when next we meet,*' Lil quoted.

'You realise that in the play, that means the next day… when they get married.'

'It's a dramatic timeline,' Lil said, waving her hand. 'But the sentiment is clear.'

I already had visions of Lil in a white dress, a veil trailing to the floor, and I tried to focus on more immediate issues.

'How long will we write to each other?' I asked.

'Until the season changes,' she replied cryptically.

Shakespeare had a lot to answer for.

1st January

Dear Lil,

I just left your house and I thought I'd start my letter tonight.

This isn't exactly how I expected us to bring in the new year. But then, nothing over the past few weeks has turned out as I expected.

I'm sorry for letting you down, and not being the right kind of boyfriend. But I hope I can learn, and change, and that you believe it's possible.

I've always been so challenged by your faith. You didn't have the advantages of growing up in church, or a faith-filled family, but you still shine like the brightest of stars. God's work in your life is evident, and now He's drawing in your sister, and your mum too. Cling onto the truth that there's purpose behind the pain of what you're going through.

You're someone who understands grace, otherwise you wouldn't have responded so kindly to me tonight. Thank you. I know you're grappling with what your father has done, and how you feel, but just remember what you told me: God is big enough to handle your struggles.

I'm going to keep telling myself that, too.

Love, Sam

1st January

Dear Sam,

I found your letter on the mat this morning when I came downstairs. The house is quiet, so I've been able to read it and think about what I should write back.

I spent some time praying last night after you'd gone. It helped. I feel some sort of peace about this messy situation. Even though there's so many unknowns, I do trust that God is working it all out for our good.

Thank you for your honesty. Even though it was hard to hear, I'm glad you told me.

Remember you don't have to fight this battle alone. The guys who helped you on the day of your accident… God sent them at just the right time. Be honest with them, and ask for their help and support. We're not meant to carry our burdens alone. There's power in confessing your sin, bringing it into the light.

I feel stupid for writing that I miss you already, but I do. I know you would come round in an instant if I asked you to, but I want to stay strong and stick to what we agreed. It's for the best.

I hope this time of physical separation can help us both to process what we really want.

I hope you don't give up on me, Sam.

Love, Lil.

4th January

Dear Lil,

I unpacked my rucksack when I arrived back at my student house today. The first thing I pulled out was my Bible. I sat down on my bed and cried as I thought about finding it just after my accident, reading your Christmas card, and everything that's happened since then. It was like God was reminding me that He's there, He's been there all along. He's my Good Shepherd, and I need to listen to His voice.

Things are going to be different this term. I'm going to church tomorrow with Paul and Nathan, and I'm going to tell them everything that's happened between us. I know you're right; I can't do this on my own.

I'm so grateful that God saved me, and for all the people He's put in my life. But can I say that you are the one person who is my favourite? The one person I feel I can truly be myself with?

I don't deserve you in any way, Lil. I wish I could express how much joy I feel every time I receive a letter from you. Each one is a gift of grace, treasured and savoured, reread countless times.

I still love you, and I'm going to keep writing.

Love, Sam

Dear Sam,

I've got three letters from you here and I'm only just writing a response. I've been ill in bed with flu, and I've been reading that book you sent me, The Hiding Place by Corrie Ten Boom. It's emotionally wrecked me. When I got to the part where she met a guard from the concentration camp who repented, came to faith and asked for her forgiveness, I kept reading and re-reading how she felt, and how she asked God for the strength to forgive him. Maybe I should ask God for the same thing, the strength to forgive Dad, but if I'm being really honest, I don't want to. I don't want to forgive him, because I don't feel he deserves it. Does that show that I haven't really understood the gospel? Does that show that I'm disobeying Jesus? I'm just praying at the moment that God will change my heart.

Mum and Darcy seem to be doing well, and apparently Dad's been staying at my grandparents and driving all the way over every day for his clients. He's come over a few times to see them, but Darcy hasn't talked about it much. I think she knows that I don't really want to know about it.

Honestly, what we saw that day in the car… It still makes me feel sick to think of it. I wake up in the middle of the night, my throat choking in fear. I don't even know what I'm afraid of. It's like my world turned on its axis, and I'm still experiencing the churning fall of gravity, over and over again. There are two things I'm reaching out for, to try to steady myself: God and you.

It's so strange, because if none of this had happened, and we had just had coffee in the cafe, we might not be writing to each other now. Maybe I would have had more time to be annoyed at you, to be mistrustful, and to push you away. You showed up for me, Sam, and you're continuing to show up, every time you write. Thank you.

I'm trying to rely on God more, though. I don't want to just rely on you. It's not fair on you, for one thing. Being apart like this, I've had to pray more, be alone more, and wait. The answers don't come easily, but I feel like I'm muddling my way through.

I sorted out my house for next year, and one of my friends mentioned that they knew someone in Plymouth who was finalising their placement for next year. You haven't mentioned it so I was wondering… have you made a decision yet? I know I shouldn't try to influence your decision, so I'll just say that I'll support you wherever you want to go. I don't want to get in the way, especially if you have the opportunity to go to Costa Rica.

In this dreary, cold weather, I would so love to be somewhere hot and exotic right now!

Love, Lil

28th January

Dear Lil,

I hope you're feeling better now. I made you these brownies—you have to let me know if they arrived in one piece and if they're any good!

I remember reading about Corrie Ten Boom with my family when I was younger. Her story meant a lot to us, particularly when Annabelle was ill, because she suffered with a lot of illness too, as well as her sister. In fact, I really related to her anger and helplessness when Betsy, her sister, was suffering. I know we've barely gone through any trouble compared to them, but I appreciated her honesty about the ups and downs of faith. Through it all, she held on to God. That's definitely the kind of faith I want to have.

I know I've said it before, but I really think you should talk about the situation with your dad with someone at your church, maybe a Christian counsellor. It's completely understandable that it's affected you so much. I don't want you to carry it alone.

Also, I don't think you should feel like you need to respond in the 'right' way, immediately. Give yourself time to process what happened. Perhaps it would be helpful for you to talk more with Darcy and your mum about it. Hear more from their perspective.

Sorry, I'm not trying to tell you what to do.

I've been praying a lot about my placement for next year. I want to be sure that I'm making the right decision, so I'm not going to tell you about where I'm going until we meet in person, if that's okay.

I hope it won't be too long before I can see you. I have some photos of you from Christmas on my phone and when I look at them, I have such a mixture of memories. Like you said, that moment in the car park… But there was also the moment in the car when I told you about reading your card and you wrapped your arms around me. We were both crying. It just felt so precious.

I found out more about the card, by the way. My mum slipped it into my rucksack, and it fell into my Bible. Not quite an angel, but God knew exactly when I needed to read it. I wasn't ready for it at that time.

*It's funny, I've been going to church my whole life, but it's only in the last few weeks that I've really felt **part** of it. Everything's come to life: the singing, the Bible, the sermon… I've been meeting up with Paul and Nathan to pray, and we're all going to a course at church about overcoming addictions. I always felt like God wanted me to keep all these rules, and knew that I couldn't, and then punished me anyway. I feel like I'm finally understanding grace, and it's so liberating. It's totally transformed how I feel. I want to please God, and I have the complete security that in Christ, I already do.*

In the Christian Union, we're doing a weekly study on the book of Romans. I've made so many notes! I'll try to condense them and give you the highlights in my next letter.

Love, Sam

14th February

Dear Sam,

Thank you for the roses! They are beautiful!

I'm getting a lot of questions about them, and about you, of course. One day you'll have to come here so I can prove you exist and I didn't just order flowers for myself on Valentines Day.

One day soon.

Love, Lil

20th February

Dear Lil,

Thank you for the birthday package you sent me. I can't wait to get stuck into the book about Calvin. I didn't do much to celebrate on the day, because there was a big outreach event at church and Nathan, Paul and I were helping to set up. It was really good; loads of students were there and I think we're going to run an 'exploring faith' course off the back of it. My family is coming to visit on the weekend and we've planned to go for a meal. I'm actually quite looking forward to seeing them. Things have got so much better with my parents, and it helps that I'm not running away all the time anymore.

I was really glad when you told me that you signed up for some counselling through the well-being service. I know there's no easy answers, and I'm just praying for you that God will continue to help you navigate this whole situation. Thank you for continuing to write to me; it means so much.

I hope we can see each other soon.

Love, Sam

Spring

Lil: Hey.

Sam: Hey.

Sam is typing…

Sam: You added me again?

Lil is typing…

Lil: I've missed you so much. Your letters are wonderful, but I want more than just you-on-paper. I want you in real life.

Sam is typing…

Sam: You want to meet up?

Lil is typing…

Lil: Yes.

Lil: Yes.

Lil

I tried not to overthink my outfit, but I went with a corduroy skirt, boots and a warm wool coat. The sky had finally cleared of storm clouds. Yellow daffodils nodded at the side of the road, bright clumps springing up on the verge. The trees were still bare, but green buds were appearing, if you looked close enough.

We found a town on the bus route between Plymouth and Exeter, on the edge of Dartmoor, and my bus arrived first. I sat on the bench , the tower of Buckfast Abbey a lone monument on the flat horizon. The road was deserted, and the town was quiet.

It's taken a long time to get here, God, I thought. *I hope his bus arrives okay.*

Perhaps I was thinking of an unexpected crash like in *One Day*. Thankfully, the bus pulled over, and I got to my feet, feeling slightly giddy.

Sam stepped down, and my stomach flipped to see him. His broad shoulders and lean frame looked more perfectly proportioned than when I first met him, and his smile was even more dazzling than I remembered.

He stood a foot away from me, and held up his palm.

'*If I profane with my unworthiest hand/ This holy shrine, the gentle sin is this.*'

Tears started in my eyes, and I placed my palm against his.

'*My lips, two blushing pilgrims, ready stand/ To smooth that rough touch with a tender kiss,*' I said, as he laced his fingers through mine and pulled me closer.

'That's my line,' he whispered, looking down at me.

'I wanted to say it,' I whispered back, reaching up to cup his face with my other hand.

'Do you think it's a sin if I kiss you?' he murmured.

'No,' I said, pulling him closer.

He smelled like earth, coffee and cologne. The moment our lips met, my heart ignited. He was soft, gentle… He was *Sam*. My Sam. And he was here with me, after all our time apart. Not with the hesitation of someone who wasn't really sure what they wanted, but with the steadfast certainty of being all there, all in.

'Since when do you drink coffee?' I asked.

He grinned.

'Only on special occasions.'

He reached up and brushed my hair from my face.

'You're more beautiful than I remembered,' he said.

'You're not so bad yourself,' I replied.

'I found this walk we could take,' he said, pointing towards a footpath sign. 'It takes us around the village and along the river.'

'I would expect nothing less,' I grinned.

Hand in hand, we set off along the path.

'So,' I said, 'I'm on tenterhooks. Are you going to tell me where your placement is?'

He looked sideways at me and smiled shyly.

'You want to know?'

'Of course!'

He stopped, and faced me fully, then took a deep breath. I braced myself for hearing that he would be in South America for the next year. I mean, I couldn't expect him to shape his plans around me when we were only writing to each other…

'I'm going to be here, in Dartmoor,' he said.

I blinked.

'Pardon?'

'My placement's here,' he said.

I was still speechless.

'I'm not trying to pressure you in any way,' he added, hurriedly, 'but this is my way of saying: I choose you, Lil. There's never been anyone else for me. If you want me to wait for you, I will. I want to be here if you need me.'

I started to laugh and sob at the same time. He wrapped his arms around me and hugged me.

'I feel like I've spent too much time apart from you,' he said. 'I couldn't choose another year away.'

'I don't want to ruin your opportunities,' I said, sniffing and brushing tears away from my eyes.

'You are the best and brightest opportunity I'll ever have,' he said tenderly, taking my face in his hands. 'You are a light in my life, Lil. I never want to let you go. I only hope that I can prove myself to you now, that I can be a light to you, instead of dragging you into darkness. If you can be gracious enough to give me a second chance.'

'Sam, this is us,' I said. 'You don't need to prove yourself to me. I know that you've repented and you're walking with the Lord now. Your letters showed me your heart. You don't have to be perfect; I'm certainly not. It's about being two sinners at the foot of the cross together.'

'That's where I am,' he sighed. 'Lil, I've been honest with you, and I've been going to the support group and everything, but I can't promise you that I'm never going to fall, that I'm never going to slip up or hurt you.'

'Whatever happens, we're in this together,' I told him, lifting his hand to my lips to kiss it. 'As long as we don't die at the end.'

'So we're rewriting the story?' Sam teased, raising his eyebrow. He knew how purist I was about literature.

'We get to rewrite our story every day,' I said.

It was true for my parents. They were still separated, but they had both been seeing a relationship counsellor. Mum had called me up to apologise for working too many hours, and said she was making changes. I hadn't spoken to Dad, but I got the impression that he was trying to win Mum back. I wasn't sure exactly what to think about that, but I knew that I couldn't expect perfection from Sam, or burden him with unrealistic expectations.

'"*Their sins and lawless acts I will remember no more. And where these have been forgiven, an offering for sin is no longer needed,*"' Sam quoted. Sam quoting Scripture was new, but at the same time, felt wholly natural. I could see how much he'd changed in just a few months.

'I've been reading through Hebrews,' he explained. 'It just really struck me, the finality of what Jesus did. There is no more offering to be made. I don't know why I always felt like I had to go around in sackcloth and ashes. I didn't know how to take my sin to the cross and leave it there.'

'It's not easy to do that,' I said. 'And we still need genuine repentance.'

'Absolutely,' he said, nodding. 'You know those notes I sent you on Romans? I heard this great sermon on chapter 6, '*Shall we go on sinning so that grace may increase?*' It was just such a bold, clear message about the need to get serious about sin and rely on the Holy Spirit to form new habits and patterns.'

He continued to outline the teaching, and I realised that the conversation hadn't stopped while we'd had this time apart. Unlike our previous separation, this time our letters had carried on exchanging news, ideas, thoughts and feelings. Even though we hadn't seen each other in person, I knew what Sam had been ruminating about, what his focus had been. To hear him talk about the Bible… I wouldn't get tired of that.

If he was doing a placement so close to where I lived, I'd be able to see him a lot more often. Our relationship could finally get a proper second chance.

'I'm sorry if you found it hurtful that I didn't want to see you these past few months,' I said. We'd reached a stile and Sam was helping me over it.

'I understand you needed the space,' he said.

I climbed down and stood in front of him. His face was open, with nothing hidden or guarded.

'I know that you've been through a lot,' he continued. 'I'm sure you're still dealing with all of that.'

His eyes searched mine, with concern. I looked at him sadly.

'There are no easy answers,' I said. 'But I didn't want you to think that you'd committed some unforgivable sin. Because you haven't.'

We held each other's gaze.

'When I said I loved you,' Sam said, his voice huskier now, 'I meant it. I love you, Lil. I love you enough to give you space when you need it, to be there when you need me, to pray when you need me to pray… I want to be all of it for you.'

'You already are,' I smiled, reaching up around his neck to pull him closer. 'I love you, Sam, not if and when you're a better person, or when you've sorted out your mess. I love you in your mess and in my own mess, because that's the only way that human love can work.'

'Two sinners at the foot of the cross,' he repeated, and I could have stayed forever, basking in the way he looked at me, as though I was the most precious thing in the world to him.

This bud of love was finally ready to blossom.

Christmas

Sam

Going back to Glastonbury Tor was a risk, but I hoped it would pay off.

Yes, there were some not-very-wholesome memories from that day, three years ago. Yes, it was likely to remind Lil of our horrible, pre-Christmas breakup. But I wanted to redeem it. I wanted to celebrate the journey God had taken us on, with all its ups and downs, all the twists and turns, because Calvin was right: God's will is irresistible. We may have sinned and I may have strayed, but God was still God. It blew my mind.

We were both at home for Christmas; Lil back from Exeter, preparing to graduate in the summer, and I'd just finished the first few months of my placement in Dartmoor. I was loving it. I was outdoors in the forest or on the moor every day. I'd had the opportunity to run some schools' workshops, and it had been so much fun teaching the kids how to build a den, make a fire, and forage. I still had my final year to complete, but my boss knew about a potential upcoming role for running Forest Schools, and said she could try to get me a place on their training course. Considering how fragmented and meaningless my life had felt just over a year ago, it was only God who could have woven all these pieces into place so perfectly.

And there was Lil. We'd seen each other fairly regularly after our first meeting in the Spring. In the summer, we'd both lived at home and worked. I went back to the cafe, and Lil was temping.

When term restarted in September, and I began my placement, we could meet up at the weekends and sometimes in the week too.

We called each other every day. Things had settled down, worked themselves out somehow. Well, I attributed that to God, too.

Annabelle knew I was going to propose, and I just hoped she would manage to keep her mouth shut. After all, there was the possibility that Lil might say no. I knew that I still had a year of uni left, but Lil would be working and if we rented a small place together, I thought it would be better than another year of commuting to see each other. I hoped Lil felt the same.

When the day turned out to be full of sunshine, against a blue sky, I felt like it was God's seal of approval. I didn't tell Lil where we were going, and when I turned to follow the signs, she gave me a curious look.

'Are we going where I think we're going?' she asked.

'Possibly,' I hedged.

She shook her head and laughed. I took this as a good sign.

It was not deserted, like when we'd been here before, but it wasn't overly crowded either. I parked up and we tightened our scarves. I took her gloved hand in mine.

The air was cold, but not unpleasant, and the leaves in the shade were still anointed with frost. Last time we'd walked this path, we'd been battling wind and sleet.

'It's nice to be dry this time,' Lil remarked.

'We might actually see something when we get to the viewpoint,' I said.

Lil chatted about Darcy's latest boy fiasco (there were many), and I felt the red box burning away in my coat pocket. I kept compulsively checking it was still there. Would she like the ring? *God, please help me to get my words out right. I want Lil to know how special she is to me.*

'Apparently Dad's coming over on Christmas Eve,' she said, looking down at the ground.

I squeezed her hand.

'How are you feeling about it?'

'I think I should see him,' she said, lifting her head to look at me again. 'I just don't know what I'm going to say to him.'

'Maybe just being there will be enough,' I said.

I was trying to be supportive, but I was also trying to calculate the perfect spot. The monument itself was not going to be very private, but the path was full of people coming both ways.

'How about we go off the path for a bit?' I said, hoping that she didn't suspect anything.

'Sure.'

We walked onto the grass, and my palms felt sweaty. Maybe I should have left my gloves behind.

'I mean, if he says sorry, I don't know what I'm going to say back,' she said.

She was wearing a cute bobble hat, and her red hair was spilling around her shoulders, over her wool coat. Gingerbread.

'You don't have to say anything,' I said.

'It'll be awkward,' she said, frowning.

I shrugged.

'It was always going to be awkward.' We walked a little further, and then I tugged at her hand to stop. 'What do you want him to say and do?'

She wrinkled her nose as she thought.

'Not be unfaithful.'

'He hasn't seen Sal, has he?'

'He says he hasn't.'

Her tone was skeptical.

'The problem is, he can't change the things he's done in the past,' I said. 'He can only change what he does now.'

She said nothing, but looked at me, as if wanting me to continue. I swallowed.

'In a way, that's why we're here,' I said. 'I wish I could rewind the clock and do everything that happened three years ago differently. But I can't. I can tell you though that I'm sorry, that I've changed, and I want to make the right choices now.'

'I know,' she said softly, squeezing my hand.

'Lil, I know I don't deserve your love. I'm just so grateful that we're standing here now, together, in this place. It shows how gracious God is, and it shows that we can rewrite the story.'

'*My bounty is as boundless as the sea,/ My love as deep; the more I give to thee,/ The more I have, for both are infinite,*' Lil quoted, leaning closer.

'I was going to say that,' I murmured.

'It was my line,' Lil argued playfully. 'You've got plenty of good ones you can still use.'

'*Did my heart love till now? Forswear it, sight!/ For I ne'er saw true beauty till this night.*'

Lil smiled, and I wanted to kiss her, but this was The Moment and I needed to get the ring out of my pocket, but I also still had my gloves on…

'Sorry, this isn't very romantic, but will you hold my gloves?'

Lil took them, laughing and rolling her eyes, while I unzipped my pocket and finally drew out the box. Her face changed instantly as her eyes widened in realisation. She looked up at me and clapped her hand over her mouth.

'Sam!' she said.

I opened the box.

'Will you marry me, Lil?'

Tears shone in her eyes as she nodded.

'Yes!' she said, her face breaking into a smile.

She flung her arms around my neck, almost knocking the box onto the ground, and pressed her lips to mine. I felt too distracted by holding the most expensive piece of jewellery I'd ever bought in my hand, so I pulled back and held it out to her.

'Let me try it on you.'

'I'm still holding your gloves,' she said, laughing and waving them. 'And I've got gloves on.'

'Chuck them on the floor,' I said impatiently, grinning. 'They don't show it like this in the movies!'

She tossed my gloves aside and pulled off her own, shoving it into her pocket. I slid the ring over her finger, the diamond catching the light and sparkling.

'It's beautiful,' she breathed.

'You're beautiful,' I said, closing the empty box and putting it back in my pocket.

I pulled her close for a proper kiss, finally unhindered. She smelled of oranges and cinnamon. I could spend the rest of my life kissing her.

'This Christmas is going to be a lot happier than three years ago,' Lil said, leaning her forehead against mine.

'Definitely.' I paused for a moment. 'Can I get my gloves back now?'

Back in the car, I thought about the conversations we were going to have when we arrived back home. I knew Darcy and Annabelle would squeal and want to be bridesmaids. My parents and Julia would hug us, and each other, and start making plans. I wasn't sure if Bryan would be in the picture or not. I thought about the two Christmas cards we'd written to each other, and how I could frame them as a gift for our first married Christmas next year. Perhaps I could write a caption... Which *Romeo and Juliet* quote should I choose? Maybe I should just write all of our favourites around the cards.

'Listen!' Lil said, turning up the volume on the radio.

It was *Winter Wonderland*.

'*Later on, we'll conspire*,' she sang. 'This is perfect!'

Maybe it was time to move on from Romeo and Juliet. Maybe I should just write *In our story, we don't die at the end.* Hmm, that was a bit morbid. What was it that Lil had said?

We get to rewrite our story every day.

Now that was perfect.

Yay! You've finished this book.
Do you think you could leave a review?
Just one line from you can make a big difference and means so much to an indie author like me.
If you can, leave a review on Amazon and Goodreads.
Thanks so much!

ACKNOWLEDGEMENTS

This is my first foray into Christian fiction, and I have two writers who inspired me to tell this story. Heather Miekstyn and Drew Taylor, your books really spoke to me, and made me think about the need for stories about making mistakes, and finding grace, particularly in the context of sexual purity.

Having lived through the *I Kissed Dating Goodbye* culture, I wanted to explore some of the nuances of healthy boundaries vs legalism. The problem is always the human heart. And yet, for all our brokenness, love is a beautiful gift from our heavenly Father. I hope this story captures that.

I want to thank Andy, my husband, for yet another stunning cover, and also for reading and providing much-needed critique on this story. I carried Sam and Lil in my heart and I'm so excited now that others can share their story, but I couldn't have got here without Andy's help, feedback and support.

To my lovely team of ARC readers, thank you for being willing to read this at one of the busiest (though most wonderful) times of the year. I hugely appreciate your support.

Thank YOU, reader, for getting this far. I pray that you'll know the power of God's love for you.

About the Author

Sophie Toovey loves reading and writing romance. She's an English teacher who drinks too much tea, and a total Jane Austen geek. She lives in Wales, in the UK, and enjoys smart romcoms where there's a bit of grit and realism. She writes clean, closed-door romance with kisses only. Sign up for her newsletter at sophietoovey.com and receive a free ebook of *I Want You Back*, a contemporary retelling of *Persuasion*.

Connect with Sophie
Listen to audio chapters for free on YouTube
Instagram @Sophie_Toovey
Twitter @SophieToovey
TikTok @sophietoovey

The Castle

A YA contemporary romance set in a reality TV show

Read on for a free excerpt

People who say that winning isn't important, it's the taking part that counts... They've never <u>had</u> to win anything. They've never had to fight for something.

I want this. I'm going to fight for this. And I'm going to win.

1

It was all Nanny Mo's idea. She's always sniffing around for opportunities, and she wouldn't let this one rest until I had sent in the application.

"Just think, a scholarship to drama school!"

"But it's reality TV," I said, thinking of every inane programme the girls at school would talk about.

"It's a means to an end," Nanny Mo reasoned. "You're young and you've got nothing to lose."

I didn't really think too much more about it. It was only when they contacted me and said I was being shortlisted that I started to take it seriously. I hadn't told my parents about it, so Nanny Mo had to cover for me. At least I turned eighteen already, so I didn't need them to sign anything.

As I packed my bag and took a final glance at our cluttered living room, the faded orange sofa clashing with the lime green rug, it started to sink in that I was going away. I closed the front door and breathed a sigh of relief.

———

On the coach, I looked through all the documents on my phone. I had to zoom right in and even then I could barely read the small print. Certain phrases jumped out:

'*At* The Castle *you are expected to stay in character at all times…*

you will be provided with medieval costumes…

every room is fitted with cameras…

when you complete outdoor activities, a crew will be in attendance.'

I scrolled on, looking for the part that made my heart race: the scholarship section.

'At the Julia Carter School of Performing Arts, we are passionate about recruiting the best students from all backgrounds. We will award a full scholarship place to one outstanding candidate. The candidate will have shown consistency in playing their assigned role throughout their time at The Castle, *and a high standard of excellence in their two main auditions. The televising of the selection process enables us not only to scrutinise each candidate's performance, but also to fund our scholarship programme.'*

It was certainly a Faustian bargain: sell your soul for the indignity of Big Brother style surveillance—with the mirage-like pot of gold at the end of the rainbow.

I turned to my character profile. There was very little to go on —it felt like taking part in a murder mystery party.

You are Scarlett.
Your character type: rebel.
Your core value: determination.

That was it.

There was small print—again—detailing that all activity in *The Castle* was unscripted, but characters would be prompted into certain scenarios—namely, your two main auditions.

'Your main audition will be a highly dramatic scenario and you will be informed when, where and with whom it will take place. It is imperative that all candidates follow instructions, as failure to do so could have negative consequences upon storylines affecting other characters. Once you have successfully completed your first audition, you will unlock your character's

middle name. All characters' names will be required to complete the Quest in the grand finale, which will be broadcast live from the castle.'

I put the phone down, beginning to feel a faint sense of nausea. What if I messed it up, and made a fool of myself on TV?

I couldn't think about that.

Instead, I needed to focus on Scarlett. The name didn't sound very medieval. I was going to have to remember not to sound modern in the way I spoke. How did people in medieval times speak, anyway? I opened my audiobook app and decided on Shakespeare as the next best thing. Listening to *Much Ado About Nothing*, I fell asleep.

Long journeys were the bread-and-butter of my childhood… literally. My parents were musicians and most weekends, we'd be gunning down the motorway to some kind of gig.

They varied in quality.

We lived in Manchester, so there was no shortage of live music venues around us, and in nearby cities like Liverpool and Birmingham. My parents loved pubs, and it felt like they knew everyone within a fifty-mile radius. But they couldn't survive without the holiday park gigs. We'd drive for hours to get to some crummy entertainment lounge in a seaside town well past its sell-by date, and they'd play covers and impersonate Elvis, Fleetwood Mac… I enjoyed the 90s music nights, because they played all the indie rock which was probably their music of choice. Growing up in Manchester, you learn Oasis songs before you learn 'Happy Birthday'.

Sometimes I enjoyed the perks of a holiday park, like a dip in the pool or a round of mini golf. Maybe we'd buy chips and ice cream. But as I got older, I grew weary of the stale smell of faded upholstery, and the garish commentary of the Guy with a Microphone. I would do my Maths homework on a sticky table, ringed with beer glass stains, and read my English books, tuning out of the disco.

One weekend, I was ill, so I stayed with Nanny Mo while they went to Skegness. Once I felt better, by the Saturday afternoon, it was blissful to lie on the sofa watching TV, and eat a home cooked meal that wasn't fish fingers and chips. Soon I asked to stay behind most weekends. I usually found an excuse like a Science test to revise for, but I think my parents knew by that point that I was just fed up with it all.

Maybe we were fed up with each other.

This way, they could live the music lifestyle they wanted, without me dragging them down, and I could stay sane and get semi-decent grades in school. We both made choices, and whenever I felt disappointed that they hadn't chosen me, I reminded myself that I hadn't chosen them, either.

When I woke up, the scenery had changed from the urban tower blocks of Birmingham to the rolling hills of the Malverns. Soon, we'd be crossing the Severn Bridge into Wales.

I'd probably been to Wales a handful of times, to Prestatyn or Trecco Bay, and I'd seen my share of castles. They were usually on the coast, and in ruins. What made this programme so compelling was that it was set in a *living* castle, built in the nineteenth century, but designed to look medieval, complete with fairy turrets. Officially, it was called Castell Seren, which Nanny Mo translated for me as Star Castle.

'Ooh, that's a sign!' she said triumphantly.

My name is Stella: Latin for star. My parents obviously projected their desires for fame onto me when they chose it.

I checked my phone and Nanny Mo had texted.

You'll be amazing. So proud of you xxx

I smiled, then used my camera to check my face. My hair, down over my shoulders, was a bit dishevelled, and my skin looked pale. I'd put red lipstick on this morning in honour of my character's name, but its vibrancy was draining the colour from the rest of my complexion. My mascara was holding up, and the thick eyeliner I'd used with light eyeshadow succeeded in looking vintage, but I didn't look *medieval*. Well, that's what the stylists were for.

The coach pulled into a service station, near Cardiff, and a guy in a T-shirt and jeans moved forward to meet me.

'Stella?' he asked. 'I'm Chris. I'm here to drive you to the castle.'

I didn't have much luggage, because we were barely allowed to bring anything. Our costumes were provided, we weren't allowed technological devices, so I simply had a hairbrush, basic toiletries, and my notebook.

Chris led the way to his car, an ordinary Ford Fiesta, and I wondered what the budget for this programme was. What did I expect: a limo? After all, this was the first series. Clearly, the drama school hoped it would do well enough to keep going, and keep their scholarship programme funded. As we left the motorway, we went in the opposite direction of the city, high up into the forest. Definitely not a limo-friendly route.

On the way, Chris gushed about the setup.

'It's incredible, exactly like going back in time. Tapestries, fires burning, bows and arrows…'

I smiled. It was the sort of thing my History teacher would have loved.

'What happens when we arrive?'

'I'll take you to the Ladies' Quarters and the team will prepare you.'

I gulped.

The road started winding up a steep hill, and I gasped as four turrets emerged from the forest. It was just like a fairy tale and the pictures did not do it justice.

'Here we are,' Chris said, grinning.

Castell Seren had smooth stone walls, narrow windows and several conical towers. It stood proud and tall, surrounded by thick woodland.

We drove through the gates, and there was a car park with an outdoor toilet block. He pulled up and I scrabbled to stand in the dusty gravel. It looked magnificent.

'It's quite something, isn't it?' he said.

'Yeah,' I agreed, shielding my eyes to look up to the top tower.

It was early September, and the haze of summer was lasting long enough for the sun to feel warm on my skin. Kids were back in school, most of my friends were going to university, and I was going to live in a castle for a reality TV show.

Surreal doesn't cover it.

I carried my holdall, feeling as though I'd just landed in Narnia. The door was thick, solid wood, grooved with age, and with iron bolts. I walked in, and the musty smell of time and fireplaces surrounded me.

My breath caught in my throat as I looked at the intricate panelling, the carved patterns, the rugs and tapestries. The ceiling rose in a large dome, ornately painted, and with a huge chandelier. There was a long dining table in the centre of the room.

'This is the Great Hall,' Chris explained, leading me through another door. 'And this is the drawing room.'

This room was smaller, round, with another stunning domed ceiling. There was a fire, and wooden seats like pews, but also an upper balcony area, where there were windows all around. I couldn't wait to explore.

'The Ladies' Quarters are just through here.'

He led me to a narrow staircase, and at the top was a dark corridor.

'The cameras aren't live yet,' he said, as we approached the door. 'We only start officially once everyone's here and in costume. But this is the last time I'm going to call you Stella. From the moment you enter this room, you are Scarlett. You can't tell any of the other actors your real name. Okay?'

I nodded, feeling my stomach twist with nervous anticipation. He gave me a reassuring smile, then knocked at the door.

'Come in,' a voice called.

I took a deep breath and stepped forward.

2

I was in a large boudoir. The walls were jade green, with golden flourishes. The fire was bright and radiating heat. The floor was packed with people. I could just about see four beds, but there were dresses, make up, and luggage strewn everywhere.

'Hi.' A girl in a black T shirt and skinny jeans came up to me. 'Are you Scarlett? I'm Mags.'

I nodded dumbly, hoping that I remembered to respond to a different name every time someone called me.

'Great!' she grinned, her eyes sparkling under heavy black eyeliner. 'Let's begin your transformation.'

She led me to a rail with long dresses.

'Here are your clothes.'

I looked nervously at a girl standing by the next bed, dressed in a blue floor length dress.

'Hello.' She spoke formally, with an accent like my grandma. Not Nanny Mo, but my mum's mother, who lived in High Wycombe and said 'super' without a trace of irony.

'Hello,' I returned, then my attention was pulled back to the dresses. Red, purple, blue, bottle green. 'That one,' I pointed. 'It's like the colour of ivy.'

'Good choice.'

Mags started to help me put my luggage down and take off my clothes.

'You're allowed to wear your own pants,' she said. 'But no bras. The bodices are designed to give your chest support. Start by putting on the undergarment.'

The thin white cotton layer formed a vest shape and its length was down to my knees. Then I stepped into the ivy dress and Mags showed me how to button the bodice. The material felt velvety and luxurious.

'Wireless microphones are sewn into your clothes, on the neckline,' Mags explained. 'We'll arrange your hair so that the front section is pulled back, so we don't get rustling over the mikes.'

I pulled up a section of my hair to test out the style, tossing the rest over my shoulders. It was almost black in some lights, but reddish gold when it caught the sun.

The girl in the blue dress was watching me.

'How were your travels?' she asked when I caught her eye. She had long, golden hair and piercing blue eyes with an edge of sharpness.

'Okay.' I shrugged.

'You shouldn't say that,' she said immediately, with a frown. 'You should say, acceptable but tiring, or long and arduous, perhaps.'

She had a distinctly superior air.

'You don't want your language to be anachronistic, you know.'

I felt my cheeks begin to sting with embarrassment, but as she looked around the rest of the room with a haughty manner, the girl opposite me gave me a warm, genuine smile. She was having her hair styled too, long, black and glossy. She was Chinese, and her skin was radiant.

'I love the colour of your dress,' she said. She was wearing a russet red gown.

'Thanks,' I said gratefully. 'Yours looks lovely too.'

'Well I'm complaining about mine.'

A loud voice cut in, with a London accent. I twisted slightly to see a tall, Black girl in a primrose yellow dress. She looked like a supermodel with her height and lithe shape, and striking features.

'This shade is hideous. I feel like a canary.'

'I think it looks stunning on you,' the girl in the red dress said admiringly. 'I'm sorry you don't like it. I'd offer to swap but mine would be far too short for you.'

'You can't swap clothes.' Mags glanced up from her make up bag. 'They're all made to measure. Plus it's against the rules.'

My throat constricted. It was all becoming real.

'Right everyone, stand still where you are please. It's time for briefing.'

In the centre of the room, a woman commanded our attention, holding a clipboard. She had curly red hair and wore a shirt with jeans that looked slightly too tight to be comfortable. The noise of the room settled, and everyone turned to face her.

'I'm Liz, and I'm the Assistant Director of *The Castle*,' she said, with a broad smile. 'Welcome to our candidates. Gwen—'

The proud looking one in the blue dress.

'Mel—'

The nice once in red.

'Carreen—'

The canary).

'—and Scarlett.'

There was a beat of disconnect in my head before I realised that was me.

'Well done to our team—the girls are looking fabulous—and it is nearly time for the warm-up activity. I'm going to run through some important information now, so please be fully attentive.'

She cleared her throat, and glanced around the room to check that everyone was listening.

'At *The Castle*, you are playing a role. You are living in the fourteenth century. You are expected to stay in character at all times; you will be observed not only for your main auditions, but in all other activities. The success of the TV show depends upon a believable performance. If anyone ceases to give a believable performance, not only will they have lost their opportunity for a scholarship, but they may also be withdrawn from the programme. I am sure this will not be necessary.

'Your clothes, most of your belongings, and any technical devices must be handed over to be locked in the Vault. If anyone is caught using contraband materials, they risk expulsion from the programme.

'This week has been carefully structured to make the best entertainment for viewers, and the best opportunity for you, as actors, to shine. There are different story threads running through the week, involving different characters. Please follow any instructions you receive. It is of the utmost importance.

'Your aim is to unlock your character's middle name, which is needed to complete the Quest in the live finale.

'You will notice there are staff around you in the castle. The staff in costume are servants and will be catering and cleaning for you throughout this week. Crew members and stylists will be dressed in their own clothes. Please keep your interactions with them to a minimum, and as much as you can, pretend that they are not there. If there is a cameraman, don't look directly at the camera. The show needs to feel authentic and as if the viewer is a fly on the wall.

'You have all gone through a rigorous process to get this far. Congratulations. Enjoy yourselves! I think you are in for an amazing week.'

We clapped, though my stomach was queasy again. It didn't feel real. Then we sent our last messages, checked our phones for the final time, before handing everything over to be locked away.

'I hope you're proud of me, Nanny Mo,' I thought, as the Vault door clanged shut with finality.

3

Now that we were all dressed and styled, the boudoir had emptied of staff, and the four of us were left to wait nervously until we were called for the warm-up activity.

'Good luck everyone,' Mel said.

'I think this week is going to be a rollercoaster,' Carreen commented. 'Makes me nervous to think what they've got in store for us.'

'I've never been anywhere like this before,' Mel said. She seemed to be one of those people who talked when she was nervous.

'My eighteenth birthday party was in a castle,' Gwen said.

I wasn't sure if she was in role or not. But it didn't surprise me.

'How many people were there?' Carreen asked.

'About two hundred,' she replied nonchalantly.

'That must have been amazing,' Mel said in awe.

'That's not exactly how I celebrated my eighteenth,' Carreen said wryly.

'What did you do?' Mel asked.

'Consumed so much alcohol that I don't remember much of it.'

'What about you, Scarlett?'

I looked up to see Gwen staring at me again.

'What was the question?' I stalled.

'How did you celebrate your eighteenth?'

Memories of my party in the bar where my Mum worked came to mind, and Dad playing his guitar. How could I make it a bit more fourteenth-century?

'With music,' I said cryptically. 'I have minstrels in my family. Not the chocolate kind.'

Carreen and Mel laughed. Gwen didn't smile.

'Ready, ladies?' Chris asked. 'We may need to do several takes as you enter the room, so be prepared.'

A cameraman and assistant were walking backwards ahead of us, to get the best angle and capture our expressions as we met the boys for the first time. We assembled in a line at the door. Mel squeezed my hand.

Awkwardly, we all trooped through the dark panelled corridor, and then had to wait while the crew readied themselves in the drawing room, before we were called in.

We stepped into the drawing room, and three boys were standing there, waiting for us. The cameras were snaking around, and it was disorienting as I tried to focus on the actors, not the crew. I wasn't supposed to *look* at the cameras, but I was afraid of bumping into them if I didn't.

'Cut!' Liz called.

I hadn't even noticed her; she was by the wall on the same side as the door.

'I think we need to do another take, and Dave, move slightly to the right with Camera three.'

We moved back into the corridor, and it took another two times before Liz was happy to continue.

'Now, in keeping with medieval manners, boys will bow and girls will curtsey.'

Once the cameras were ready, the three boys bent forwards, with their left arms out behind them. They were dressed in smart tunics, with gold lining the collar and sleeves, and belts around their waists. We curtsied, holding our skirts out, and then we each had to sit on a wooden chair. They were arranged in a circle with the cameras behind, at different vantage points, but I began to realise the complexity of getting all the shots without other cameras in view.

I had no idea how they were going to pull off the live finale without being able to do multiple takes.

'So this is our warm-up,' Liz said, coming to stand in the middle of the circle. 'We're all warming up as well as you guys. Hopefully by the end of tonight you'll have a really good idea how things will run at *The Castle* when we're filming specific tasks or challenges. As you know, there are cameras installed all over the building which will pick up footage as you go through your day. Your microphones will always be on. But the tasks will be the focus on the episodes, and we've decided that Charles will lead the tasks, still in character, of course.

'I will give you all a briefing of what the task is about, and what we want to happen, and then when we start rolling, Charles will explain the task to you, for the benefit of the audience.

'In this warm-up activity, we want each of you to introduce yourselves to the group… and to the audience as well. Charles will lay out some cards, and each card pictures an animal. Your task is to pick the animal which best represents your character, and explain why to the group.

'We want this to be lively, fun and give you a chance to emphasise who your character is. First impressions are very important.'

I looked across at Mel, who seemed nervous. I settled my hands in my lap, trying to look relaxed, while I stared at each of the boys in turn. A large part of winning was going to be assessing the competition.

While Liz checked positioning and spoke to the crew, the boy opposite me cleared his throat.

'So…' he said, with mock-awkwardness, and a few people laughed. 'I'm Charles, if you didn't know that already, and I had a very difficult time getting here today.'

He was Black, with a broad, white smile, and the other boys must have known about his journey because they grinned as well.

'My—er—*horse* got injured on the way here,' he said, catching himself in time.

I smiled at him. He seemed a genuinely likable sort of guy. When he smiled, his whole face lit up with a bright warmth, and already he seemed right at home. He had dark eyes and black chin-length hair, with corkscrew curls. His hair bounced as he moved, and he seemed full of vibrant energy. If he was leading us through

the tasks, they must have chosen him because he would manage to
pull off a semi-presenting role, along with staying in character and
putting everyone at ease.

'Ready?' asked Liz. 'Start rolling.'

'Welcome to *The Castle*,' Charles said confidently. 'My name is
Charles and I've got a game so that we can all introduce ourselves.
Without further ado…'

He produced seven large square cards and laid them out on the
floor in the middle of the circle.

'We've got the cat, the dog, the lion, the peacock, the squirrel,
the horse, and the hawk. You need to choose one animal and
explain what it has in common with your personality. The
downside is that if someone chooses an animal, it cannot be chosen
again. I get to go first because I had a sneak preview… Sorry.' He
gave an unapologetic grin. 'I'm going to choose the hawk, because
I'm majestic and once you win my trust, I'll never desert you.'

He picked up the hawk card and placed it at his feet, then sat
back on his chair.

'Cut!' Liz called. 'Great, we'll do one more take.'

It gave me a lot of time to think, the stop-start nature of filming.
When Liz was happy, Charles moved on to the next person.

'I will now nominate Lance to go next.'

The boy on his right grinned and ran a hand through his hair,
which was tousled with blond streaks in it. He had a pale, angular
face, and his eyes were a mix of grey and blue.

'I'm Lance,' he said, and his accent sounded Irish. 'I'm going to
choose the lion because it feels manly… and I'm courageous. I'll
fight for you to the death.'

I stifled an eyeroll then caught a glimpse of Gwen, leaning
forward on her chair hungrily. She seemed transfixed with him.

'Who would you like to choose to go next?' Charles asked him.

He looked around the circle.

'I'm going to ask the lady in red, because that's my favourite
colour,' he said, grinning suggestively at Mel.

Mel flustered beside me.

'Well, thank you,' she said, clearly chuffed to be chosen. I looked smugly at Gwen, who was suitably piqued. 'I'm Mel, and I am going to choose the squirrel. A squirrel mother will rescue each of her children from danger, transporting them to another location, at great risk to herself. Sometimes squirrels even adopt other squirrel babies who have lost their mother. I am also caring and willing to risk my life to help others.'

How random that Mel knew so much about squirrels. I also felt a jarring prod of guilt as she spoke. Would my character be willing to risk herself for others? *Rebel* and *determined*. Hmm.

'We'll do another take,' Liz said. 'Mel, make sure you speak slowly.'

Once it was Mel's turn to choose, she said,

'I'd like to ask the gentleman on the other side of Charles.'

This boy didn't look quite so self-assured as Lance, or as relaxed as Charles. He cleared his throat, and shifted in his seat. His legs were long and his shirt was loose over his thin frame. He reached out and took the horse card.

'My name is Ash,' he said. 'I'm like the horse, because you can always rely on me. Unless you're Charles.'

There was more polite laughter and Charles pretended to look offended, before joining in.

'Sticking with dress colour, I'd like to nominate the lady in yellow,' Ash said.

Carreen made a face.

'I didn't choose this colour, by the way,' she said. 'Right, then, I'm Carreen. I'm going to choose the cat. I'm very loyal. If you treat me nicely, I'm yours forever.'

This was beginning to sound like *Blind Date*. Just Gwen and me left. I was going to be stuck with whatever she discarded.

'Gwen, you can go next.'

Gwen smiled coolly, and my heart sank.

'Well, there's actually two vital aspects to my personality that you all need to know, and for this I need to take both of the cards.'

She snatched them both up and brandished them like a lottery ticket.

'Firstly, the dog, because I'm always hopeful. And secondly, the peacock, because my beauty brings joy wherever I go.'

The guys laughed awkwardly, and I didn't hold my eye roll back this time.

'Maybe you could just choose one so that the lady in green has one?' Charles pressed, obviously keen for fairness, and shooting a glance at Liz.

'Don't worry,' I said, throwing Gwen my best patronising stare, 'I am quite able to improvise.'

Looking around, I spotted a chess board. I jumped up and grabbed the Queen.

'I am best represented by this Queen,' I said, holding it proudly. 'I make my own rules and I go wherever I want to. No one can stop me.'

Everyone broke into applause, except Gwen. *Check.*

'Cut!' shouted Liz.

'Don't you want to do another take?' Gwen asked, looking alarmed.

'I think we got what we needed,' Liz said, with a grin.

She turned to Chris and said,

'Ashleigh will definitely be happy with that.'

Maybe this wasn't so hard after all.

4

By the time we moved into the Great Hall for dinner, my head was beginning to ache. The strain of being Scarlett, watching everyone else, being constantly aware of the cameras and the crew… It was so much harder than I thought it would be. It was a relief to eat because then I didn't have to say anything. I had to measure every word so carefully, and it didn't help that I felt like Gwen was just waiting for me to make a mistake.

I definitely hadn't made it easier to be friends with her, but what else was I supposed to do? She was clearly the biggest threat out of the girls to me with her uncanny poise. I wasn't here to make friends; I was here to win.

The meal contained three courses, and servants brought all the food in: soup, roast beef, and pudding. I was so relieved the food was good. Things felt more relaxed around the table; I sat next to Mel and we giggled about Lance's constant tousling of his hair so it looked unstyled when it very clearly was. Ash was directly opposite us, and he was very interesting to talk to. He shared facts about the castle and made speculations about what activities we would be doing, and told us what the boys' quarters were like.

'We were told that our room is not as fancy as yours,' he said. 'We don't have the gold gilding and everything.'

'You must have more space than us, if there's only three of you,' I pointed out.

'Yes, I suppose so,' he said.

After dinner, I was ready to retreat, but we had to do a photo shoot in the drawing room. They wanted images for all their publicity, so we did some painstakingly arranged group shots and individual ones too. Finally Liz thanked us all and gave us a final notice before we could be dismissed.

'Breakfast will be served at eight o'clock and your first activity will begin at nine. As you have no clocks, you need to listen out for the bell which will ring to summon you. Servants will come in to wake you and help you to dress. Get a good night's sleep. I'm excited for all the fun we're going to have this week.'

Wearing a fourteenth century nightgown, all I could think as I collapsed into bed was, *'how on earth am I going to do this?'*

In the morning, I felt more positive and ready for the challenge. Two female servants, who looked around thirty years old, came in with their aprons and hats on. One of them helped me into a lavender cotton day dress, and as the sun was shining, I felt excited about exploring the castle and the grounds more. Our first activity allowed us to do just that: it was a scavenger hunt.

'The boys can work together and the girls can work in pairs. Use the map to navigate your way around the castle grounds and visit each of the checkpoints,' Liz explained. 'First team to find the flag wins.'

We filmed Charles explaining the task, and when we were given the green light, Mel and I paired up and darted off inside the castle. We found the checkpoints in the Great Hall and the drawing room first, before we raced outside to begin tracing the path leading into the gardens. There were checkpoints at the arbour, the fountain, and the aviary, and everything in this area was beautifully sculpted and in its place. The air was sweet with the scent of honeysuckle and rosemary, and even though it wasn't the most comfortable experience, running around in a long dress, the cotton fabric was light and the sun was warm on our faces.

The only checkpoints remaining were in the woodland. We followed the path until it changed into a dustier track, under the shade of the leaves. There were several checkpoints to find and these were more hidden, a bit like trying to find a geocache somewhere.

A small crew stayed with us the whole time, filming our progress. I felt a thrill of exhilaration as I located the final checkpoint and said to Mel,

'Right—let's head to the courtyard!'

We weaved through the trees and one of the servants came into view, carrying a large sack, about twenty feet in front of us.

'Hey,' Mel said, reaching to touch my arm. 'Do you think we should offer to help him?'

'He's a servant.' I shrugged. 'It's his job.'

Right at that moment, I saw him twist his head to the side, as if he'd heard me. Then a second later, he stumbled and fell to the ground.

'Oh!' Mel gasped, running up to him. 'Are you all right?'

I reluctantly caught up. This injury was all too conveniently timed to make us lose. The camera crew were loving it, zooming right in.

'We need to get back first, then we can ask the guys to come back and help him.'

'What's your name?' Mel asked, as the guy dropped hold of his sack and placed both hands around his ankle. His head suddenly rose and his eyes pierced mine with a sharpness I didn't expect. His eyes were a dark colour and his hair was cropped short at the sides, but had a longer fringe which looked as though it needed to be swept slightly to one side. Just the right amount of untidiness to look attractive, in contrast to Lance's carefully arranged style.

'Gareth,' he said.

He was still looking at me. I raised an eyebrow.

'Are you really hurt?' I asked skeptically.

He felt his ankle and winced, a bit like a Premier League footballer.

'We'll help you,' Mel said firmly, glaring at me.

'Thank you.'

He took Mel's arm and rose up to stand. He was tall and broad shouldered. It would probably take six of us to carry him.

'I can limp,' he said, then his eyes flicked to the sack.

'Scarlett, you take the sack.' Mel could certainly be assertive when she wanted to be.

'Mel—' I began in protest.

'It matters more than winning.'

I shook my head and sighed. As I grabbed the sack, heavy with potatoes, I caught the glimpse of a smirk cross Gareth's face.

'You better have a real injury,' I muttered. 'I know bad acting when I see it.'

That got rid of the smirk, and I saw his jaw set. We made our way back to the courtyard, and Ash, Lance and Charles waved the banner under our nose in victory. That was irritating enough in itself, but they seemed particularly childish and immature. Particularly when a tall, dark *man* stood beside them.

As much as I scowled at Gareth, he didn't look at me again. Something about his presence was magnetic, and the way his jaw twitched, I think he knew I was staring at him.

5

After lunch we were told that we would have a Welcome Ball that evening, so in the afternoon, we were going to be taught how to dance. We all assembled in the drawing room, and all the furniture had been pushed back to create space in the middle of the room. A woman in costume came in to teach us the steps.

'It's all quite simple, don't worry,' she reassured us. 'Now, I need you to pair up. Boys, select a partner.'

Ash chose Mel, Lance chose Carreen, and Charles was closest to Gwen and looked at me apologetically.

'Oh, I didn't realise there wasn't an even number…' the dance teacher said.

'Do you need another boy?' Liz called across the room. 'Hang on one second.'

I stood there awkwardly, trying to look as though I didn't care that I didn't get chosen. When clearly I did.

'We have a servant who's willing to step in,' Liz's loud voice announced, as she entered the room—with Gareth.

'Oh no,' I said, looking at Mel for help. She shrugged.

'My lady.' Gareth strode up to me and bowed, one arm folded across his torso and one behind his back. The movement was precise, and when he straightened up, his chest was directly in my eyeline. I moved my eyes up to his face, and his eyes sparked with something. They were a warmer shade of brown than earlier.

'I thought your foot was injured,' I said accusingly.

'I will fight the pain for your sake.'

His mouth was set firmly, but his eyes were dancing. In the background, I noticed Liz whisper something to Chris. He looked over at Gareth and me, and nodded. Apparently he was a producer for the show.

The lesson began. The dance reminded me of a mixture of country dancing and a ceilidh. We started with simple steps, claps, and changing positions, and it gradually became closer, and more complicated. When Gareth took my hand, his grasp was firm, with just the right amount of pressure. Soon I was touching his shoulder, and his strong arms encircled me and guided me along the line.

The teacher gave instructions for a turn movement, and Gareth lifted our joined hands in the air and spun me swiftly, catching me neatly and lowering me into a dip. He held me there for a second, frozen in time, as I held my breath and felt the heat radiating from his skin, so close to mine as he leaned over me.

'Camera one!' Liz called, and the moment was broken. 'Do that again, please. Yes, just Gareth and Scarlett.'

He blushed faintly, but he did it again, ignoring the camera zooming into our faces.

'Hold that pose a little longer,' Liz said.

Her voice seemed oddly distant as I stared into Gareth's eyes.

'Got it!' Liz said.

Gareth released me and I ran my fingers through my hair, tidying it unnecessarily for something to do. Gwen glared at me. I gave her a sweet smile in return. It was nice that I wasn't the wallflower anymore, stuck on the side, and Gareth was actually quite a good dancer.

We resumed the routine as a group, and it felt more relaxed, the more we practised.

'Your ankle seems to be much better,' I commented, with a wry smile.

'Amazing what rest can do.'

I tried to detect irony in his tone, but I also had to concentrate on where I was stepping.

'Didn't think servants got much of that,' I said, as a light challenge.

He laughed, and his teeth were surprisingly white.

'I'm glad we're not totally medieval when it comes to human rights.'

'And toilets,' I added.

'Indeed.'

He stepped forward, to my side, then we moved around on the spot, his hand on my waist. I tried to ignore the effect of his proximity, although I was stupidly conscious of his touch.

'Do you like the castle?' he asked, in a low tone.

His voice had a slight edge to it. I looked at his face again.

'Dancing gives the opportunity for private conversation,' he continued. 'I doubt anyone can hear us over the music.'

'So you want me to tell you all my secrets?' I teased. 'Who I like, and who I dislike?'

'I wonder which list I'm in?'

'Not my best actor list, that's for sure.'

He laughed again, as he turned me round, then pulled me in closer, crushing me against him for a long moment.

'I'm not here to compete, you know,' he said, as I looked at him, trying to shake the thought out of my head of what it would be like to kiss him.

Then he released me and bowed. The dance was over.

═══

I was in the boudoir, preparing for the evening events, when a servant came in with a note for me. I unfolded the paper to read:

So this was it. I read and re-read it and then burned it in the fire. Ash was likeable enough, if you wanted to speak about historical artefacts. But a passionate kiss? I couldn't help feeling this was going to go down like a lead balloon.

I spent time preening in front of the mirror, vanity getting the better of me. I looked good in my evening gown. It was a royal blue colour, and accentuated my figure. My hair was pinned up and I knew I looked attractive. Anyway, surely Ash had been given information too. It must be his first audition as well. He may not like it, but he would have to go along with it.

I hoped.